Created by
WARREN MURPHY
and RICHARD SAPIR

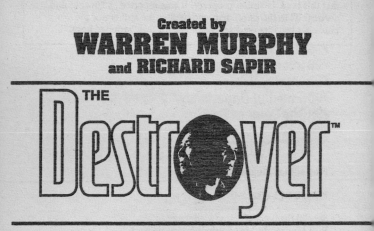

THE

Destroyer™

LAST RITES

A GOLD EAGLE BOOK FROM
WORLDWIDE®

TORONTO • NEW YORK • LONDON
AMSTERDAM • PARIS • SYDNEY • HAMBURG
STOCKHOLM • ATHENS • TOKYO • MILAN
MADRID • WARSAW • BUDAPEST • AUCKLAND

First edition August 1995

ISBN 0-373-63215-0

Special thanks and acknowledgment to
Will Murray for his contribution to this work.

LAST RITES

Printed in U.S.A.

For Brian Murphy, King of the Emergency Room,
who came up with the idea.

And for Maureen A. Murray, who came up with me.

Not to mention the Glorious House of Sinanju,
P.O. Box 2505, Quincy, MA 02269
[willray@cambridge.village.com]

AN ANNIVERSARY MESSAGE
FROM THE CREATOR OF
THE DESTROYER

In an age where breakfast was yesterday and everything—families, cars, homes, value systems—is discarded as casually as moist Kleenex, anything manmade that hangs around for a quarter century is probably worth an extra look.

And so is this Destroyer book, Number 100 in an unbroken string that started back in June of 1971.

When Dick Sapir and I wrote about the adventures of Remo and Chiun for the first time, we certainly never considered such longevity possible. Hell, we didn't even know we were writing a series until the original publisher asked for a second book.

Early on, we realized we did not want to write the same story over and over again, so, to the consternation of a lot of publishing suits, we began to use The Destroyer as a vehicle for humor and social comment and also to satirize the whole action-adventure genre. This turned out to be a good decision because a few years later, when most of the other wham-bam-thank-you-ma'am series had bitten the dust, we managed to hang around because nobody else was doing quite exactly the stuff we were turning out. It's my hope that this book you're now holding in your hands continues to live up to that promise. But let me know, because when it no longer does, we're outta here.

The plot for this book was suggested to Dick Sapir a long time ago by a young boy who was born on the exact same day the first Destroyer was written and who thus came this close to being baptized Remo. Dick died obscenely prematurely and never got around to writing the story, yet many years later, here it is, and I suppose that is telling us that good ideas never die.

Fortunately neither do our memories of good men—to one of whom, Richard Ben Sapir, who knew that dreams come in different sizes—this book is lovingly dedicated.

Warren B. Murphy,
August 1995

PROLOGUE

They had laid her out in the narrow oaken bed to die.

Everyone knew she was to die. She was old. Very old. She had lived a useful and productive life as a bride of Christ, but now that life had ceased to be useful, and her senses were shutting down.

A priest had given her the last rites of the Catholic church, sprinkling holy water over her thin frame with an aspergillum. He had spoken the words in the familiar Latin, commending her immortal soul to her savior. Incense candles were lit.

But she refused to die. The windows were curtained to keep out the harsh sunlight that tormented her even through the milky cataracts that had robbed her of almost all sight. She could hardly hear. She had not strength to walk. Food seemed not to nourish her.

There was no quality to her life, and although no disease ravaged her work-worn body, there was no hope for recovery. Her vitality had been used up. Some say she had begun to fail many years ago, after the fire.

Yet she lay in her deathbed, shrouded in white linen, blind eyes fixed on the cracked ceiling of Our Lady of Perpetual Care Home for the Infirm, fingering the black beads of her rosary. Her thin lips writhed soundlessly.

The sisters who took care of her in lieu of nurses thought she was saying her Hail Mary's. She was not.

She was counting her charges, reflecting on their destinies. A virgin, she had no sons or daughters to call her own, and so the lost and abandoned offspring of others became hers.

Each bead groped between her fingers brought to mind a name. Most she had lost touch of. Some had visited her often in days gone by. Many were lost. In France, in Korea, in Vietnam and more obscure places whose names no longer mattered, their bright promise had been spent like so many precious coins.

No one visited her now. She had retired long ago—so long ago that even the youngest boy had grown old enough to have adult children and adult cares and no time in a busy life for an old woman who had taught him the best she could.

She had never imagined growing this old. The infirmities were almost unendurable. She wore her skin like shellacked paper stretched almost to the breaking point. The slightest bump to the backs of her hands where the skin was especially shiny created a black bruise that seemed never to heal.

Another bead crawled between her fingers. And another. There was no order to the boyish faces that came to her mind's eye. They came unbidden, spoke in their authentic voices and seemed to be saying goodbye.

Then came a face that brought a clutching twinge to her heart and a wave of inexpressible sadness filled her breast.

She remembered him as a boy. Not even ten. She preferred to remember him as a boy. She had known him as a man, but she always thought of him as a boy. Just as when she dreamed, she did not dream of the rectory where she had dwelt for most of her adult life, but of her childhood home. Many people dreamed that way, she had read.

The boy had·sad eyes the color of tree bark. He had not been the smiling kind. A serious boy. "The Window Boy," they used to call him. For hours on end, he would press his face to the orphanage window, looking out into the wide world he did not know, waiting, ever waiting.

He was waiting for the parents he never knew. The parents no one knew. The parents who might or might not be alive. She had told him that. Still, he waited.

But no one ever came for him. No one ever cared.

My failure, she thought bitterly. My one failure.

Some children are placed and some are not. That is a truth as hard as concrete and as eternal as the promise of resurrection.

Perhaps if a proper home had been found, things might have turned out differently for that one sad-faced boy. But they had not. It was the boy's own fault, in a way. He had resisted all efforts to place him in a good, loving home. He stubbornly waited for his true parents, who never came.

When he had matured, he was full of such promise. A policeman. It was a surprising choice. Perhaps not so surprising upon reflection. A wronged boy who wanted to set the whole world right. He had been an honest boy, too.

It was such a shock when they had convicted him of that murder.

The boy she had known would never have slain. But he had been a Marine. Had served in Vietnam. Vietnam had changed so many of them. They came back lean and hollow cheeked and with a spiritual emptiness deep in their eyes. It was, she had long ago concluded, Vietnam that must have changed him so. Although he returned to exchange his green uniform of war for his blue one of peace, no doubt he had been changed by the green.

It had been such a bitter day when the state executed him. To Sister Mary Margaret Morrow, it had felt like losing flesh and blood.

Now, with her body failing and her senses all but shut down, Sister Mary Margaret lay in expectation of death, refusing to die and wondering why.

She had no unfinished business on this earth. None whatsoever.

But the good Lord refused to take her, and all she could think of was an orphan boy who had gone bad many many years ago.

A boy named Remo Williams.

She wondered if she should ask for him at the gateway to Heaven. She was certain he had died in Christ, in the end.

1

By the time he took the last turn on the trail from Yuma and Red Ghost Butte hove into view, William S. Roam began to feel as if he were riding across the dying planet Mars.

Red Ghost Butte was the color of raw brick. Everything around it was red. The sun burned overhead like a red, resentful orb. The sandstone hills were red. But Red Ghost Butte was reddest of all.

Although he had grown up in these rusty hills among the blowing sands of this low corner of Arizona, he had been away long enough that the red receptors of his eyes were overwhelmed by the sheer ferocity of the color of desolation.

All at once he felt ill, weaving on his hand-tooled saddle as he piloted his horse through the low desert toward Red Ghost Butte and what lay beyond.

Even his horse seemed red. It was chestnut colored, more brown than red, but under the blazing Arizona sun, it seemed to absorb the infernal redness all around till its hair smoldered.

Though sick, Bill Roam pushed on. His people needed him. He had nothing to bring but the white man's money and an empty fame that had come too late in life. But they were his people, and he had a duty to them.

Last Rites

He looked like a cowboy in his pink shirt and denims. His boots were hand-tooled Spanish leather, bought in Mexico City with a Visa Gold credit card. His white Stetson was pure Hollywood. The silver points of his turquoise-studded bola tie clinked together with each gritting hoof fall. His legs were long, and his muscles under his denim jacket were like lean, knotted ropes. Seven feet would catch his height. Only God could calculate his age.

He was no cowboy. His face was as red as the land that had formed him, as eroded as the sandstone mesas that dotted the endless red desolation. His eyes wore a permanent sun-squint, and their color was the color of the red-brown clay that lay under the red sand to nourish the corn that was life.

After three more miles, his red receptors shut down. The red of the sand and the sun faded, washed out, and he felt twenty times better.

The corral-style fence came into view, its gate as wide open as all outdoors.

"Pick it up, Sanshin," he told his horse, urging it along.

The horse began cantering. The red never bothered him. Horses don't see color. Horses don't know heartsick. Horses are lucky, he thought.

Bill Roam rode through the gate, past a weathered sign. There were two words that had been burnt into the sign with a heated poker. The first word began with an *S.* That was the only letter still visible. The second word was Reservation.

The first hogans began appearing. Every door faced east as tradition demanded. Every dome roof sported a stovepipe. And every third roof had a satellite dish pointed to the vaulting blue sky.

"I can see where my money went," he muttered without bitterness.

An Indian in a red-checker shirt and ragged Levi's stepped out of the first hogan, took one look and came back with a pump shotgun. He squinted up the long barrel.

"This is reservation land, white man."

"You wouldn't know it from the sky dishes, Tomi."

The pump gun all but fell from the brave's sunburned hands.

"Sunny Joe. That you?"

"I come back."

"We thought you'd deserted us forever."

"You got no call saying that. I been sending money right along."

"Hell, you know we got millions in that bank account we don't ever touch because it came from Washington."

"My money still good around here?"

"You know it is, Sunny Joe."

"Swap you a silver dollar for a cold one."

"Coming right up, Sunny Joe."

Bill "Sunny Joe" Roam kept riding. Tomi caught up on foot. Walking backward to keep pace with the chestnut horse, the spurs on his Reeboks jingling, Tomi handed up a cool Tecate, saying, "Keep your silver dollars, Sunny Joe."

"Sounds like you got plenty of these firewater cans," said Bill Roam, popping the tab.

"I like to keep the dust from my mouth these days."

"How is the dust these days?"

"It's killing us off, Sunny Joe. You know that, else you wouldn't have come all the way from that opulence you enjoy."

"I know," said Bill Roam gravely. "That's why I come back."

And he knocked back the entire can without pausing for breath.

"It's the death-hogan dust. It's powerful strong now."

"I hear they call it something else now," said Sunny Joe.

Tomi spat. "White man's words. White man's science."

"I hear they call it the Sun On Jo Disease."

"What do whites know?"

"How many dead, Tomi?"

Tomi grunted. "How many living is a shorter answer. Just a few of us left. We're dying, Sunny Joe. Not all at once. But it's catching up. The death-hogan dust is bound to devour us all before too long."

"That's why I come back."

"To save us, Sunny Joe?"

"If I can."

"Can you?"

"Doubt it. All I got is money and fame. What do the death spirits care about either?"

"Then why'd you leave all that to risk inhaling the dust of death, Sunny Joe?"

"If my people are going to perish, I aim to die with them. After all, I'm the last Sunny Joe. And what have I got left at my age? Just too much money and useless damn fame."

Sullen Indians began collecting behind the horse with every hogan they passed. Some were drunk. Most were skeptical. A few jeered.

"Show us some magic, Sunny Joe."

"I'm fresh out of magic, Happy Bear."

"Did you meet any famous white guys in the white lands, Sunny Joe?"

"Yeah. Stallone. Schwarzenegger. Any of those?"

"Any and all. But I wouldn't trade a one for the least of you ornery redskins," Roam answered.

"People say you turned apple."

"Do I look like an apple to you, Gus Jong?"

The Indians fell silent.

When they passed a hogan and no one emerged, Bill Roam would ask, "Who died there?"

And as he heard the names, he hung his head and squeezed his dry eyes.

"Ko Jong Oh gather up his red soul," he said softly.

"You look tired, Sunny Joe."

Old Bill Roam's eyes sought Red Ghost Butte standing in the shadow of the great Chocolate Mountains.

"I am tired. Damn tired. I'm an old man now. I have come home forever." And lowering his voice to a dust-dry whisper, he added, "Forever to dwell with the spirits of my honored ancestors, whom I revere more than life."

2

His name was Remo and he couldn't tell if he was dreaming or not.

He knew he had been asleep. In the quiet darkness of the summer night with the faint salt tang of the Atlantic Ocean coming in through the open window of his unfurnished bedroom, he wondered if he was still asleep and only dreaming.

Remo was a Master of Sinanju, and so did not sleep like other men. A part of his brain was always awake, eternally aware. He slept deeper than other men, woke up more refreshed than other men, but still his sleep was deeper. Rarely now did he dream. Of course he did dream. All men dreamed. Even men who had been elevated by the discipline of Sinanju—the first and ultimate of the martial arts—dreamed. But Remo rarely remembered his dreams upon waking.

If this was a dream, Remo knew he would never forget it. If this was a dream, Remo understood it was important.

For in the fitful darkness of his room, where moonlight showed on and off through rifts in the summertime clouds, a woman appeared in the room.

The portion of Remo's brain that never slept, which monitored his surroundings even in the deepest part of sleep, became aware of the woman the instant she appeared at the foot of the tatami mat on which Remo slept.

That the woman did not enter the room through the door or a window startled the never-dormant portion of Remo's brain, and he snapped awake like a mousetrap tripping.

Remo sat up, dark eyes adjusting to the darkness of the room.

At this point he wasn't certain he was really awake. The ever-vigilant part of his brain—which had warned him of the presence in his room—went dormant as his other senses kicked in.

They told him he was alone in the room. His hearing detected no heartbeat, no faint, elastic wheeze of lungs, no gurgle or hum of blood coursing through miles of veins and blood vessels. His sense of smell trapped the airborne scent molecules tumbling around the still air, separated sea salt, car exhaust and mown grass and told him there were no danger smells present.

Almost every sense told him he was alone. Except sight. He could see the woman. She was looking down at him with a calm face that was an oval framed in long dark hair. It was a cameo face. Young but ageless, beautiful but not breathtaking.

Her eyes were very sad.

She stood barefoot at the foot of the reed mat, and while her face was clear, her form was something even Remo's powerful eyes could not read. She did not appear to be clothed. Yet there was no impression of nudity. She might have been some cosmic angel beyond the concept of skin or cloth.

Remo reached out with a bare toe to touch the woman.

His foot disappeared into a darkness so absolute he had to yank it back.

Then the woman spoke.

"I was only watching you sleep." And she smiled faintly. For all its hesitation, it was a warm and generous smile. "You are so handsome as a man."

"Are you really my—mother?" Remo asked in a voice that cracked on the last word.

Her sad eyes shone. "Yes. I am your mother."

"I recognize your eyes."

"Do you remember me?"

"No. But I have a daughter. Your eyes are like hers."

"There is shadow around your daughter."

"What!"

"That is not for you to worry about now. One day you will face this shadow. You will face many things you do not understand." She closed her eyes. "We have been apart nearly all of your life. But that too will change. When you die, my only son, you will die unknown. But they will see fit to bury you in Arlington National Cemetery under the name that belongs to you, but which you have never heard."

"'Remo Williams' isn't my real name?"

She shook her head slowly.

"What is my name?"

"You must discover that for yourself."

"Tell me your name, then."

"*He* will tell you."

"My father?"

"You have not yet found him."

"I've been trying, but—"

"I have told you that I lie buried by Laughing Brook."

"I can't find any Laughing Brook. It's not on any map or in any atlas or guide books."

"Laughing Brook is a sacred place. It does not belong on any map. And I have told you that your father is known to you."

"I don't know who that is. I've racked my brain—"

"You must not stop searching in your mind, in your heart or in the world of flesh and earth."

"Just tell me his name," Remo pleaded.

"I am sorry."

"Look, if it's so freaking important for me to find him," Remo said hotly, "just tell me his name."

"I would not be a fit mother if I led you by the hand long after you have learned to walk."

"Then give me another hint. Please."

"Sometimes he dwells in the land where the Great Star fell. Other times he dwells among the stars."

"What does that mean?"

"Search for him south of Great Star Crater or among the other earthly stars."

"I don't know what an earthly star is."

The woman closed her dark eyes. "I am permitted to show you a vision."

And in the formless space between her face and her bare feet, the darkness congealed. Dim shadows darkened, took form. Patches of moonlight bent themselves into artful, impossible shapes.

Gradually a picture resolved. There was no color, just blacks and grays. A night image.

"What do you see, my son who is not known to me?"

"A cave ..."

"Look deeper. What do you see in the cave?"

Remo peered into the vision. The cave was dark, but his eyes took in the ambient light, amplifying it.

He saw at first a pitiful thing wrapped in a blanket. The blanket had color once. But now it was faded and tattered. In the blanket was a bundle of desiccated sticks and patches of dried brown hide, and above the bundle, tilted to one side, lolled a human head, shriveled, wizened, eyes withered shut above a sunken nose and a mouth that appeared to have been stitched shut.

To the bald, drum-tight skin of the head clung dirty tatters of hair.

"I see a mummy," said Remo.

"Does the mummy have a face?"

"Not much of one," Remo admitted.

"In death, do you see whose face the mummy wore in life?"

Remo's eyes took in the ruined mask of parchment skin and dead bone for a long time. He swallowed once, hard.

And turning his head away, Remo squeezed his eyes shut and said nothing.

"Whose face?" the woman insisted.

"You know whose face," he said thickly.

"You will visit this cave soon. You have only to take the first step."

"I don't want to go anymore."

"You seek your father. You seek the truth."

"Not if it costs me—"

"You have searched with your eyes and your brain. You have not yet searched with your heart. His eyes look down upon you, although he does not see you."

"What does *that* mean?"

"My people are the people of the Sun. Your people are the people of the Sun. Find the people of the Sun, and you will find understanding and the peace you have sought all your life."

"I—I can't."

"You will. Listen to the mother you have never known. You will enter this cave, and all will be revealed to you. Do not be afraid. There is no death. You are no more alive than I am. No more conscious than your most remote ancestor. And I am no more dead than my genes that you carry in your body."

And with a last wistful look, the apparition faded from the room.

Remo did not sleep the rest of the night. He lay flat on his back looking up at the ceiling, trying to convince himself that it had all been a bad dream.

But Masters of Sinanju, the absolute lords of their own minds and bodies, did not experience nightmares. And Remo knew that his worst fears were only days away.

THE MASTER OF SINANJU was making longevity tea for breakfast.

The water boiled happily in its celadon teapot while the ginseng strips and crushed jujubes and raw pine nuts waited patiently in their individual bowls. Warm sunlight streamed through the kitchen window as the Western sun shed its good radiance upon the loose imported green tea leaves.

The Master of Sinanju would have preferred an Eastern sun, but he lived in difficult times. Yet they were not terrible times, he reflected as he bustled around the kitchen with its electric stove and running water and other Western conveniences.

As he prepared the morning meal, he hummed a song from his village of Sinanju in faraway Korea. The song made him feel closer to his village. But in truth, he was not unhappy.

True, he dwelt in a barbarian land. True also, he dwelt with a son who was not only adopted, but white and large of foot and nose and blankly round of eye. A ghost-faced white.

But the Master of Sinanju had known harsher times. He had experienced the bitter comfort of his village during the difficult days when he had no son, no heir, no pupil. Only the awesome responsibility of his village and the cold knowledge that the five-thousand-year tradition, of which he was the last caretaker, had come to an ignominious end.

In those days he had tasted the gall of failure, the sure knowledge that he had let down fifty centuries of ancestors, and faced his final days alone.

Those had been the darkest hours of his life. How could any event seem more distasteful? How could any ignominy make that one pale into insignificance?

So he happily prepared longevity tea in the warm morning sunshine and, although his pupil should have arisen with the sun, Chiun didn't go upstairs to awaken him.

"Remo will appear in due time. He is a good son, if pale."

But Remo didn't appear. And when the water had bubbled down to trace metals, the Master of Sinanju simply put on a fresh pot and resumed his wait.

Longevity tea is worth waiting for. And so are good sons.

THE HUMMING had long since ceased and the teapot had grown cold when Remo Williams padded barefoot into the kitchen, the lines and planes of his strong face unhappy. His deep-set eyes were like burn holes above his high cheekbones.

"I have made longevity tea," said Chiun, Reigning Master of Sinanju, not turning from the stove.

"I'm not hungry."

"That is good, because I have thrown yours into the sink."

"That's okay," Remo said absently, taking a tumbler from a cupboard and holding it under running water.

He drank two glasses of the metallic-tasting water, and the Master of Sinanju still didn't turn around.

"I have wasted the entire morning," Chiun said abruptly.

"Doing what?"

"Being happy."

"That's not a waste."

"When one spends an entire morning thinking well of inconsiderate boors, it is a waste. It is a betrayal."

Remo said nothing.

Chiun whirled. "Do you know what time it is?"

Remo didn't have to look at the wall clock in the shape of a black cat whose rocking tail swung in constant opposition to its shifty cartoon eyes. "Ten thirty-two," he said, setting the empty tumbler in the stainless-steel sink. His wrists were freakishly thick.

"Why did you keep me waiting?"

"Couldn't sleep."

"If you could not sleep, why fritter away the morning on your back?"

"Because I was afraid to get out of bed."

The Master of Sinanju stopped, his mouth a perfect O. "Why?"

Remo hesitated.

"Why do you fear morning?" Chiun pressed.

And when Remo turned, there were tears in his dark, deep-set eyes. One rolled down the curve of a high cheekbone. "You're going to die," he said.

"Possibly," Chiun admitted, searching his pupil's troubled features.

"You're going to die soon, Little Father."

A dark cloud passed over the Master of Sinanju's features. "Why do you say that?"

"I don't want to be left alone in the world."

And seeing the pain deep in his pupil's eyes, the Master of Sinanju dropped his anger like a mask and padded toward Remo.

"What troubles you?"

"I don't want to talk about it."

Chiun clapped his long-nailed fingers together. "Speak!"

The doorbell rang.

"I will answer it," said Chiun.

He came back a minute later with a heavy plastic mailing envelope and laid it on a kitchen counter carelessly.

"What's that?" asked Remo.

"Nothing."

"How do you know?"

"It is only for you and it is from Smith."

"Could be important."

"It is not. The look in your eyes is important."

"I'd better make sure," said Remo.

And because he was showing interest through his pain, the Master of Sinanju allowed his pupil to open the package.

It was a Federal Express pouch, made of a plastic called Tyvek that was so tough it could not be torn or damaged even by truck drivers flinging it carelessly at doors. Houses were now wrapped with Tyvek before siding was nailed in place. It could be cut with sharp blades but not torn by human hands, no matter how strong.

Remo tried to find the flap, got confused and impatiently grabbed the pouch at both ends, popping it apart like a paper sack.

Out spilled a fanfold stack of green-bar computer paper. Remo glanced at the top sheet briefly.

"What is it?" asked Chiun.

"Nothing," said Remo, dumping the stack of paper into the trash bin.

"It is from Smith. How could it be nothing?"

"Because it is," said Remo.

The Master of Sinanju lifted the stack from the trash and examined the top sheet. It was a list of names.

Williams, Aaron
Williams, Adam
Williams, Alan
Williams, Allen
Williams, Arthur

"What are all these names?" he wondered.

"Just names. Forget them."

"Ah," said Chiun, understanding dawning in his hazel eyes. "You demanded of Smith that he seek out a suitable father for you, and this is the list of culprits."

"It's a stack of wastepaper. Get rid of it."

"If you no longer care to seek your wayward father, perhaps I will do so. If only to congratulate him for ridding himself of so intractable a son. Then I will present him with a bill for raising you.''

''Stuff it,'' said Remo, storming from the room.

3

Dr. Harold W. Smith began his day as he always did.

He parked his beat-up station wagon in his assigned parking spot at Folcroft Sanitarium, nodded to the lobby guard as he strode to the elevator and rode it one floor up to his office.

"Any calls, Mrs. Mikulka?" he asked, and Mrs. Mikulka crisply informed him that no, there had not been any calls, a fact that should have been obvious inasmuch as it was six in the morning.

Harold Smith liked to get an early start on the day. Some people were that way, so no one considered it unusual that the director of a sleepy sanitarium in Rye, New York, should approach his boring job with the same brisk urgency as the head of a major TV network.

Smith shut the office door behind him and entered his sanctum sanctorum, an office overlooking Long Island Sound.

The office reflected his personality. Spare, frugal, unassuming. If Smith had chosen the wall paint, it would have been gray, like the three-piece suit he habitually wore. Like the pale grayish cast of his skin. But because Folcroft was supposed to be a warehouse for the chronically ill, the walls were a vapid hospital green.

The office might have been furnished in the 1960s from prewar castoffs. Except for the desk. It gleamed darkly, like an altar of obsidian, out of place in the slightly shabby room.

A Spartan block, the desk sat before the picture window framing the sound. The leather executive chair behind it was cracked with age, and the springs creaked when Harold Smith dropped his spare frame into it. But the desk was new.

Smith absently tightened the knot of his hunter green Dartmouth tie and reached under the lip of the slab of black tempered glass that served as a desktop. He found a black button and depressed it.

Deep in the desk, under the glass and canted so that it faced the man behind the desk but was invisible to anyone else, a phosphorescent amber screen came to life.

Smith brought his gnarled fingers up to the edge of the desk. A touch-sensitive keyboard lit up. Smith input a string of characters, and the amber screen went through its sign-on cycle.

Smith waited patiently, his patrician face glued to the screen. Behind rimless glasses, his gray eyes watched the familiar process. The virus-check program automatically executed. When it was complete, Smith watched for an on-screen warning light.

There were none. No emergencies. Only then did he relax.

Smith called up the Constitution data base, reading it word for word as he had for the three decades he had operated out of Folcroft, not as its chief administrator, but as the director of CURE, a government agency so supersecret only the President of the United States knew it existed.

"We the people of the United States, in order to form a more perfect union..."

Smith finished his reading, closed the file, and called up the wire-service news digests. Two floors below, in Folcroft's basement, giant mainframes and optical WORM-drive servers toiled night and day, trolling the net, culling information that might indicate a threat to U.S. security, warning signs of domestic disorder or global peril—all of which fell under the secret CURE operational guidelines.

There had been another overnight Amtrak derailment. This time outside Baton Rouge. It might be simply another example of incompetence on the part of the government-funded company that ran the nation's aging railroad system, but there had been a great many such derailments of late. Smith captured the news digest and dumped it into a growing electronic file marked "Amtrak."

If these derailments continued, it might mean a matter for CURE to look into.

There had been an overnight political assassination in Mexico, according to Notimex. This was the third in recent months. The situation south of the border was difficult but not explosive. At least not yet.

After reading the extract, Smith dumped it into the Mexico file.

Other items flashed on the buried amber screen. Another American fishing boat had been seized in Canadian waters. The new premier of North Korea continued his courting of the UN, even while making veiled threats against South Korea. The situation in Macedonia still festered.

Problems but no crises. No mission for CURE, Harold Smith reflected.

Which was a distinct relief, because CURE had no enforcement capability at present. He was on strike and vowed to remain on strike until Harold Smith had found his parents.

It was ironic, thought Smith as he turned in his chair to face Long Island Sound with its sun-dappled waters and scooting skiffs. Remo Williams had been selected to be CURE's enforcement arm precisely because he had no living relatives. There had been other candidates, all collected by the very mainframes that still hummed in the Folcroft basement, but only Remo had all the qualifications to fulfill the mission.

When CURE was set up in the early 1960s, there had been no thought of an enforcement arm. A new President of the U.S. had taken up residence in the White House full of hope—and discovered the nation faced its greatest crisis. It was tearing itself apart. The laws of the nation were no longer enough to hold society together. The Constitution had been made obsolete by lawless forces.

That President had faced as stark a choice as Lincoln had a century before. Take drastic action or forfeit the nation.

Two options had presented themselves. Declare martial law or suspend the Constitution.

The President had wisely done neither. Instead, he had plucked an obscure information analyst named Smith out of the CIA and installed him as head of CURE with a mandate to clean up the nation and preserve American democracy even if it meant riding roughshod over the Constitution of the United States.

Which Harold Smith did with a grim relentlessness over the course of CURE's first decade. And it was the reason why, at the beginning of every work day, he dutifully read the most sacred document in American history. It was a reminder of his awesome responsibility and a kind of silent act of contrition. Harold Smith believed in the Constitution. He just didn't believe in sacrificing the greatest democracy in human history to the inflexible demands inscribed on a sheet of parchment paper. Nor did he believe that the great democratic experiment called America had failed abysmally.

By the end of that first decade, a new President had assumed the office and found the tide of lawlessness had only worsened. He had given Smith the broader responsibility of creating an enforcement arm.

Smith had plucked an obscure patrolman with a single tour in Vietnam to his credit—who nevertheless fit an exhaustive list of criteria—and had him killed.

Harold Smith's fingerprints were not on file in the killing of patrolman Remo Williams, the last man executed by the State of New Jersey. He had arranged it all by telephone calls and whispered orders. Others had done the dirty work.

A badge was stolen. A pusher was beaten to death with a baseball bat in an alley in the Ironbound section of Newark, New Jersey, and when the sun rose, it was Remo Williams's badge that was found at the scene of the crime, Remo Williams who was arrested by Newark detectives, Remo Williams who was rushed through a show trial and found guilty of premeditated murder.

Everyone believed Remo was guilty because everyone knew that the State of New Jersey would not execute one of its own law-enforcement officers unless there was absolutely no shred of doubt. Twelve honest men found Remo Williams guilty, never dreaming they were unwitting participants in a conspiracy that reached all the way to the Oval Office. They only knew that

Remo Williams had to die. It was as obvious as the color of the sky.

Remo Williams never understood he had been framed and railroaded through a corrupt justice system. Not until the day after the smothering black leather hood had been jammed over his head and the searing juice poured through his jerking body.

He'd lost consciousness in the death house of Trenton State Prison and woke up in Folcroft Sanitarium, where it was all explained to him by CURE's lone field operative in those days, a one-handed man named Conrad MacCleary.

The chair had been rigged. The trial had been rigged, the jury bought off. His fingerprints and other life records had been pulled from every file.

"Won't work," Remo had said after it was all laid out for him.

"We were thorough," said MacCleary. "You have no family. Few friends—what cop has real friends except other cops?—and the blue brotherhood didn't exactly stand by you here. You were too honest. And honest cops are always the first ones they hang out to dry."

"Still won't work," Remo Williams insisted stubbornly, feeling the bandages on his face from the plastic surgery used to change his appearance.

"Why not?" asked the man with the hook for a hand.

"I grew up in an orphanage. Maybe I don't have a family, but I had a zillion brothers."

"Saint Theresa's burned down two weeks ago. Fortunately, there was only one casualty. A nun. Seems she contracted smoke inhalation or something. Understand you knew her, Williams. Sister Mary something?"

''You bastard.''

''You're all alone in the world, Williams. And there's a hobo with no name lying in your grave. Just say the word, and we'll swap you for him and no one will know any different.''

Remo Williams had accepted his new life. He had been given over to the last pure-blooded Master of Sinanju and transformed by long training, arduous exercise and monkish diet until he himself was a Master of Sinanju, a martial-arts discipline so old it was said that all other fighting arts were descended from it.

For many years, seeming never to grow older, he had served America in secret. The man who didn't exist working for the the agency that didn't exist. America's enemies wilted before this silent, implacable human weapon.

And now he wanted out. Forever.

But before he got out, Remo was calling in an old obligation from the man who had robbed him of his old life and set him on the new.

The trouble was, Harold Smith had done his job too well so many years ago. Erasing all traces of Remo Williams's existence had been easy compared to erasing other men's existences. Consequently, two decades later, absolutely no trace remained.

The orphanage had burned down to the ground with its scant records. Smith had read Remo's record long ago, before the orphanage was consumed. The skimpy account told of a baby boy, not many weeks old, left in a basket on the doorstep of Saint Theresa's Orphanage. A note attached to the babe's swaddling clothes told his name. Remo Williams. That was all. No explanation. No back trail.

Even Smith's computer file on Remo, maintained over those long years, had been lost when Smith was forced to erase all CURE files during an IRS seizure of the sanitarium in the recent past.

Smith had hit a brick wall. Remo Williams might well have never existed—just as Harold W. Smith had intended all along.

Only now Harold W. Smith very much wanted to locate Remo Williams's parents. The contract between the CURE and the House of Sinanju was due to be renewed in the coming months. And without Remo, CURE might as well shut down.

The blue contact telephone rang. Smith scooped it up and said, "Yes?"

"Hail, O Emperor of understanding and enlightenment. I crave the boon of your clear-seeing mind," said a squeaky voice.

"Go ahead, Master Chiun."

"Remo is acting strangely."

"More strangely than usual?"

"He received your package."

"It was the best I could do. It is a printout of all U.S. males whose last name is Williams and whose dates of birth fall within the parameters that would permit them to parent someone Remo's age."

"He threw these names away, unread."

"Why?"

"I do not know why," Chiun said, a testy quality creeping into his tone. "That is why I have called you. Why would these names cease to interest Remo?"

"I have no idea. Last week he appeared very eager when I told him I was compiling such a list."

"Yet now he scorns these names. Scorns the very thing that has obsessed him for many seasons."

"Master Chiun, barring a miracle, I do not believe I can ever locate the information Remo seeks."

"That is good."

"You have expressed those sentiments before."

"And I express them now."

"In the past you made representations suggesting you know something about Remo's past. Something you refuse to divulge."

"I do. Remo is Korean."

"I think that unlikely."

"Remo's father is Korean. Possibly his mother, as well."

"Why do you say that?"

"It is very simple. Remo is outwardly white, but he has taken to Sinanju like no pure-blooded boy of my village ever has. Therefore, he cannot be white. Entirely white. He is Korean. And if he is Korean, his father must be Korean, for it is well-known that Koreanness—true Koreanness—can only be passed from father to son."

"I see," said Harold Smith vaguely, recognizing that the Master of Sinanju had lapsed into the prejudice and superstition of his ancestors.

Smith changed the subject. "What do you suggest we do? The next contract expires in the fall. It is bad enough that Remo considers himself on strike, but once the contract lapses, there is no predicting what he will do."

"Remo must never be allowed to find his father," Chiun said suddenly.

"Why not?"

"Because," said the Master of Sinanju in a strange voice, "if he does, he may never forgive me."

"What do you mean by that?" asked Smith.

But the Master of Sinanju had already hung up.

Harold Smith replaced his receiver and turned his chair around to face Long Island Sound. He steepled his fingers as a sour expression settled over his slightly sharp features.

All his life he had traded in information. Hard fact was his currency. On hard fact he made countless life-and-death decisions. Harold Smith believed that like the radio transmissions of his long-ago youth, the facts of Remo's lineage not gone forever, but were speeding through the galaxy. If one could take a radio far enough into deep space, fifty-year-old broadcasts of "The Shadow" and "The Green Hornet" and "I Love a Mystery" could be received as clearly as if it were 1939.

Somewhere out there was a document, a file, a newspaper account or even a human brain that held the secret of Remo Williams.

It was just a matter of finding it and recognizing it.

4

Remo Williams walked the sands of Wollaston Beach thinking that all the important places in his life were by the water. Newark. Folcroft. Sinanju. And now Quincy, Massachusetts.

There was a spanking wind off Quincy Bay. White sea gulls hung in the air like kites, feet dangling, heads craning and twisting down to spy food scraps. Once in a while one would drop to catch a fish or root among discarded food on the curved smile of sand that was the beach.

Remo was walking north, toward the place where the sand became rock and then salt marsh. Beyond it was the Hummock, a hump of trees and brush that was also known as Arrowhead Hill. There the Moswetuset Indians had dwelt until the white man came, some say to despoil a vibrant culture. But the tribe that had given their name—if unwillingly—to the State of Massachusetts had left behind only a hill not much more prominent than a garbage dump. Beyond the Hummock the blue towers of Boston, a city not among the nation's largest by any means, reared gleaming to put the ancient seat of the Moswetusets to shame.

As he walked, Remo thought about another beach, more rock than sand, fronting the inhospitable slaty waters of the West Korea Bay, thousands of miles away.

On that beach a fishing village called Sinanju stood as it had for over five thousand years. Almost no one in the West knew of it. But it was from this village that the Masters of Sinanju—the premier assassins in human history—had ventured forth to serve the great thrones of the ancient world.

From Egyptian and Chinese dynasties history had long forgotten to the Roman Empire—which, by Sinanju standards, fell in the recent past—the House of Sinanju had been the preeminent historical power. Preeminent but unsuspected by historians and thus unrecorded. In their way, the Masters of Sinanju kept the peace. For when an emperor had an assassin at his disposal, he could crush his rivals, internal and external, thereby preserving his domain. Costly and ruinous wars were prevented this way. Lives were saved. Armies were not wasted on bloody combat. Kingdoms were made stable.

At least that was how the Master of Sinanju had explained it to Remo.

That village was old when the Moswetusets were learning to chip flint. It would still be standing when Boston had sunk into rubble. If Chiun had his way, Remo would one day take over the village as the first white Master of Sinanju.

It wasn't exactly how Remo had envisioned his life when he left the orphanage to seek his fortune. In those days his dreams had a different size. A policeman's salary, wife and kids and the traditional clapboard house with a white picket fence. Houses like that were all over America. Remo had never lived in one. Not for long, anyway. The simple dreams had always eluded him.

He couldn't see himself living in Sinanju. Ever. But the years had made him more part of Sinanju than America.

Newark, the city of his youth, was no more. Riots and neglect and the grinding passing of time had obliterated it.

This city was only the latest in a long string of places where Remo had lived since shedding his old life in that other place on the water, Folcroft Sanitarium. Remo might live here another year, or even ten. It would never be home. There was no home for an orphan who had never had a family. Not in the comfort of the past. Not in the uncertainty of the future.

Remo walked on. Having come from nowhere, he was not concerned that his path was aimless.

He became aware of the Master of Sinanju padding alongside him long after Chiun had joined him. Remo had been looking down at the sand, not up at the world and the sky.

"You are a duck that walks," Chiun squeaked.

"I'm a duck that walks," agreed Remo.

"A target for any who would do you harm."

"That's called a sitting duck."

"For a Master of Sinanju to walk along so oblivious to danger, you might as well be sitting."

"I'm in no danger."

"It is when you are most lulled that danger rears its water-buffalo skull."

"That's 'ugly head.'"

"There is no difference," Chiun said dismissively. "What troubles you, Remo?"

"I don't belong anywhere."

"You belong to me."

"And after you pass on?"

"Why this preoccupation with death?"

"It's my trade," said Remo bitterly. "I never wanted to be an assassin. I'm sick of death."

"This has troubled you these last few months. Something new troubles you today, my son."

Remo held his tongue for a full minute before speaking. "She came to me again last night," he said softly. "My mother."

"That hussy!" Chiun hissed.

"I thought you said she didn't exist."

"She is a fragment of your imagination, therefore she is a hussy. Because what other kind of woman would spring unbidden from your white mind?"

"She's real. She told me to keep looking for my father."

"And so, like an obedient son, you have stopped?"

"She showed me something else."

"What is that?"

"A vision."

"An hallucination," spat Chiun.

"You didn't say that when I saw the Great Wang that time years ago."

"Seeing the Great Wang was the last passage of a Master in training to full Masterhood."

"Yeah, well, it was good to get all those dippy rites of passage over with. The Night of the Salt. The Dream of Death. The Master's Trial. It was getting to be like puberty every three years."

"There is still one other rite you have not yet undergone."

"What is it? The Dance of the Dippy Duck?"

"No. The Rite of Attainment."

Remo regarded the Boston skyline. "Never heard of it."

"It is necessary to prepare a full Master for the final stage in his responsibilities to the House."

"What's that?" Remo asked without interest.

"It sanctifies a full Master so that upon the retirement of his teacher, he can assume the title of Reigning Master of Sinanju."

"You planning on retiring?"

"No."

Remo stopped suddenly. He turned to face the Master of Sinanju. He was rotating his thick wrists, something he did when agitated. They were as unalike as two men could be. Remo towered over the old Korean. His white T-shirt and gray chinos were casual while Chiun's riotous scarlet-and-lavender kimono belonged in a Chinese wedding party. One ageless, the other ancient.

"Little Father," said Remo.

Chiun searched his pupil's troubled features. "Yes?"

"That vision she showed me. It was of you."

Chiun brightened. "Me. Really, Remo?"

Remo frowned darkly. "Why are you suddenly interested in a vision of a woman you say you don't believe in?" he asked tightly.

"Because the vision mentioned someone of importance. Namely, me. Continue, Remo. What did she say about me?"

"Nothing. She showed me a cave."

"What was in this cave?"

"You were."

"What was I doing?"

"Decomposing."

The Master of Sinanju stepped back as if struck by a blow. He narrowed his hazel eyes. "She lied!" he shrieked.

"She said I had to find my father and when I did, I would enter that cave and discover the truth about myself."

Chiun gathered up his wispy chin whiskers in a pout.

"You'd been dead a while, Little Father. You were a mummy."

"How did you know it was me?" Chiun challenged.

"It was your face, your hair, your bone structure."

The Master of Sinanju made a fist of his face, the deep seams and wrinkles gathering tighter and tighter like parchment wrinkling as it absorbed water.

"When did she say this evil day would come to pass?"

"She didn't. Exactly. Only that it would be soon if I kept looking for my father."

"You must not seek out that man, Remo!" Chiun said, waggling a stern finger in Remo's face.

"That's exactly what I was thinking."

"And you must go near no caves."

"That goes double for you, you know."

Chiun stroked his tendril of a beard thoughtfully. "And we must seek out a place where that busybody woman can vex you no longer."

"I'm quitting CURE, Little Father."

"Yes, yes. Let me think."

"For good this time. I mean it."

Chiun fluttered his winglike kimono sleeves like an ungainly, flightless bird. "Yes, yes. Of course you do."

"The organization can dragoon someone else if they want. Let 'em make an enforcement arm out of Arnold Schwarzenegger, for all I care. I've done my time, paid my dues. It's time to move on."

"We must pack."

"To go where?"

"You must trust me. Do you trust me?"

"Sure. You know I do."

"Then come. For I have been neglectful in my duties to the House. You have been a full Master long enough. It is time that you undergo the Rite of Attainment."

And the Master of Sinanju ran down to the lapping waters of Quincy Bay, leaving no sandal prints in the loose beige sand.

Remo followed, likewise leaving no trace of his passing.

When they reached the bay, it was in unison. They seemed to step up onto the calm water as if mounting a shifting ledge of rock. The water supported them. They ran out past the anchored sailboats and rounded Squantum headland, where legend had it Captain Miles Standish first met Squanto, the Indian who taught the pilgrims how to survive their first harsh New England winter by planting corn.

"Where are we going?" Remo asked as they ran under the long bridge to Moon Island and entered Boston Harbor, water barely splashing under their feet.

"There," Chiun said, pointing north.

And on the other side of Boston Harbor, Remo spotted the fat concrete radar tower of Logan Airport. A 747 was lifting off in their direction, trailing a dirty fan of exhaust.

"I thought you said we had to pack first."

"Pack!" Chiun spat. "There is no time to pack! Make haste, O slugabed."

"So, WHERE ARE WE HEADED, Little Father?" Remo asked after the Boston-to–New York City TWA passenger jet lifted off over Boston Harbor.

"That is a surprise."

"If we're going to Sinanju, I'm grabbing my seat flotation cushion and getting off here."

"We are not going to Sinanju."

"Good."

"You do not deserve to visit the Pearl of the Orient."

"Oyster of the Yellow Sea is more like it," muttered Remo.

Chiun had the window seat and was looking out.

"Wing holding up?" asked Remo.

"I am not looking at the wing."

"What are you looking at, then?"

"There!" said Chiun in the high, squeaky voice he used when excited. "Behold, Remo."

Remo leaned over to see out the window.

The wheels were up, and the TWA 747 was swinging back over land. They were south of Boston. Remo recognized the sinuous Neponset River separating Boston from Quincy.

Then he saw it.

Nestled beside the T-shaped high school was the unmistakable place they called home. Even from the air it stood out.

Once it had been a church. A real-estate developer had come along and replaced the stained glass with vinyl-clad replacement windows, added doghouse and shed roof dormers to the roofline and converted it into a sixteen-unit condominium. The Master of Sinanju had acquired it from Harold Smith two contract negotiations back.

"Castle Sinanju," said Chiun proudly. "Look how it dwarfs all lesser domiciles."

Remo folded his lean arms. "If I never see it again, it'll be fine with me."

"Philistine," sniffed the Master of Sinanju.

The 747 leveled off at two thousand feet and followed the coastline south. Remo recognized the hook of Cape Cod, the seat belt light winked off and he settled down to enjoy the flight.

A black-haired stewardess came up and leaned so far down, her cleavage almost plopped into Remo's lap.

"Sir, you look like a strong man. We could use a strong man in the galley."

"Is there a problem?"

The stewardess looked up and down the aisles. "I don't want to alarm the other passengers. If you could just follow me."

"Sure," said Remo.

"It is a trap," warned Chiun.

"On an airplane?"

"There are traps and there are traps," sniffed Chiun.

Smiling, the stewardess led the way to the galley and, when Remo entered, she ran the curtain shut.

"What's the problem?" asked Remo.

"My uniform zipper is stuck." And she turned to present her shapely back to him.

"It's all the way up."

"I know. Could you get it down for me?"

"If you say so," said Remo. The zipper came down easily, and the stewardess wriggled out of her uniform, turned and gave Remo the full sunshine of her radiant smile.

"What's this?" he asked.

"Your free initiation."

"Into what?" Remo asked suspiciously.

"The Mile High Club."

At that moment the curtain drew back and a honey blond head poked in. "What's going on?" the new arrival hissed.

"He's just helping me with my uniform zipper."

The blond stewardess looked from the stewardess in her underwear to Remo and slipped in. "My panty hose are sagging. Do you think you could do something with them?"

"I don't do panty-hose realignments," said Remo.

"You don't?" The blond stewardess looked stricken.

The other stewardess crooked her fingers and looked as if she wanted to gouge the blonde's eyes out. "He doesn't," she said tartly. "He's strictly a zipper man. Now, get back to serving peanuts."

"Can I watch?" wondered the blonde.

"No!" Remo and the first stewardess said together.

"How about I just close my eyes and listen?"

"This is a private party," the first stewardess hissed.

"This is no party at all," said Remo. "Excuse me." And he exited the galley.

Four hands reached out to pull him back but ended up clutching at empty air as Remo glided back to his seat and turned to the Master of Sinanju.

"You were right, Little Father. It was the oldest trap in the world."

"You resisted?"

"I don't take advantage of women who are drunk on my Sinanju pheromones."

"Unless they are hung like cows."

"Women are not hung. Men are hung. The expression is 'hung like a bull.'"

"Cows hang lower than bulls."

"Okay, cows are hung, too."

"They drag their udders through the grass."

"I get the picture."

"Just like the white women you fancy."

"I don't fancy stewardesses. Stewardesses are always hitting on me. That's another thing I don't like about my life. I can have any woman I want. They can't resist me. It's no fun. Where's the chase?"

"Coming up the aisle," said Chiun, nudging Remo with a bony, silk-covered elbow.

The entire complement of stewardesses bustled up the aisle, their reproachful eyes fixed on Remo.

"We're on strike until we get some satisfaction," one said.

"Don't look at me," returned Remo.

The stewardesses then sat down in the middle of the aisle—including the one still in her underwear.

"No satisfaction," she announced, "no peanuts or drinks for anyone." And she gave a clenched-fist salute.

"What's going on here?" a passenger demanded.

The underwear stewardess pointed an accusing finger at Remo and said, "That man disrobed and abandoned me."

"Shame on you!"

"I was helping her with her zipper," Remo said.

"Looks like you got carried away."

"And didn't have the balls to finish what you started," a little old lady added.

"Skirt teaser!" another woman accused.

"Remo, we will never get any peace unless you satisfy that poor waif," said Chiun.

"She's no more waif than I am Steven Seagal."

A passenger went forward to the crew compartment, and the copilot came back wearing a stiff expression.

He had to step over three stewardesses in order to reach Remo's seat.

"I understand you've been bothering the stewardesses."

"Not me," Remo said defensively.

"It is a federal offense to tamper with the crew of a commercial carrier, sir. Especially in flight."

"Okay, okay, I'll do it. Anything to get some peace and quiet." Remo stood up. "Is that all right with everybody?"

The stewardess in her underwear piped up from the floor. "Yes!" It was very a enthusiastic yes.

Reluctantly Remo escorted her to the galley, and the stewardess stood with her eyes closed and her cleavage thrust forward as if on a serving platter.

"You may begin wherever you like," she murmured.

Remo lifted her left hand by the wrist and turned it over.

"Oooh, I feel shivery already."

"Me, too," Remo said without enthusiasm.

Holding the underside of her wrist up, Remo began tapping on it methodically.

"Whatever you're doing, keep it up."

"It's called foreplay."

"I never had foreplay like this."

"And you never will again," said Remo.

"Oh, don't say that!"

Remo continued tapping, achieving a rhythm and bringing it higher and higher until the fleshy face of the stewardess began to tighten like a fine clock being wound.

This was the first in the thirty-seven steps to sexual fulfillment the Master of Sinanju had taught Remo long ago. There was a sensitive nerve in the human wrist, unsuspected by Gloria Steinem, that could be manipulated until a woman achieved a delicious kind of whole-body orgasm.

At least that was how it sounded to the expectant passengers and crew of the TWA 747 when the stewardess's screams of pleasure began rolling down the aisles and back up again like a very long wave sloshing between two stone jetties.

When Remo stepped out from the galley, he was greeted with a standing ovation.

The other stewardesses began lining up with expectant faces.

"Sorry. One orgasm per flight," said Remo, brushing past them and sliding back into his seat, next to the Master of Sinanju, who sat with his hands clapped over his delicate ears.

"It's over," Remo told him.

Chiun removed his hands. "It is disgusting what these white women will do."

"Actually she tended more to olive skinned."

"Green is not a healthy color, but for a white it is healthier than the fish-belly coloring you unfortunate people are cursed with."

Twenty minutes later they landed at Kennedy International Airport, and no one got off. Instead, the empty seats filled up.

The black-haired stewardess was carried unconscious out of the galley and poured into a jumpseat, where she smiled dreamily all through the flight over the Atlantic.

"So, where are we going?"

"Iberia."

"Oh, yeah? What's in Iberia?"

"Us. Provided the wings do not fall off."

TWO HOURS over the Atlantic, Remo had read every magazine and was bored. The stewardesses started looking at him with appealing eyes, and they kept moistening their lips with their tongues until their mouths became pale and their tongues turned assorted Maybelline colors.

So Remo pretended to sleep in his seat. And because he was bored, he willed himself to drop off.

Remo Williams dreamed.

In the dream he was standing before a cave. It was an impenetrable black maw, but as he stood before the opening, mists began rolling toward him with a hungry eagerness.

Remo tried to peer past the white swirl to see what was making mist emerge from a cave, but he saw only more vapor.

The mist was white, vaporous, ghostly. It shone with an inner luminance.

And deep within the cave, Remo heard the approaching sound of a beating human heart.

"Who's in there?" Remo asked in his dream.

The heartbeat continued its approach.

In his dream Remo's own heartbeat began to accelerate. He willed it to stabilize.

"Who's in there?" Remo repeated.

The mist suddenly regathered, intensified and filled the cave entrance like flowing cotton spiderwebs.

When it was as opaque as milk, it started to swirl outward. Remo dropped into a defensive posture, legs bent at the knees, hands hovering at his belt line, right hand a fist, left a spear point of stiffened fingers.

When the man stepped out, he seemed to be clothed in mist. Smoky tendrils clung to his lean, wiry form.

"Who the hell are you?" Remo asked.

"I am the first," he said in a hollow, dead voice.

"The first what?"

"The first," repeated the tiny man dressed in mist.

"What do you want?" Remo demanded, keeping his guard up.

"You must best me. If you can."

Remo grunted a confident laugh. "I could take you with both hands tied behind my back."

"That you must prove," said the man dressed in mist. Only then did Remo get a good look at his face.

It was Asian. The man had no eyes. The loose skin of his eyelids were sunken hollows and stitched shut with catgut. He advanced purposefully.

Remo watched his movements, and the phrase that came to his mind was *cream puff*.

The eyeless man walked right into a nerve punch that compressed his entire rib cage, exploded the air from his lungs and laid him flat on his back.

As the mist from the cave strove forward to wash over him, the blind Asian intoned, "I was only the first."

"Good for you," said Remo, eyes snapping open.

"WHAT IS GOOD FOR ME?" asked Chiun, turning in his seat.

The dull whine of jet engines filled Remo's ears. "Nothing. I was dreaming."

"Quickly!" Chiun clutched Remo's arm. "What did the hussy say this time?"

"Let go of me. She didn't say anything. I didn't dream of her. Not that last time was a dream."

"You dreamed?"

"Yes."

"Sitting here next to me with a full six hours of sleep from last night and another ten minutes on top of that, you dreamed?"

"Yes, I dreamed. Break my saber in two and tear off my chevrons, I dreamed."

Chiun regarded his pupil with narrowing eyes. "Of what did you dream, Remo?" he asked, thin voiced.

"Nothing."

"Speak!"

"A cave. I dreamed of a cave."

"You had another vision?"

"I don't think it was the same cave. Anyway, I didn't go in to find out."

"Good. If you dream of that cave again, do not enter it. If you disobey me, then do not tell me what you saw in that cave, for I do not want to know. Unless it is very important, of course."

"Something came out of the cave."

"What?"

"A guy."

"Guy? What kind of guy? Speak his name."

"He didn't give one. He challenged me to a fight for no reason."

"And what happened?"

Remo shrugged unconcernedly. "What do you think? I laid him flat with one shot."

"Ah," said Chiun. "Good. You killed him."

"Nah. I just laid him out."

"Why did you say 'Good for you' in your sleep?"

"He said he was only the first."

Chiun's eyes suddenly thinned to unreadable slits.

"What did this man look like, my son?"

"He was Asian. Looked like someone gouged his eyes out and stitched the lids shut."

Chiun nodded to himself. "Was this man Korean?"

Remo shook his head. "Maybe. But he was covered in mist."

"Mist?"

"Yeah, mist. There was mist coming from the cave. It clung to him. That was the weird part. He was dressed in white mist. Wonder what that means."

"Why should it mean anything?" snapped Chiun.

"I read an article about dreams a few months back," Remo said. "Scientists say they're the unconscious mind's way of processing the day's events, mixing them with fantasy and crazy stuff so the brain can work through its fears and concerns."

"Pah. White superstitions."

"You should talk. You think I'm the reincarnation of Shiva the Destroyer."

"You are."

"And of an old Sinanju Master named Lu."

"You are Lu, too."

"I'm Remo Williams and I haven't had a real dream about Sinanju that I can remember since the Dream of Death. That's gotta be over ten years ago."

"You are who you are. Just because you do not understand who you are does not mean you are not what you are."

"I can understand the cave. It's my brain working through the vision. But who was the eyeless guy and why was he wearing mist instead of clothing?"

"Perhaps he was a poor vagabond in search of a home."

"I wish I understood dreams."

"I wish I understood whites," said Chiun, dismissing the subject with a careless wave of his clicking fingernails.

But when Remo glanced over at him a few minutes later, the Master of Sinanju's wrinkled visage was tense with a dark foreboding.

5

When Remo deplaned, the TWA stewardesses were all lined up at the exit door, tears in their eyes.

They waved him goodbye, patting him on the back, wishing him a happy stay in Madrid, and felt his strong lean biceps wistfully.

One gave him an affectionate pat on the backside, and when he and Chiun reached the terminal, Remo sensed he was being followed.

"Little Father, are those stewardesses following us?"

"No," said Chiun.

"Good."

"They are following *you*."

"Rats."

Outside the terminal a fight started over who would share a cab with Remo.

"No one's sharing a cab with me," said Remo, pulling spitting and clawing stewardesses off one another and making two piles.

Instantly the stewardesses pulled nail files and pen knives and held them to their pulsing throats.

"I'd rather die than not share a cab with you," one sobbed.

"Me, too."

Remo threw up his hands. "Okay. Okay. I surrender. Everybody into the cab."

There was a scramble to enter the cab. Remo obligingly held the doors open for the eager stewardesses. When the back seat filled up, he held open the front passenger's door. The driver was pushed out the other side by the crush of perfumed, uniformed bodies.

A stewardess reached out and clapped his cap over her head, rolling up the driver's-side window to prevent him from recovering it.

"Everybody comfy?" asked Remo.

"Yes! Oh, yes. Yes, yes, yes, yes."

"Good," said Remo, going from door to door and welding them shut with the high-speed friction of his rubbing palms.

He left the trapped stewardesses fighting the windows open so they could squeeze out.

"What the hell's going on?" Remo complained to the Master of Sinanju as they walked away. "I always have problems with loose stewardesses, but never this bad."

"You are obviously baiting them with your manly allures."

"That's another thing. What about my rights as a man? That first stewardess all but tried to rape me, but I had to satisfy *her*. If it was the other way around, I'd have been the one up on charges."

"Aggressor."

"Get off it."

When the next cab in line pulled up, Chiun entered and told the driver in perfect Spanish, "Pompelo."

"*¿Que?*" said the driver.

"Pompelo," Chiun repeated. And when the driver continued looking blank, he added, "San Fermin."

"Ah," said the driver. He hit the gas just as Remo's foot left the pavement. Remo got the door shut in time to see the airport Exit sign flash by.

"Where are we going?" he asked Chiun.

"To a pleasant little town below the Pyrenees."

"What's it called?"

"It was founded by one of Pompey's sons. The cross-eyed one, if I recall the scrolls of my ancestors correctly."

"Do you recall a name?"

"Pompelo."

"Never heard of it. I've heard of Pamplona, but not Pompelo."

Chiun made a face. "These modern Iberians cannot even pronounce the names of their better towns. Pah."

The cab took them out of Madrid at high speed and through lush, climbing Spanish countryside. The early-July air was brisk and invigorating. There were many white churches along the way.

On the way, Remo saw a road sign that read Pamplona—300 km.

"That's two hundred miles."

"If we are going to Pamplona. We are not. We are going to Pompelo," said Chiun.

They drove for nearly four hours through hills and valleys with the Pyrenees always looming off to the east. When the mountains petered out into a flat plain, they reached their destination.

It was a plain-looking city dominated by industrial smokestacks and the brick of factory buildings.

Remo said, "The sign says Pamplona."

"It is really Pompelo."

As they entered town, it became clear a festival of some sort was in progress. The streets were clogged by cars, tourists from all nations staggered about in various stages of inebriation. Soon traveling by car became more trouble than it was worth.

In perfect Spanish, Chiun paid off the driver and they got out in a broad plaza that reeked of history.

"What's going on?" asked Remo as two men stumbled by wearing red sashes and long ropes of garlic hung around their necks.

"Some pagan festival," sniffed Chiun as a man in an ordinary suit coat and an exaggerated papier-mâché head the size of a suitcase staggered by.

"I'm not in the mood for festivities."

"It is a Christian celebration, dedicated to a Moorish saint called San Fermin."

"I didn't know there were Moorish saints."

"The Moors once ruled this land after the Christian upstarts had pulled it down from is lofty Roman greatness. It was inevitable that in a moment of weakness one would succumb to carpenter worship. Perhaps while we are here, you would like to light a candle to San Fermin."

"No, thanks."

"Good," said Chiun, leading Remo to a street stall where a vendor sold an assortment of red cotton sashes and scarves.

After bickering with the merchant, the Master of Sinanju purchased one of each item and offered them to Remo with a polite dip of a bow and an air of quiet ceremony.

"Don these."

Remo examined the items critically. "What are they?"

"What do they look like?"

"A red sash and matching scarf."

"Then you should know which to wrap around your neck and which goes about your flabby middle without instruction from me."

"My middle is not flabby," said Remo, snatching the limp swatches of red cotton from Chiun's fingers.

"You have gained over an ounce in the last five years. I suspect you of sneaking sweets when my back is turned."

"Your back is never turned," said Remo, tying the sash around his waist so the broad end hung over his right front pocket. The red scarf went around his neck with a quick tie.

"Now what?" he asked.

Chiun beckoned with a crooked yellow finger. "Follow."

At what appeared from the outside to be a stadium, Chiun bought them tickets and they took front-row seats among a growing crowd of drunken revelers. Many were passed out in their seats.

"We going to see a bullfight?"

"*You* will not," said Chiun.

"Huh?"

And the Master of Sinanju leaped without warning into the dirt-floored ring.

"What are you doing?" demanded Remo, jumping down to join him.

He looked around warily. There was no sign of any bulls or horses or matadors. In fact, the more he looked around, the more Remo was reminded of a rodeo ring. At one end a wooden corral gate lay agape. It led out of the ring and up a narrow chute obviously meant for the bulls.

The Master of Sinanju ignored his pupil and instead went padding about the ring, his head bowed, his eyes intent on the ground upon which he walked.

"What are you looking for?" asked Remo.

"Shush," said Chiun, continuing his perambulations.

When he reached a certain spot, Chiun indicated it with a pointing fingernail. "Dig."

"For what?"

"Dig, and the what will reveal itself."

Shrugging, Remo dropped to one knee and began scratching dirt away from the spot where the Master of Sinanju pointed so sternly.

From the stands they were watched. But not challenged.

Remo used his hands to spank away the loose dirt that had been pounded dry by the tread of men and the hooves of beasts. When he reached the darker, moister subsoil, he used the tips of his fingers to excavate. A pile formed, pale at the base but darker as it grew.

When there was a tiny mountain, Remo's fingernails scratched metal.

"Found something," he said, lifting a dirt-caked disk to the hot Spanish sun.

"Clean it," commanded Chiun.

Rising, Remo gave the disk a flick as if flipping a coin. The disk spun upward, shedding the accumulation of grit through centrifugal force. Then it landed in his open palm. It was a thin bit of hammered metal with the profile of a man on one side. An inscription ran around the rim.

"Looks like an old Roman coin."

"A denarius," corrected Chiun. "Did the vestal virgins who reared you teach you Latin?"

Remo looked at the inscription. It read J. CAES. AUG. PONT. MAX. P. P.

"Yeah. It says, 'Julius Caesar Augustus Pontifex Maximus.' I don't know what the 'P. P.' part stands for."

"*Pater Patriae*. Father of his Country."

"Just like Washington," grunted Remo.

"Once the Roman Empire extended to the far corners of the earth. Now all that is left are ruins, countless worthless coins in the dirt and idle eaters of pasta and makers of pizza."

"Meaning?"

"You must find the meaning for yourself. For it is time for you to run."

"Run where? I thought we came to see a bullfight."

Chiun examined Remo critically. "Let me straighten your scarf, for it is on wrong."

"It's fine," said Remo, nevertheless letting the Master of Sinanju adjust his scarf.

When it was retightened, it covered his eyes completely.

"Now I can't see," Remo complained.

"Can you hear?"

"Of course I can hear."

Then a dull whoosh like a rocket going up came from a mile or so away.

"You must run toward that sound," said Chiun.

"Why?"

"You will know when you get there. Let me point you in the proper direction." Remo felt himself being spun in place. "Do you remember the open gate?"

"Yeah."

"Run through it. Follow the cobbled path. Do not stop. Do not allow any obstacle to dissuade you from your path. There will be barriers on either side to keep you on the correct path."

Chiun gave Remo a quick shove and said, "Now go!"

Remo ran. His memory guided him to the open gate at the far end of the ring, and when the dirt beneath his feet became wood and then cobblestones the size of loaves of bread, he switched from a flat-footed run to a toe sprint that propelled him lightly from cobble to cobble.

His other senses guided him along. He heard cheers. They swelled. A few shouted Spanish at him, he didn't understand.

"¡Estúpido! ¿No te das cuenta de que te estas equivocado?"

The cobbled pathway twisted and turned as Remo ran through a world of smells. There was bread and coffee and liquor and the sweat of human beings worked up in a frenzy of excitement.

Far ahead he heard the sound of another rocket. Then a rumble. It grew nearer. The cobbles, connected to one another by mortar, communicated an impending vibration that grew and grew the farther Remo ran.

Something was coming his way. But Remo couldn't stop to worry about it now. He had a goal. He didn't know what it was all about, but the Master of Sinanju had given it to him. And his training wouldn't let him turn away until he reached it.

EVERY YEAR Don Angel Murillo looked forward to the Festival of San Fermin.

And every year he was glad when it was over. The foreigners with their drinking and their drugs and their lack of appreciation for the glorious art of bullfighting were difficult to stomach.

But he took solace in the running of the bulls. Always in the running of the bulls.

It was Don Angel's responsibility to oversee the running of the bulls so foolish men, both Spanish and otherwise, did not ruin the glorious event.

The rules were firm. From the moment the first rocket was fired from the town hall to set the runners on their way to the firing of the second rocket, announcing that the bulls had been released from their corrals at the bottom of Calle Santo Domingol, no man intending to stay ahead of the bulls could call attention to himself or incite the brave bulls in any way that brought harm to others.

If a man stumbled before the rushing hooves, that was his privilege. If the horns caught him and hooked him upward, well, that was what the horns of the bull naturally did. Everyone knew that. Even drunken Princeton students.

It was strictly forbidden for a runner to do anything to cause a bull to deviate from the barricade-lined nine-minute run to the bullring. Or injure an unsuspecting runner or bystanders.

Don Angel Murillo was stationed at the barricade along Dona Blanca de Navarra to see that none of these things happened.

When the first rocket was fired, the runners were off and the first cheers went up. When the second rocket arced smokily upward in the bright blue sky, the rattling drum of hooves made the very ground vibrate and the souls of men and woman thrill with anticipation.

Don Angel Murillo was looking up toward the town hall in heart-pounding anticipation of the first red-sashed runners in white pants when a man in gray chinos wearing the scarf of San Fermin, the patron saint of Pamplona, and the red sash of a runner came flying up the course.

He was going in the wrong direction. This was not only very definitely against the rules but very strange indeed.

More strange undoubtedly was he fact that he wore the scarf over his face, obscuring his vision.

"*¡Estúpido!*" Don Angel called in Spanish. "Do you not know you are running the wrong way?"

Then around the corner came the first stumbling wave of men, and behind them the snorting black bulls of Pamplona.

A WALL OF MOVING FLESH jumped around the corner. Remo heard their feet and hooves mingle and blend into a mass of sound as great as the mass of flesh and bone he faced.

The panting of men mixed with the snorting of bulls. Remo recognized that the brutes were bulls. This was Pamplona, made famous by Ernest Hemingway for the running of the bulls, despite whatever name the Master of Sinanju called it.

Calculating the closing distance, Remo flashed ahead, knowing he had a better chance of surviving if he shortened the ordeal's duration.

Men were stumbling and pressing themselves up against the barricades as the bulls pounded down the straightaway.

Remo fixed on the heartbeat of one man who ran ahead of the pack and made for him.

The man tried to swerve from the unexpected obstacle, but Remo was too fast for him. Leaping off the cobbles, Remo used his shoulder for a catapult. Remo launched himself over the heads of the other runners and toward the mass of bulls.

One foot touched an undulating back, rebounded, and the other jumped off the bullish rump.

After that, his feet took him from bull to bull, so tightly clumped there was almost no space between them. They were running in a bunch. No stragglers. No mavericks. And though they were moving fast, especially if one was trying to keep one step ahead of them, to Remo's highly trained reflexes they might as well have been grazing.

His toes bounced him from back to back with such grace the spectators lining the barricaded runway exploded into spontaneous applause. And then Remo alighted back on the cobbles and was racing toward the place where he had fixed the sounds of the rockets.

When he reached it, he sensed a broad plaza and a rowdy crowd who shouted Spanish compliments.

"¡Bravo! ¡Bravo!"

"¡Magnífico!"

"¡Viva San Fermín!"

"¡Tienes duende! ¡Se siente tu duende!"

Remo reached up to remove his scarf when a third rocket pistol banged back the way he had come.

"What the heck does that mean?" Remo muttered, wondering if he was supposed to run back the way he had come or not.

"It means," squeaked the Master of Sinanju, suddenly at his elbow, "that you have braved the first *athloi*."

Remo snatched off his scarf.

Chiun stood looking up at him, his face unreadable.

"Athloi?"

"Yes."

"Is that a Korean word?"

"No."

Remo looked back down the road he had come. "That was the running of the bulls I just screwed up, wasn't it?"

"Yes."

"You're supposed to run ahead of the bulls, not into them."

"Any fool can be trampled. A Master of Sinanju requires a greater test of his grace."

"I think my intelligence was just tested, not my grace."

"And you may be correct, for you lack all graces," spat Chiun.

"What are they saying about me?" Remo asked as the crowd surged drunkenly toward them.

"That you have *duende*."

"What's that mean?"

"Some say it means grace."

Remo grinned. "I like the Spanish. They recognize quality when they see it."

Chiun didn't return the grin. Instead, he turned away with a swirl of kimono skirts. "Come. We are through here."

"We just got here."

"And now we are leaving."

"But we just got here."

"Pah. I am glad too that my ancestors did not survive to see the town that Pompey's son founded become a den of besotted Christianity."

And they melted into the alleys and byways around the great square, often leaping over the sprawled figures of drunken tourists.

"Where to next?" wondered Remo.

"Hellas."

"What did you say?"

"I said Hellas."

"That's good," said Remo. "For a minute I thought you said we were going to Hell."

"We are not yet going to Hell," said the Master of Sinanju. "For you, however, there may be no difference."

6

Remo got off the Olympic Airways plane in Athens, Greece, wearing a T-shirt that read I Ran With The Bulls Of Pamplona, a red baseball cap that sported bull's horns and a fan club consisting of an assortment of Greek stewardesses—along with one cow-eyed steward who ardently tried to interest Remo in an alternative life-style.

Remo ducked into the nearest men's room, which took care of the stewardesses, and locked the lovestruck steward in a toilet stall.

When he emerged again, the stewardesses were singing his praises in a kind of Greek chorus.

"You are so manly," one cooed.

"For an American," another amended.

"Do you like Greek women?" asked a third.

"Greek women," Remo said, "should be neither seen nor heard."

The collection of Greek stewardesses looked at one another with baffled black-olive eyes.

"I like women who are hard to get," Remo clarified.

"Hard to—"

"Very hard to get," said Remo.

"If we are hard to get, will you seek us out?"

"Only if you're completely out of my sight," promised Remo.

The stewardesses made themselves scarce, and Remo and Chiun sought a cab.

"You are learning," said Chiun as the cab took them away.

"Not what I want to learn. Why are we in Athens?"

"You have your Roman coin?"

"Yep."

"We must find you a Greek coin."

"Why would I want a Greek coin?"

"Because you failed to discern the meaning of the Roman coin."

Remo shrugged and watched the city go past. The driver drove like a maniac. Remo wondered what it was about European capitals that made the taxi drivers drive as if suicidal.

"Where to, guys?" the driver asked, turning his head. His breath filled the back seat with a commingled grape-leaf, onion, olives, lamb and feta-cheese odor.

"Piriaévs," said Chiun.

The driver seemed to know where that was and redoubled his speed, banging around narrow corners like a caroming billiard ball.

He took them to the waterfront smelling of creosote and tar, where small, flat octopuses hung drying on lines like wash. There the Master of Sinanju engaged a seamfaced Greek trawler captain in fluent Greek. Some gold changed hands, and Remo was waved aboard.

"Where are we going this time?" Remo asked once on board.

"*You* are going sponge diving."

"What are *you* going to be doing?"

"Hoping you do not take all day because we have to be in Kriti by nightfall."

The trawler was ancient and barnacle encrusted. It muttered out into the brilliant blue Aegean and its many sun-drenched islands.

When they reached an island that stood out from all the others by its crusty gray-and-white streaked homeliness, the boat stopped and dropped anchor.

Chiun faced Remo, saying, "There are sponges below us. You must find the two largest and bring them back."

"Why?"

"Because your Master has told you to do this."

Remo hesitated. Then, stepping out of his shoes, he somersaulted from a standing position from the aft deck and into the water. He went in like a dolphin, with hardly a splash.

The Greek sea captain happened to be in midblink when Remo left the deck, so to his slow brain and eyes, it was as if Remo had abruptly dwindled into his shoes. He knelt to examine the shoes, found them empty but still warm with the vitality of the man who had stood in them just a moment before. The captain crossed himself fervently.

THE AEGEAN WAS AS BLUE below as it had been above. Remo arrowed through the crystalline water and found the bottom.

A ghost-gray octopus went flowing past, tentacles spread like a flower, two touching the bottom to guide itself along.

It saw Remo with its sleepy, human-looking eyes, went from gray to a livid green in a glimmering and pulled itself into the safety of a broken ceramic pot, so that one near-human eye peered out warily.

Remo swam on. Fish he did not recognize swam and darted by.

The sea bottom was silty, and when he touched it, sediment curled up in brownish obscuring clouds.

Remo found a bed of sponges and began picking through them. They were of all sizes and shapes but the largest ones were easily the size of both his hands joined together. He found one he liked and spent a casual five minutes looking for its mate.

Meanwhile, carbon-dioxide bubbles dribbled from one corner of his grim mouth at a rate of one every quarter minute. The lack of oxygen bothered Remo not at all. His training had expanded his lung capacity so that once he charged them, he was good for over an hour underwater. More if he didn't exert himself. Since there was no rush and he knew Chiun would be critical of his choices if he wasn't careful, Remo took his time finding two matching sponges.

"THESE ARE THE BEST you could find?" the Master of Sinanju demanded when Remo's head popped up alee of the fishing boat, hands held high, the sponges upraised for his inspection.

"You saw how long I was down there."

"You were playing."

"I scoured the bottom for the best sponges," Remo insisted. "These are them."

Chiun turned to the boat captain and gave him a withering stare. "You and your greedy kind have taken all the best."

The boat captain shrugged. He was still trying to figure out how Remo had gotten into the water in the first place.

Chiun turned back to Remo. "Take your sorry prizes to that isle and do what has to be done."

"What's that?"

"You will know what the moment you step onto its shore."

Remo turned. The isle was a hump not bigger than a city parking lot. Sea gulls and other ocean birds circled it. Some alighted, paused and flew off again.

They made no attempt to peck or claw its surface for food scraps. Not surprising, Remo saw. There wasn't a shred of vegetation on the thing.

Remo saw why when he reached the place. The water at the edge was gray and scummy, the smell rank.

"Wanna throw me my shoes? I think I'm going to need them."

The shoes plopped obligingly into the water, only to sink from sight.

"Damn," said Remo, diving after them.

Putting them on underwater, he surfaced and recovered the sponges, which bobbed in the grayish water.

Remo jumped straight out of the water and onto the crusty shore. His feet splashed up grayish-white goo.

"What do they call this place?" Remo called back.

"In Greek you would not understand the words. In English it is called Guano Isle."

"Why aren't I surprised?"

"If you are not surprised, why do you dally?"

"Because I have a sinking feeling what these sponges are for now."

"What are sponges for?"

"Not for eating."

"Good. If not for eating, what then is their purpose?"

"Cleaning," Remo said without enthusiasm.

"You may begin now. You have until sundown."

Remo started at one end of the isle, standing in water so he wouldn't have to kneel. Seabirds eyed him with hostile intent. Occasionally one dropped a present where he stood.

Soon Remo was covered in malodorous stuff. He kept scouring.

"This is starting to feel like the twelve freaking labors of Hercules," Remo complained.

And from the sponge trawler the Master of Sinanju burst into brief but polite applause.

"Why are you applauding?"

"Because you are half through with your noble chore."

"What's noble about being hip deep in bird shit?"

"The knowledge that you are conveniencing the seabirds of the next century who will have a clean nest to feather."

"Bulldooky," Remo grumbled.

"No. Gull guano."

When Remo was finally finished, it was late. The sun was going down, and the lights of Athens were coming on. High on the hill called the Acropolis, the many-columned Parthenon burst into radiance like an ivory shrine.

Remo raised his tattered sponges to the night sky. "Hallelujah. I'm done!"

A sea gull dropped a spatter of gray and white just in front of one ruined shoe.

Keeping his face triumphant, Remo eased one foot over the offending blot.

"I saw that," said Chiun.

Reluctantly Remo dropped to one knee and cleaned up the spot. He flung the sponge at the offending bird, and it dropped into the water, flustered and chastised.

As he climbed off the isle, other seabirds came along.

Remo tried shoo them away. They shooed. But they also came back.

"You cannot leave as long as one spot remains," Chiun called out.

"The minute I turn my back, there's going to be more than one spot."

"This is your *athloi*."

"I thought cleaning the isle was my *athloi!*"

"No. You had to scour Guano Isle in order for the *athloi* to commence."

"That wasn't the freaking *athloi?* This is the freaking *athloi?*"

"Yes," intoned Chiun. "This is the freaking *athloi*."

"Damn."

Remo looked up. The white sea gulls were hanging in the wind, just like sea gulls the world over.

"We could be here all night," he warned Chiun.

"You do not have all night. There is still the coin to find."

Remo made his voice resolute. "I say we pack it in and find that all-important coin."

"You cannot leave until you have completed the *athloi*."

"Can't leave tonight? Or can't leave ever?"

"Ever. That is the rule."

"Who made up this rule?"

"The Great Wang."

"He wouldn't do that to me."

"Take it up with him."

"He's been dead for three thousand years."

"Dawdler," spat Chiun.

Grumbling, Remo looked around the isle. It appeared to be made of rock and maybe some old coral. It was hard to say. A lot of it was porous. That might have been the nature of coral or the corrosive effect of centuries of gauno action.

The porous stuff broke off under his weight, so Remo willed his mass to adjust. Then he had a thought.

Going to one end of the isle, he stamped hard. This had two results. It spooked the hovering sea gulls and it broke off a chunk of isle, which dropped into the now-very-white water.

Grinning, Remo repeated his action after moving back a pace. Another section of isle dropped into the water to sink from sight.

"What are you doing?" the Master of Sinanju shrieked as the west end of the island began to crumble into the Aegean.

"Completing my freaking *athloi*," Remo retorted.

"What about future Masters?"

"I'm doing them a favor. They'll thank me."

"This is against the rules, as well."

"When the Great Wang tells me so, I'll stop," said Remo, redoubling his efforts.

"You are willful and disobedient!" Chiun accused.

"Maybe. But I'm also getting off this stupid rock."

By midnight the isle had been reduced to the size of a trash-can lid, and Remo realized that he was going to drop himself into the befouled water sooner or later. So he took a deep breath, jumped up as high as he could and brought both feet stamping down on the last pitiful remainder of the isle.

It pulverized and dropped Remo into the water.

Eyes closed, he swam toward the bobbing boat.

When Remo surfaced, Chiun glared down at him angrily.

"You are filthy."

"But triumphant."

"You have desecrated a shrine of Sinanju."

"Let's just get out of here. I'm exhausted."

Chiun shook his aged head. "You cannot climb aboard as you are. You must swim." And before Remo could protest, Chiun directed the trawler captain to weigh anchor.

The chain rattled up, and the screws began churning gray-white water. The trawler bubbled away.

Remo followed at a brisk pace, swearing all the way.

After a while he noticed they weren't swimming north toward the Acropolis, but farther south into the island-dotted Aegean Sea.

"I don't like where this is going," Remo grumbled to himself.

And back from the muttering trawler came the Master of Sinanju's squeak, "How can you say that when you do not know where you are going?"

"Because I know you."

"You wish."

And Remo wondered what the Master of Sinanju meant by that.

7

Four hours later the Greek sponge trawler put down anchor within sight of a sprawling island.

"Oh, no," said Remo, treading water with tired arms. "I'm not cleaning that! No way."

"This is not your *athloi*," returned the Master of Sinanju. "Come, but do not profane this worthy vessel's deck with your soiled tread."

Chiun padded toward the bow and Remo swam around the boat, keeping pace with him.

At the bow the Master of Sinanju pointed toward the dark and rocky shoreline and said, "There is a sea cave in that inlet."

"I'm not going into any cave. And you know why."

"I am not in this cave, so do not fear to venture within."

"What am I supposed to do?"

"Enter this cave," said Chiun, "and find your way to the other end." He pointed down the coast, to the south. "I will await you at its exit."

"Sounds easy," Remo said reluctantly.

"Therefore, it cannot be easy."

"What's the name of this island anyway?"

"That will become obvious even to you once you enter the cave that awaits you."

Remo struck out for the cave. As he approached, the sea lapping against the shore made weird sobbing sounds, like an old woman crying.

The sea floor came up to scrape Remo's questing hands and bare feet. It felt like coral, but when Remo reached shore, he saw it was a gray-black volcanic rock.

He walked up to the cave mouth and listened. All he heard was the incessant sobbing, and when he compressed his eyelids to squeeze out all but necessary moonlight, the black cave mouth remained black and foreboding.

"Here goes," Remo said, entering the cave.

Wide at the mouth, the cave became more like a tunnel the deeper Remo passed into it. The feel of porous volcanic rock against his bare soles was unpleasant, but as his tough soles became accustomed to it, he soon put it out of his mind.

The ceiling sloped downward. Remo was forced to bend his head to keep walking.

Thirty feet in, the tunnel branched off in two directions. Remo paused and tried to figure out the right way to go. After a moment he realized that one branch went south toward where the cave exit was supposed to be.

Then again, since this whole test was Chiun's idea, the most logical choice was probably the wrong one.

Remo took the northern tunnel, suppressing a grin of confidence.

It evaporated when he came to a blank wall before a quiet pool. In the darkness his feet discovered the pool. There was no sign of any secret walls or other exits.

Grumbling, Remo backtracked and followed the southern branch.

After about the same distance, it too stopped at a blank wall. Only this time there was no pool.

"Don't tell me I blew it," said Remo.

He felt the walls for levers or catches. Finding none, he padded back to the north tunnel.

When he reached the pool, he knelt before it and touched the water with his fingertips. It was cool to the touch. He brought the moistened tip of one finger to his nose and sniffed.

No scent of poison or predators.

Sighing, Remo slipped into the pool feet first, knowing if there was something lurking in the pool he stood a better chance of survival if it bit off a foot and not his head.

The pool swallowed him. There was no light, of course—any more than there had been in the tunnel—but Remo's trained senses enabled him to feel his way down.

The pool led to a watery shaft, like a well. But it took a sudden horizontal jog and became an underground river.

Remo hesitated. He hadn't expected this. There was no way to tell if the river ran very far or not. Did he have enough oxygen in his lungs or not?

After a moment Remo decided to chance it. He swam south, the logical direction, keeping his movements to a minimum to conserve air and energy. There was a current, so he surrendered to it, knowing it would do most of the work for him. This helped conserve oxygen, too.

Remo knew when the tunnel ran out because he bumped his head. There was almost no warning. He couldn't see. There wasn't even any ambient light down here for his eyes to capture and magnify. The current had begun to slow. Remo had run out of tunnel.

Recoiling from the unexpected obstacle, Remo got reoriented and tried feeling for a way out. He found no shaft leading up. Nor one down, either.

There was a hole about the size of his hand in the end of the underground tunnel. The water was flowing on through that. But it was too small for a man, and when Remo attacked it with his fingers, he excavated a distance of about a foot, only to find the tunnel remained narrow as far as he could feel.

Treading water, he let the bubbles dribble from his mouth as he considered his next move. He might have enough oxygen to keep digging. Then again, maybe this wasn't the correct way.

In the end the low glow of fear deep in the pit of his stomach forced Remo to retrace his swim. He swam hard, against the current, using up precious air faster than he planned.

At the juncture below the shaft, he was forced to stop and think ahead. Go up and recharge his air or swim the other way?

He decided to go for the air.

When his head popped up at the top of the pool, he immediately sensed a presence.

Remo went very very still and let the sounds of the presence come to him.

The predominant sound was breathing—heavy, moist and brutish. He tried to resolve the darkness in the area where the thing hovered. It was impossible. There was nothing to work with.

So Remo closed his eyes. His energies redirected themselves toward his remaining senses.

The overall impression was of an upright being—a biped. But its heart action and working of the lungs was greater than that of a man. And the breathing was that of a brute.

The creature—whatever it was—snorted once, and Remo reacted as he was trained to. He went for the sound.

The thing, amazingly, retreated faster than Remo's thrust.

Remo came out of the water and moved in on it. Where the carotid artery pulsed more loudly than any other point in the circulatory system except the heart, Remo attacked. He employed a simple but effective blow. A lateral slice with the side of his hand.

The blow, designed to sever the head so swiftly the target never knew what hit him, was clean. So clean, Remo thought as the body fell with a surprisingly soft thud, that he hardly felt the strong muscles and cables of the neck give before it.

The head fell into his hands, and instinctively Remo snared it.

He discovered he had grabbed it by a thick, short horn and, startled, dropped the head. In his mind's eye, he visualized a bull's head.

But the thing he had killed was a biped.

He decided to leave the corpse alone.

Filling his lungs to full capacity, Remo returned to the pool and swam north against the current this time.

It was a long swim and he began to tire. His oxygen held out, but he had been swimming half the night. While he had reserves of strength to draw upon yet, the first tendrils of fatigue had insinuated themselves into his nerves and muscles. He sensed lactic acid accumulating in his muscles and willed his body to ignore the approaching fatigue.

More than a mile along, the tunnel began to curve. Remo used his hands to guide him, walking along the bottom of the tunnel the way he had seen the Aegean octopus do it earlier in the day.

The tunnel twisted in several directions, and only the magnetic crystals in Remo's brain—crystals present in most higher animals including man—enabled him to keep track of his polar orientations.

Remo found himself swimming in the same direction as when he had started along this branch of the cave when a fragment of loose, current-borne volcanic rock bounced off his shoulder.

Instantly all his senses went to full alert. Another tumbled past. And while he was wondering what could have disturbed solid rock without disturbing the water or setting off warning vibrations, Remo swam smack into a blank wall.

Damn! he thought, panic raising. He had maybe five minutes of good air left. Quickly he began feeling the rock.

Then there was a small hole, the size of a quarter in the end of the tunnel. Otherwise, it was a dead end.

A dead end and a fifteen-minute swim back to the pool where life-giving oxygen waited.

Remo thought fast. Maybe there was a branch trail. As soon as the thought came, he realized eddies in the current would have indicated a side tunnel. There was no side tunnel. He had struck another dead end. A complete dead end.

Two dead ends, and the Master of Sinanju had told him to follow the cave to its southern exit.

I must have missed it, Remo thought angrily. Smart-ass that I am, I must have gone right past it. But where and when?

With no hope of swimming back in time, his brain wrestled with the problem. *What could I have missed? How could I have missed it? It's impossible.*

Unless Chiun faked me out.

Three minutes of oxygen burning in his lungs, Remo began to consider the possibility that the Master of Sianju had lied to him.

Can't be. He wouldn't do that. He said to meet at the exit. There has to be an exit. Remo visualized the Master of Sinanju pointing southward. And he was facing north. The other tunnel had pointed south.

Then a thought struck him. It came to him with a great cold clarity.

I'm on Crete. That thing with a bull's head was the Minotaur. I'm on Crete. This is the labyrinth. I'm on Crete.

And in his mind, the voice of Sister Mary Margaret came to him, telling him how Theseus used his wiles to find his way out of the minotaur's labyrinth.

Damn. I should have realized this was Crete. But even a thread won't save me now. Goodbye, Little Father. I hope wherever I'm going I'll meet my mother.

And in his mind's ear he heard the crisp, no-nonsense voice of Sister Mary Margaret repeat the legend of Theseus: *With only simple thread, Theseus retraced his way out of the labyrinth of the Minotaur and found salvation.*

That's it! That's what I missed.

Furiously Remo attacked the quarter-sized hole at the end of the tunnel. Volcanic rock turned to powder under the hydraulic force of his compressing fingers. The water became gritty to the touch.

When Remo broke through, he shot ahead like an arrow, against the current. He was down to ninety seconds of usable air. If he was wrong, it would all be over soon. He would lose control, thrashing and flailing like an insect as his body surrendered to the inimical watery environment it was never meant to plumb.

One minute of oxygen remained. He began counting the seconds as he reached out to use the jagged roof to pull him along. A few more yards, he thought. If I'm right, it's just a few more yards.

He was out of oxygen when his questing fingers lost all purchase.

He shot upward and felt the blood rush from his head and brain. Everything started to go dark.

He was wondering how it could get any darker since he was already in impenetrable darkness when he completely lost consciousness.

WHEN REMO AWOKE he found himself floating. And breathing.

For a moment he wondered if he could be dead. But the coldness of the water and the sweet-stale tang of cave air told him otherwise. He drew in a full double lungful and charged every lobe of both lungs.

"I'm alive," he whispered.

Hoisting himself out of the pool, Remo used his bare feet to feel for the body of the fallen Minotaur. It was gone. Only the coarse-haired head remained.

Remo picked it up and tucked it under one arm. It wasn't much of a trophy, but it was better than facing the Master of Sinanju empty-handed and wearing complete failure on his face.

When Remo emerged from the sea cave, the Greek fishing trawler still lay at anchor. And the Master of Sinanju stood stiff-faced at the entrance, his hands tucked into his scarlet kimono sleeves.

"I thought you said you'd meet me at the exit," Remo said.

"And I have kept my word," said Chiun.

"You pointed south when you said that," Remo said hotly.

"And if I had scratched my nose instead, would you have emerged from one of my nostrils?"

"That's not funny. I came this close to drowning."

"Master Nonja nearly drowned too. But he did not and you did not and that is that."

"This is Crete, isn't it?"

Chiun looked pleased. "Kriti." He gestured to the object tucked under Remo's arm. "And I see you have bested the Minotaur."

Remo lifted the bull's head to the moonlight. For the first time he got a clear look at it. The head was definitely bullish. It was also hollow and made of hardwood covered in scratchy black fur. Its nostrils were twin bovine flares, and the horns were tipped with hammered silver. The eyes were two polished gems that reflected the moonlight with a greenish-red smoldering.

"It's only a stupid helmet."

"Do not insult the proud skull of the mighty Minotaur," said Chiun, snatching it from his pupil's fingers.

The Master of Sinanju carried it down the shore and stepped on a black horn of volcanic outcropping. A shelf cracked open, revealing a boxlike cavity into which he deposited the Minotaur head.

When Chiun took his foot off the horn, the shelf dropped back into place, showing no seam.

Remo pointed an accusing finger at him and exploded, "You were the Minotaur! You made your heart and lung action sound different, didn't you?"

"I admit nothing of the kind."

Chiun padded past him toward the waiting trawler. Remo followed angrily.

"That's why there was no body when I came back. You'd taken off."

"Next you will tell me that I was also the Santa Claus of your youth."

"Santa didn't visit the orphanage much," Remo said glumly. "You old fake."

"Rest assured that the Minotaur will live again if there are any Masters of Sinanju after you or I."

Remo went on. "The water tunnel was a circle. If I broke through from either direction, it would lead me back to the pool and the Minotaur."

"Gi the Lesser realized this without having to break the labyrinth. Now you have ruined it for future Masters."

"Sue me."

They entered the water and got on the boat. Chiun didn't object, but the Greek sponge captain didn't look very happy when he saw the wet footprints Remo tracked all over his deck.

As they beat back toward Athens, Remo laid himself out among a coarse pile of dragnets and said, "I don't think I would have made it without Sister Mary Margaret."

Chiun eyed him coldly. "Why do you say that?"

"I heard her voice telling me how Theseus did it. He used string."

"If you had employed string, you would have cheated."

"That's not the point. She said Theseus used string to retrace his way out of the labyrinth of the Minotaur. Not to find the exit. But to retrace the way he came. That meant the entrance was also the exit."

"That is obvious," Chiun said in a chilly voice.

"Even then, I couldn't be sure. But there was another way I figured it out."

"And what is that?"

"I remembered you pointed south. You didn't say the exit was south. You just pointed. That meant technically you didn't lie to me."

Chiun said nothing.

"I knew if my life was at stake, you wouldn't lie," Remo went on. "You wouldn't lie to me about something that important."

And the Master of Sinanju went to the bow and stood there like some troubled figurehead, staring across the Aegean toward Athens, where the floodlit Acropolis gleamed like an ancient pharos.

Among his nets, Remo Williams succumbed to sleep and dreamed fitfully.

HE FOUND HIMSELF FACING a pleasant little Asian man dressed in the garb of rural Korea. They were in a place of rolling hills touched by the pink blossoms of the flower known as rose of Sharon in the West, which the Koreans called *mu-gang-hwa*.

The man greeted him with the ancient and traditional greeting of the Korean countryside.

"Pam-go-sso-yo?"

"Yes, I have had rice today," Remo answered in his best Korean.

"Good," said the pleasant little man. He smiled. It was an infectious smile despite the man's lack of a full set of teeth. Remo couldn't help but smile back.

So when the pleasant little man tried to take Remo's head off with an unexpected snap kick, Remo was caught off guard. He evaded the strike only because his body was trained never to be caught unawares.

"Hey! What's your problem?"

"I am the second."

"The second what?"

The little man bowed politely. "My name is Kim."

"Big deal. So's every third Korean's."

"Your reflexes are exquisite," said the little Korean pleasantly.

"Thanks. Why did you try to kill me just now?"

"I wanted to see if it was true what they say."

"What's true?"

"That a big-nose, round-eyed white had mastered Sinanju."

"What's it to you?" demanded Remo.

"It is a point of family pride."

"What family are we talking about?"

"Your family." And the little man dropped into another bow. He bowed so low he vanished from sight with a tiny pop like a cork letting go.

WHEN REMO WOKE AGAIN, he got up and found the Master of Sinanju watching the lights of Athens from the bow.

"What was the name of the second Master of Sinanju?"

"I have taught you that," Chiun said coldly. "You should know."

"Was it Kim?"

"There were many Masters named Kim. 'Kim' is a common name in my land. It means metal. It is like your 'Smith.' "

"Answer my question."

"There was Kim the Younger, Kim the Elder, the Lesser Kim and the Greater Kim, as well as several unremarkable Kims. But yes, the second Master was named Kim. The Lesser."

"I just had a dream about him."

Chiun said nothing for a very long time. Abruptly he turned away from contemplating the lights of Athens and said in a cold, remote tone, "We are about to make landfall, and I have no time for your unimportant dreams."

Remo stood alone on the deck wearing a hurt expression on his strong face.

HE WAS STILL WEARING IT when they climbed the hill called the Acropolis and looked down upon the white city of Athens below.

Chiun began pacing amid the ruins until he found a spot he liked. "You must dig."

Remo looked at the spot. "How do you know this is the right spot?"

"Dig," repeated the Master of Sinanju sternly.

So Remo dug. This time he used his bare big toe to disturb the earth, not dropping to his knees until the glint of metal peeked up from the ancient soil.

"Got another coin," he said.

"A drachma."

Remo stood up. This time he cleared the dirt of the coin by tapping each side once with a fingertip. The dirt flew off as if vacuumed away.

One side had the profile of a man with a winged helmet.

"Hey. This looks kinda like one of those old Mercury-head dimes I used to see when I was a kid."

Chiun raised an eyebrow. "You recognize Mercury?"

"Sure. He was the Greek god of—wait a minute. Wasn't he Roman?"

"The Romans took their gods from the Greeks."

"Oh, right. Who did the Greeks get their gods from?"

"Hither and yon. The Egyptians and the Koreans mainly."

"I don't remember any Korean gods except that bear that was supposed to be the first man."

"As usual, you have gotten everything confused. The face on that coin is Hermes, whom the Romans called Mercury."

"It's coming back to me. Zeus was Jupiter. Ares was Mars. Hercules was.... What was Hercules?"

"A drunken wastrel."

"No, I meant what was his Greek name?"

"Heracles."

"I never liked that name," Remo said thoughtfully. "He was always Hercules to me."

"The vestal virgins who raised you filled your mind with useless junk. You know no Korean tales but those I taught you."

"Is there a point to all this carping and criticizing?"

"If there is, you are too dense to see it," snapped Chiun, who started down off the mountain.

Remo followed him down. "That's it? We climb this mountain, dig up an old coin and we're on our way again?"

"Yes."

"How about we check into a hotel for a few hours? I'm beat."

"You have had six entire hours of sleep. And a nap. You cannot be tired."

"I must be getting old."

"You are getting lazy, and there will be no hotel. We are going to Giza."

"Isn't that in Japan?"

"You are thinking of the Ginza. Giza is in Khemet."

"Never heard of Khemet, either," grumbled Remo, taking a last look back at the crumbling Parthenon and thinking how much it reminded him of Washington, D.C.

" 'Khemet' means 'Black Land,' " said Chiun.

"Still never heard of it."

"That is because the rulers of Khemet threw away their brains."

Remo looked his question, but the Master of Sinanju said nothing.

8

On the plane Remo fell asleep.

A darkness filled his mind and, after a time, it churned and boiled and out of this darkness stepped a man wearing the robes of ancient Egypt and the face of a sad pharaoh. Despite his pharaonic attire, he was unmistakably Korean.

His mouth parted and the words coming out were doleful and hollow. "History has forgotten me."

"Who are you?" Remo asked.

"Wo-Ti was my name."

"Was?"

"I served Pharaoh Pepi II all of his days."

"Good for you," said Remo.

"His days numbered ninety-six years. And because I was pledged to guard his body, I did not see the village of my birth for the remainder of my days. The world still remembers Pepi II, but not Wo-Ti who ensured his long life."

"Where is this place?" asked Remo, seeing all around him only a blackness so intense it seemed to vibrate.

"This is the Void."

"Yeah. I thought so. Pleasant. Do all Masters of Sinanju end up here after they go?"

"The Void is not a place of bitterness, unless one brings bitterness into the Void with him. Remember that. When you drop your body, leave all bitterness behind you to lie moldering with your bones.''

"I'll try to keep that in mind," Remo said dryly.

Wo-Ti lifted gnarled hands and flexed them with a warning crackling of cartilage. "Now we must fight."

"Why?"

"Because you have failed to recognize me."

"What kind of cockamamy reason is that?" said Remo. "I never met you before."

"That is no excuse." And Wo-Ti lashed out with a stabbing finger Remo checked with one thick wrist. The opposite hand flashed out. Remo caught it with his other wrist and stepped back.

"This is ridiculous. I gotta be three times younger."

"And I possess three times your experience. Defend your life."

Wo-Ti made two fists like mallets of bone, and Remo copied his posture, stance and blocking moves.

Their fists orbited each other, feinting, circling, withdrawing just on the verge of connecting. No blow was struck. This was not a contest of strikes or blows. Each man knew from the way the other reacted that his blow would fail if launched, and, knowing this, wasted no effort.

It was the purest form of Sinanju fighting, a training exercise that could only be undertaken by two full Masters. Any lesser human being would not survive the first three seconds. It was called Lodestones, because the closed fists acted like magnets, attracting and repelling by turns, but never touching. To either land or receive a blow brought disgrace to both combatants equally. For contact signified that both teacher and pupil had failed in their duties to the House of Sinanju.

It took Remo back to his earliest days of training, when Chiun would land many blows and become enraged at Remo for allowing it.

"How long does this go on?" he asked Master Wo-Ti.

"When you can tell me the lesson of my Masterhood."

"What if I don't remember?"

"It will be as much of a disgrace to you and your teacher as if your fist struck my body or my fist struck yours," said Wo-Ti, probing for an opening.

Remo thought hard. Trouble was, it was nearly impossible to do Lodestones and concentrate on anything else.

Wo-Ti. Wo-Ti. Why was Wo-Ti important? Remo thought.

It hit him in a blaze of insight.

Yeah. I remember now. Pharaoh Pepi II had the longest reign of any emperor in history, thanks to Wo-Ti. And all because Wo-Ti promised Pepi I he'd watch over his son for the rest of his life.

"A Master should never serve a succeeding emperor!" Remo said quickly.

And without another word, Master Wo-Ti dropped his guard and bowed out of existence.

WHEN REMO AWOKE there was an AirEgypt stewardess sitting in his lap staring searchingly into his eyes.

"I have a question," Remo said.

"Ask, O alabaster-skinned one."

"Where in Egypt is Khemet?"

"Egypt *is* Khemet. It is the ancient name for Egypt. You are obviously very interested in Egypt."

"Since we're about to land in Cairo, yeah."

She smiled duskily. "Then you must be interested in Egyptians."

"Vaguely."

Her fingers toyed with a lock of his dark hair. "And Egyptian women."

"In the abstract," admitted Remo.

"Have you never heard of the Mile High Club?"

"I'm a eunuch. I don't normally like to admit it but I notice you're fingering my zipper even though we just met, so I think you should know in advance."

"Perhaps if I tickle it, it will grow back."

Remo made his face sad. "Many have tried. But it doesn't work."

"You still have lips for kissing and a tongue for deeper kissing."

"Wrong again. The people who chopped it off snatched my tongue away."

"Then how do you speak?"

"Prosthetic tongue. It's plastic. Tastes like a squirt gun. You wouldn't like it."

And while the stewardess was staring with a befuddled expression lapping at her kohl-rimmed eyes, Remo reached up and touched a nerve in her neck that froze her in place. Then he gently picked her up and carried her across the aisle, still frozen in a seated position, dropping her into an empty seat. There were a lot of empty seats. These days Muslim fundamentalists were murdering tourists in Cairo with wild abandon in an effort to call down the sympathy of the world community upon their latest cause. Which, since the Israeli-Palestinian accords, seemed focused on blowing up secular poets, godless pop singers and protesting family planning.

When the jet rolled up to the gate, the remaining stewardesses were waiting to see Remo off the plane. So Remo and Chiun sat patiently in their seats until the entire plane had emptied out.

On the way out the passenger exit, Remo shook hands with every flight attendant, whispering, "I'm a eunuch. Honest. I'm a eunuch."

On his way out, the Master of Sinanju shut the cabin door behind him, giving it a smack that made the entire fuselage shake like a gaffed fish and incidentally fusing the door shut.

The sound of fists beating against unyielding metal followed them up the jetway ramp and into the busy terminal.

A smiling Egyptian man bowed Remo and Chiun into his cab outside the terminal, and Chiun slipped in first. When Remo dropped into the seat beside him, he found the driver had already been given his instructions. The cab took off, screeching through the clangor and congestion of downtown Cairo.

"Care to enlighten a tourist as to his destination?" Remo asked Chiun, rolling up his window to keep out the sulphurous smog.

"You are going to confront the dreaded Sun Lion."

"I'm not afraid of lions."

"This is a very large lion."

"How large can a lion be?" asked Remo.

The Master of Sinanju only smiled with a tight satisfaction.

UNDER THE BORED GAZES of the Cairo police Theron Moenig, UCLA professor of inexplicable phenomena, had set the four surveyor's lasers, one for each point on the compass, around the crumbling treasure of ancient Egypt men called the Great Sphinx.

The lasers were calibrated to nanometer tolerances. Set equidistant, they would detect the most minute vibrations in the great limestone idol. The great moment approached.

Theron Moenig had toiled for six years for this great moment. Six years of seeking grants, funding and specialized equipment normally used to test the structural integrity and plumb of high-rise skyscrapers. And now it was here.

He must not fail. Science looked to him for the answer to one of the great riddles surrounding the Great Sphinx of Giza.

There were many questions surrounding the Sphinx. They had been asked repeatedly down through the dusty centuries. The empty echoes of answers that were never forthcoming resounded down the decades.

Who had built the Sphinx?

Why was it built?

And who or what was represented by the giant, multiton figure of a recumbent lion with the head of a pharaoh?

Some said it wore the face of Pharaoh Khufu, who was known as Cheops to the Greeks. Others claimed the Sphinx wore the visage of his son, Khafre, at the foot of whose pyramid it reposed. Most scholars believed the Sphinx dated back to the end of the Old Kingdom. A few believed it was older than the earliest pharaoh.

Questions immemorial. The centuries rolled on, but the theories still hung in the sandy air of the desert, unanswered. If not unanswerable.

Professor Moenig had come to the land of the pharaohs not to investigate the old, unprovable theories but to pose one that had never been asked in all of history.

Has the Sphinx been moving?

It was a preposterous question, which was why it had taken six and not the usual three years to wrest a half-million-dollar grant from UCLA's archaeology department. No one ever considered that the Sphinx had moved from its original spot. It had been buried by the encroaching deserts the ancient Egyptians called the Red Land countless times. In fact, had it not been buried four and a half centuries after it was carved, and thereby sheltered from the biting erosion of the windblown sands of the desert, the Sphinx might conceivably have become even more disgracefully eroded than it was.

It was the orientation of the Great Sphinx to the Pyramid of Khufu that first posed the theory in Theron Moenig's mind. Ancient records had shown conclusively that the Sphinx lay at a precise right angle from the Khafre pyramid's eastern face. Yet a modern satellite picture showed a clear three-degree tilt away from the perpendicular.

That the Sphinx had moved over the centuries as it sat patient and brooding seemed as inescapable as it was impossible.

The Leaning Tower of Pisa tilted. Everyone knew that. Big Ben had even started leaning one way. This was known. The seas receded. Glaciers melted and tides lifted. These were facts.

But what could have caused the Sphinx to move slowly, inexorably and—prior to sensitive surveying lasers—imperceptibly from its original east-facing orientation?

Professor Moenig was determined to find out. Armed with six million dollars of UCLA money—one million of it needed to bribe Egyptian authorities—he would discover the truth.

Even if he had to live in the three-hundred-dollar-a-day Pharaoh Suite of the Nile Hilton from now until the turn of the century to do it.

Opening his sun parasol, Moenig sat down before the computer terminal that displayed the Sphinx trans-fixed by the lasers' equidistant beams and pulled a paperback book from his backpack, settling down for the long haul. The longer the better.

THE CAB CARRIED Remo and Chiun over a bridge and out of the city. They were soon on Pyramids Road, and the imposing cluster of three great pyramids bulked up through the stinking smog. Desert sands lay on either side. Camels plodded majestically along, carrying tourists and pilgrims alike.

"Now, Khufu had many sons," Chiun said suddenly, as if picking up a story left unfinished. "But only one could be pharaoh. This was in the days of Master Saja. Khufu chose Djedefre as his successor. But one of his wives schemed to install her son by Khufu, one Rama-Tut. Ignorant of Khufu's unspoken choice, she conspired with a wicked vizier to rid the world of the rival sons of Khufu. Many accidents befell the sons of Khufu, who was in those days overseeing the building of the greatest of the pyramids before you. For pharaohs believed themselves to be gods who walked the earth and who, upon death, would ascend to the stars and rule the afterlife."

"That why they built the pyramids?" asked Remo.

Chiun nodded. "The pyramids that you see are both tombs and staircases to the stars. In each structure that you see lies a shaft, facing north and slanting upward toward what was then called the Imperishable Stars—those that never set."

"Like Polaris?"

"In those days the pole star was a yellow star known to the Egyptians as Thuban, which lies at the tail of the constellation known since Roman times as Draco. Polaris has now taken its place in the sky. After we are dust, it will be the star Koreans call Chik-nyo. For not even the fixed stars in the sky are forever, Remo. But rest assured, when Chik-nyo enjoys ascendancy the House of Sinanju will yet be strong."

The hot air grew dustier with every mile. Remo said nothing. The pyramids seemed to grow before them without giving the appearance of coming closer. They were immense, their dun outlines crumbling.

Chiun spoke on. "Now, Khufu had many burdens. He fretted over his pyramid, whose construction and sanctity would ensure a happy afterlife, and he worried about the misfortunes that were felling his lesser sons. So he summoned his chief vizier and asked him if the stars blessed the ascendancy of his son Djedefre to pharaoh. And this treacherous vizier, who was in league with the wicked mother of Rama-Tut, told Khufu that Djedefre would never be pharaoh. The stars looked with favor upon Rama-Tut instead.

"These tidings troubled Khufu deeply, for he recognized the darkness of Rama-Tut's heart and trusted only Djedefre to see that after his passing his tomb would endure the centuries undefiled. So Khufu sent to Sinanju for Master Saja and presented him with his dilemma.

"'If the stars bless Rama-Tut and not my good son Djedefre, what am I to do?' he asked Saja.

"And Saja answered, 'We will foil the stars.'

"Khufu demanded of Saja what was meant, but Saja said only, 'If Sinanju can foil the stars, will you build a monument to the House that will endure through the ages?'

"'Done,' said Pharaoh Khufu. And the deal was struck.

"That night, Remo, Rama-Tut died in his sleep, and no one ever discovered the malady that ended his life. The mother of Rama-Tut threw herself into the Nile and drowned. And in the fullness of time, Khufu died and Djedefre became pharaoh, just as Saja had promised."

Remo grinned. "I think I know what got old Rama-Tut."

"Shh. It is a secret. Even now."

"That was centuries ago. What's the problem?"

"The driver may be a descendant," Chiun said in a conspiratorial voice. "Egyptians are notorious holders of grudges."

Remo rolled his eyes.

Chiun continued his tale. "When Djedefre ascended the throne, Master Saja came before him and told him of his bargain with Khufu."

"'What is your desire?' Djedefre asked Saja. And Saja replied, 'I see that your tomb is even now being laid out by your royal architects and that they quarry stone from an outcropping in the shadow of your father's tomb. Make from the rock that remains a statue of wondrous size, in the image of a recumbent lion always facing the sun and my village, which is the sun source. And give it the face of the one who ensured your assumption to the throne of Egypt. Do this to show that, mighty as Egypt is, the House of Sinanju is more powerful still.'

"'Done,' cried Pharaoh Djedefre. 'When next you see my kingdom, you will behold your wish turned to stone that will last for all of time.'

"But years passed and no more was heard from Egypt, who was in those days a great client of the House. So Saja undertook the long journey to the land of pharaohs, and when he came to Giza, he beheld the reality of his bargain from the back of a dromedary. Mighty it was, Remo. And proud as it faced the rising sun, its colors triumphant. But as Saja drew close, his boundless pride collapsed into a cold rage. For the visage of the Lion that Faces the Sun was not his own."

"Uh-oh. Djedefre welched."

"Pharaohs were notorious welchers, but we didn't know this in those days. So Saja appeared before Djedefre and demanded why the face of the Sun Lion was not his. And Djedefre replied that such was not the bargain. Saja had asked that the lion wear the likeness of the one who had ensured Djedefre's reign, and Saja had to admit that this was true. Technically. Bowing his farewells and expressing admiration for Djedefre's shrewdness, Saja returned to his village and, when in later years word came from Egypt that Djedefre needed the help of the House, Saja tore up the message without replying. And when Saja's successor received an entreaty to help succor the Old Kingdom in its waning days, that message too was ignored. Thus, Egypt fell upon evil days and it was many generations before a Master worked again for a pharaoh. And all because Djedefre was so shrewd he cheated Sinanju and in so doing lost his empire."

The cab turned off the road, and Remo saw the half-obliterated face of the Sphinx gazing over the undulating sands. It faced away from the three massive pyramids and their smaller satellite temples.

"Is that the Sun Lion?" he asked Chiun.

Chiun voiced disapproval. "It is a sad sight. Better had they left it to sleep under the sands that had claimed it."

"Better for who? The Sphinx or me?"

"Let us find out," said Chiun, paying off the driver.

"I don't like the sound of this," said Remo nervously.

Tucking his hands into his sleeves, the Master of Sinanju padded up to the gigantic Sphinx. "The sacred cobra no longer rears up from his mighty brow," he intoned. "The beard is missing. His painted headdress is forever faded. That my ancestors could see this now, they would fret and fume that this once mighty relic of a former glory has come to this."

Chiun gestured distastefully.

There were tourists walking around the Sphinx, tourists climbing the crumbling sides of the Great Pyramid of Giza.

"In the days of Wang, heads were lopped off over such desecration," Chiun observed. "Imagine, Remo, if children were allowed to run amok in the halls of your Senate."

"They do. They're called senators."

Remo grinned. Chiun frowned. Remo swallowed his grin. They continued walking, the sand beneath their feet accepting their tread without complaint and ejecting it without creating the impression of their feet.

"What are those things?" Remo asked, pointing out the tripod-mounted electronic equipment surrounding the Sphinxlike Panaflex cameras recording a Biblical epic movie set.

"I do not know."

"I think those are laser beams."

"Why would anyone want to burn holes in the Sphinx?"

"I don't think those are burning lasers, Little Father."

"Is that not what lasers do? Burn?"

"Some. Those probably do something else. What, I don't know."

They came upon a man in khaki shorts, his limbs splayed in a folding lawn chair shaded by a parasol. Before him was a portable laptop computer, and he was reading a book. Remo ducked his head to read the title. It was *Chariots of the Gods?*

"Those lasers yours?" Remo asked.

"They are," the man said in a snooty voice. A pith helmet was perched precariously on his elongated head. The letters UCLA were stenciled on the front.

"What are they doing?"

"Waiting for the Great Sphinx to move, if you must know."

"They're going to have a long wait," Remo commented.

"That is perfectly acceptable. UCLA is paying for this study."

"Do tell."

"I do. I am one of its foremost scholars. Now, kindly shoo. You are in my reading light."

"Happy to oblige," said Remo, walking away.

After he rejoined the Master of Sinanju, Remo asked, "Did you hear that screwball? He's waiting for the Sphinx to move."

"He is very intelligent for a sunburned white."

"What do you mean?"

Chiun gazed up, noting the angle of the midday sun. "It is time for the Sphinx to move."

Remo looked up at the Sphinx's noseless, wind-worn face. "This, I gotta see to believe."

"Alas, you cannot."

"Why not?"

Chiun regarded him with flinty eyes. "Because it is *you* who will move great Sun Lion."

"I can't move that."

"Why not?"

"It's too big."

"The earth is big. It moves. The moon is big. And it moves. The Sphinx is not so big, so you can move it easily."

"With all these tourists around?"

"It matters only that it moves. It does not have to move very far." Chiun's eyes narrowed cunningly. "Unless you can answer the riddle of the Sphinx," he added thinly.

Remo grinned. "Sure. Try me."

"You must not guess. You may answer only from knowledge."

"Fair enough."

Chiun regarded him thinly. "Whose face does the Sun Lion wear?"

"That's not the riddle of the Sphinx. The question is what walks on four feet in the morning, two in the afternoon and three in the evening?"

Chiun brushed Remo's protest aside. "That is the wrong riddle. That is a child's riddle. You are not a child, but a Master of Sinanju. The true riddle has been asked. Do you know the answer?"

"You know I don't."

"Are you certain? Examine the proud features. Do they not look familiar?"

"I don't know too many noseless pharaohs," Remo growled.

Chiun nodded. "Then you must move the Lion that Faces the Sun."

"What kind of test is this?"

"A difficult one," said the Master of Sinanju.

"Har-de-har-har-har," said Remo.

He began to walk around the Sphinx. It was gigantic. That was no surprise, but walking all the way around impressed Remo with its sheer immensity. He felt like a dwarf beside one of its limestone toes. How a technologically primitive people had erected it was beyond him. That it had stood there for nearly five thousand years impressed him. And as he came back to the face, so incredibly ancient, the knowledge that time had eroded its glory saddened him.

"When it was built, it must have been the greatest thing in the world," he said.

"It was," breathed Chiun.

"Now look at it."

"Yes, look at it. It is still great, but there are many great things in the world and this magnificent beast of limestone is but a honey cake set out to attract human ants and their money."

"If there's a way to move this thing, I don't see it."

"There is. And if you do not discover it, we will never see Kush."

"Suits me."

"But not me. You may begin at any time."

Remo checked the Sphinx. He looked enough like a tourist the local police didn't bother him. The other tourists ignored him. A camel spat in his direction, but Remo avoided the expectorant without turning. His body sensed pressure waves and moved him out of its path.

At the right front paw, Remo casually leaned his back against the member. His feet dug into the limestone platform on which the Sphinx was built. He pushed his body in both directions.

Somewhere a computer beeped.

"It moved! It moved!"

Remo came around the paw and said, "What moved?"

The UCLA professor was jumping up and down with undisguised glee. "The Sphinx. It moved! My instruments registered positive movement."

"You're crazy. I was right next to it."

The man squealed with delight. "It moved a nanometer."

"How small is that?"

"Barely a billionth of a meter."

"Maybe it was the laser that moved."

"Impossible. It was the beam that reacted to the movement, not the laser case."

"What direction?"

"Northeast."

"I'll go check. You go that way."

Remo ran to the rear of the Sphinx, looked both ways and leaned his back against the rump. His feet hissed as the heels sunk into the sand-dusted platform on which the Sphinx reclined.

Up by the head another beep came.

"It moved! It moved again!"

Remo came running.

"Which direction?" he asked the excited man.

"Northeast. The same direction."

"I didn't see anything."

"Something's making the Sphinx turn toward the northeast."

"Tell you what," said Remo. "You go back to the rump. I'll watch the head."

"Yes. Yes. Thank you. Thank you."

Remo took the same spot by the front paw and leaned his back against the Sphinx as if tired. His body became one with the great idol. So when he exerted pressure, it responded down to its limestone-block toes.

There came a beep and another shout of exultation.

"It moved! It's a miracle. The Sphinx is moving!"

As the UCLA professor came running back toward the head, taking Instamatic pictures every step of the way, Remo returned to his spot at the rump. This time he laid his hands against the ruin and leaned into it.

The beeping became a protracted squeal, and when Remo was satisfied, he stepped away and found the Master of Sinanju.

"That enough?" Remo asked Chiun.

"Huk moved it just as far with only two pushes."

"Huk didn't have lasers to deal with."

The UCLA professor was leaping into the air, pumping his arms excitedly. "The Sphinx moves! I've proved it. The Sphinx moves!"

"Personally," Remo called out, spanking limestone dust off his hands, "I think your equipment's on the fritz."

The man's face fell. "It's the best money could buy."

"You have all these witnesses, and no one saw a thing."

The UCLA professor got down on hands and knees, trying to see under the Sphinx. "Maybe it's on a pivot. Like a weather vane. We should dig it up. I'll bet we find a pivot."

"You know how much time and money that would cost?"

"Millions," the man cried. "Millions and millions. This is too big for UCLA. This is a Yale grant. I'll need a Yale grant. Excuse me. I have to call the States."

As he ran off, Remo asked Chiun, "Now what? Do I push it back or what?"

"No."

"No?"

"No? You mean that's it?"

"It is enough for this century. I have pushed it and now you have pushed it. If you ever sire a worthy successor, he can push it. Eventually it will face the proper direction."

"What's the proper direction?"

"Toward my village of Sinanju, of course."

"How long will that take?"

"Only another two thousand years."

Remo looked up at the crumbling face. "Think the old guy will last that long?"

"Not if these pesky tourists continue to clamber atop it."

"Not our problem. Where to next?"

"The Egyptians called it wretched Kush."

"Give me a name I understand."

"The Greeks named it Ethiopia. To the Romans it was Africa."

"I'm not up for Africa."

"We could journey to Hyperborea instead."

Remo frowned. "I never heard of Hyperborea."

"I will give you a choice. Hyperborea or Africa?"

"Is this a trick question?"

"Only to the ignorant."

Remo reached into his pockets and pulled out two coins, the Greek drachma and the Roman denarius.

"How about if I flip a coin? Heads Hyperborea and tails Africa."

"I will accept this."

Remo flipped the coin, and the face of Hermes landed up.

"Hyperborea it is. Sure hope it isn't hot and steamy like Africa."

"It is not."

"By the way," asked Remo as they sought a cab back to Cairo, "what did you mean when you said they threw away their brains?"

"When a pharaoh died, his body was prepared for entombment with preserving niter and bitumen, should he reclaim it at a later time. It was wrapped in specially prepared linen, and the organs extracted and preserved in jars. Except for one organ."

"The brain?"

"The brain."

"Why did they throw away the brains?"

"Because while the Egyptians understood the function of the heart and the liver and the gall bladder, they did not know the purpose of their own brains. And so if there is an afterlife for pharaohs, it must be a terrible place because they have no brains in their skulls to enjoy eternal dominion among the Imperishable Stars."

And amid the blowing sands of Giza, which would one day overtake Cairo itself, Remo Williams laughed softy. Until Chiun said something that wiped the smile from his face and caused a chunk of ice to settle in his heart.

"When I am a mummy, Remo, see to it that my brain reposes in the correct receptacle."

9

The flight from Cairo to Hyperborea stopped at Copenhagen, Denmark, which Remo took to be a good sign. They changed planes in Iceland, which made Remo's brow furrow with worry.

While they refueled at the Icelandic capital of Reykjavík, Remo noticed with relief that it was very green. A stopover in Greenland made him decide whoever had named both places must have dropped his notes. Iceland was green and Greenland was icy.

And when the crew changed at Godthaab, Greenland, and the Danish stewardesses who kept nibbling on Remo's ears became Eskimo stewardesses who tried to rub their cold noses against his warm one, Remo took this to be a very very bad omen.

So when the gray seas below the Air Canada's wings became choked with cakes of ice, Remo was not particularly surprised.

"We're not going to the North Pole by any chance?" wondered Remo.

"No, *we* are not," Chiun said.

"Good," said Remo.

"*You* are going to the place where only one Master of Sinanju has ventured before you."

"Where is that?"

"The moon."

"I am not going to the moon. Air Canada doesn't fly there."

Chiun waved the objection away. "It is too late for you to object, inasmuch as you are already on your way."

As the plane droned on, the Eskimo stewardesses kept up a running chatter about how they were now called Inuit but Remo could call them bandicoots if he gave them all a big hug. Preferably one at a time, but because they were landing soon, all at once would do just fine.

"Pass," said Remo, thinking furiously.

"Why do you spurn the advances of these fine, sturdy women?" asked Chiun in an undertone.

"How come you didn't ask me that in Spain or Egypt?"

"Those women spring from inferior stock."

Remo took a second look at the stewardesses who were beaming brilliant smiles in his direction like round-faced searchlights.

"These women look suspiciously Korean," he said.

"They are not. They are Eskimo."

"Inuit," called a bell-like voice.

"You know, they say Asians came across the Bering Strait and populated America."

"These women could pass for Asian," Chiun admitted. "Chinese perhaps. Or Mongol. But not Korean. Although they have their charms."

"If you like pumpkin heads perched on squash bodies."

"They are fortuitously designed for childbearing. This is a good thing for a man of your advancing years."

"My years aren't advancing that I know of. I look younger than I did before I came to Sinanju."

"It would be a correct thing for you to impregnate the three you like best in the event you do not return from the moon in this century," Chiun told Remo.

"Three?"

"Knowing you, I do not trust you not to sire another female. If not two. But if you make three with child, surely at least one boy will result."

"Pass."

"Awww," said the stewardesses in unison.

"No offense," Remo assured them. "I already have a daughter."

"And a son," added Chiun.

"The jury's still out on that one."

Remo lapsed into silence. They were flying in the general direction of the North Pole, which featured only ice and snow and cold and maybe the Fortress of Solitude. In other words, nothing useful or interesting.

Somewhere in the dim recesses of his memory, he recalled a legend of a Sinanju Master who went to the moon. Who was that?

"Shang!" Remo said, snapping his fingers. "Shang went to the moon."

Chiun clapped his hands together approvingly. "It gladdens my heart to hear that one of my lessons has stuck to the inside of your thick white skull."

"Cut it out. Besides, Shang didn't really go to the moon. He just thought he did."

"He went to the moon. So it was written in the Book of Sinanju."

"What's written in the Book of Sinanju is that Shang fell for some Japanese tart, and she hectored him into fetching her a piece of the moon, figuring if he failed, she was rid of him. So he hiked north, made it to a land of cold and ice and snow bears and, because he was ignorant of the shape of the earth, Shang thought he had made it to the moon. Actually he'd hiked across the frozen Bering Sea into what is now northern Canada. Because it was winter, there was no moon in the sky, and Shang thought he had walked all the way to the moon.''

"How did the story end?" an interested stewardess asked.

Remo shrugged. "Search me. I just remember the part of the moon. And only because it was wrong."

"Pah!" said Chiun, turning away. "You have learned nothing."

For the rest of the trip, the stewardesses tried to convince Remo that although they were Inuit or Eskimos—take your pick, kind sir—they were really just as modern and sophisticated as any woman you could find.

"Yes," said one. "We have satellite dishes in our homes. Alcoholism. Drugs and even AIDS."

"That's really sophisticated," Remo remarked dryly. "Congratulations."

The stewardesses giggled with delight, thinking they were cracking the thick antisocial ice surrounding the strange white man with the yummy, thick wrists.

So when he fell asleep, they were very disappointed.

When they deplaned at Pangnirtung on Baffin Island, the entire crew of stewardesses offered Remo a ride to any point he cared to visit, including lodgings in their very own homes, which they assured him were not igloos. Unless, of course, igloos appealed to him. In which case they would build the warmest, most snuggly igloo imaginable.

Feeling his face shrink before a polar wind, Remo muttered, "All of a sudden, I'd like to visit Africa."

"We can kayak down!" one squeaked.

In the end Remo was forced to drag them across the icy tarmac to a waiting rental agent because they had latched on to the cuffs of his pants and refused to let go.

"We wish to rent a vehicle hardy enough to travel many miles through ice and snow," Chiun announced.

"And horny Eskimo women," added Remo.

The rental agent gave them a nice deal on a snowball-colored Ford Bronco with heavy-duty studded snow tires that had chains on them for extra traction.

"Pay this man, Remo," said Chiun.

"Remo! His name is Remo!"

The rental agent peered over his counter top.

"Sir," he said in a hushed tone usually reserved for informing someone that his fly was open or toilet paper had stuck to his shoe, "you have stewardesses clinging to your pant legs."

"They think they're in love with me," Remo complained.

"They look awfully convinced of that to me," the rental agent agreed.

"Can I leave them with you?" Remo wondered.

"No! No!"

"Just until I get back?" added Remo.

"Yes! Yes! We'll wait for you! We'll wait forever."

"I was hoping you'd all say that," said Remo. "Should be back in—" He looked to the Master of Sinanju.

"Very soon or never."

"Very soon," said Remo.

"Yaaay!"

When the keys were offered to Remo, the Master of Sinanju snatched them away. "I will drive," he said coldly.

"Why do you have to drive?"

"Because you appear very tired, and I do not wish you to drive us into a glacier or off a precipice to our death."

Remo decided that made good sense, so he hopped in back while the Master of Sinanju spent ten minutes finding a position behind the steering wheel that was comfortable and didn't wrinkle his kimono.

They rattled out onto a road and into lightly blowing snow. For miles in every direction lay the snow-dusted expanse of the Arctic. They were well above the tree line, with not a spruce in sight.

On the way they passed a solitary Eskimo man hiking through the white desolation, who called encouragement after them. "Go, Juice, go!"

"You know, if we get lost in this thing, no one would ever find us. Our paint job's the same color as the terrain."

"Do not worry, Remo. *I* will not get lost."

"Good."

And Chiun did something strange. He yawned. After a minute Remo yawned, too. Chiun yawned again. And again.

Remo fell asleep in the vehicle not long after.

IN SLEEP, he was back in the Void. A sad-faced man appeared to him, wearing the baggy pastel silks of the Yi Dynasty.

"Which one are you?" asked Remo wearily.

"I am you."

"I don't remember Chiun mentioning a Master Yu."

"My name is not Yu. It is Lu."

"Lu? Oh, yeah, Chiun thinks I used to be Lu in a past life."

"That is why I said I am you."

"Funny. You don't look like me."

"We wear different flesh, but our essence is one."

"That so? If you're me and I'm you, how can we be having this conversation?"

"Because you are dreaming," Master Lu said in a reasonable voice.

"Oh, right. So. Do I have to fight you, too?"

"A man cannot fight himself. For there would be no victor—only two defeated ones."

"Gotta remember that."

"I am here to tell you that while our essence may be one and our flesh different, my blood flows in your veins."

"How's that possible? You're Korean and I'm American."

"America was not always. Your ancestors were not always American. Therefore, they were something else."

"They sure as hell weren't Korean," said Remo.

But Master Lu only smiled with a thin austerity, and as his face began to recede, Remo thought his eyes looked familiar.

Those knowing eyes were the last things to disappear into the Void.

WHEN HE WOKE UP, Remo was sitting in the back seat and the Bronco had stopped on a block of ice. There was hardly any sunlight, and it was very very cold. A steady wind blew.

"What the hell?" Remo said, opening the door. His foot touched water, and he withdrew it with haste. The water was very cold. He looked out and down. The water was gray and choppy, in addition to being cold.

The block of ice was entirely surrounded by water, confirming Remo's first sleepy impression. And it was moving south.

"Damn it Chiun! Where are you?"

As it turned out, not in the back, which contained only a wad of coarse, woolly blankets, or under the hood, which was full of cold, inert engine.

Remo scoured the horizon with his deep-set eyes. To the north lay cold, impenetrable mist and the fresh scent of snow. To the south he smelled open water and blubber.

Kneeling at the thick end of the floating ice block, Remo tested the water. So cold, it was like touching a live wire. When he pulled his finger free, it instantly acquired a coating of ice, which he knew better than to try to break off. His skin would probably crack off with it.

Sucking on his frozen finger to soften the ice, Remo returned to the Bronco. He got behind the wheel and found no key in the ignition.

Growing up on the streets of Newark had given Remo certain skills that never seemed to age. He hot-wired the ignition and got the engine going. The heater filled the interior with just enough warmth to cause Remo's muscles to relax. Then the engine conked out.

No amount of tinkering could get it going again.

The cold settled in the Bronco's interior like a frigid hand. And Remo started shivering uncontrollably. It was a mechanism by which the body warmed itself when necessary.

Remo had been taught not to shiver by the Master of Sinanju, who had pronounced it a waste of energy. But from the way things looked, he was marooned. He would shiver now and when he got bored with shivering, there were Sinanju techniques that ran the gamut from visualizing fire to hibernating that might carry him through this ordeal.

The only question in Remo's mind was why Chiun had put him in this position. It made the Cretan labyrinth look like a pie-eating contest.

Well past midnight, Remo was in the fire-visualization phase of his survival plan. It was working. He felt warm even as a night wind howled against the windshield. Windblown water had rimed the glass with a thick coating of obscuring ice. He couldn't see where he was going, even though at this time of year midnight meant the sun was hanging low to the horizon, giving the world the semblance of dusk.

So it came as a mild surprise when the ice block crashed against something and the Bronco rocked on its springs, while pressing their wet black noses to the windows.

Remo cranked the window down on the passenger's side and saw that his ice block had nudged another ice block.

"Could be my lucky break," he said.

He got out. Instantly his skin shrank over his muscles and bones. The wind was bitter and penetrating.

Remo walked over to the adjoining block of ice. It bobbed and fought against his patch, which meant it wasn't land but another chunk of floe ice.

Remo hesitated. The two cakes were clashing, but nothing said they'd stay joined forever. He looked back.

He couldn't afford to lose the shelter of the Bronco, so he went back and released the emergency brake.

After that it was easy to roll it onto the other block.

Remo reconnoitered the new block. It was flat for a hundred or so yards but soon grew vertical. A peak of snow-dusted ice lifted into the star-touched sky, the top obscured by a mist of ice crystals.

I'm on a freaking iceberg, he decided.

Remo searched his memory for what he knew of icebergs. They broke off from the Arctic ice pack and drifted south, sometimes taking years. This was not an encouraging thought. On the other hand, when they hit warm water below the polar regions, they could melt into nothing. This was even more discouraging to contemplate.

From somewhere in the vicinity of the peak, came a low, mournful growl.

Remo listened. After a while the growl came again.

In the course of his reading, the phrase *blue growler* had stuck with Remo. It was a kind of iceberg that made growling sounds under the stresses of intense wind and cold and water.

Maybe he was on a blue growler.

Except there was nothing blue about the ice and snow. It was definitely whitish. Not bluish. Nothing bluish about it. Maybe they were only blue under strong sunlight.

The growl came again, and this time it sounded organic.

Remo decided he'd look into the growling.

Climbing the iceberg meant exposing himself to high, subfeezing winds, but there was no smarter way to do this. He started up on foot, switched to all fours, and to gain the slippery summit he poked fingerholds into the ice with stabbing thrusts of his forefingers.

From the peak Remo saw the polar bears on the other side as plain as day. They looked surreal—as surreal as the animated polar bears in the soft-drink commercial.

Casually they looked up at him with big wet eyes. Remo gave them a friendly little wave, and one, encouraged, tried to clamber up the iceberg after him. He kept losing his purchase, sliding back on his white rump and spinning when he reached flat pack ice.

When they started to walk around the summit, Remo decided he needed to protect his only shelter.

Climbing down was harder than climbing up, even with prepunched fingerholds. Halfway down Remo was forced to slide on his stomach in emulation of the bear. He came up on all fours, still sliding, and skated on two legs the rest of the way.

He reached the Bronco one step ahead of the loping bears.

Grabbing the door, Remo tried to open it. Stuck. The lock was frozen. Remo gave the lock a quick knuckle strike and tried again. It came open with only a minor hesitation.

He slid in, and was pulling the door shut when a huge white paw swiped in, holding the door open.

Remo slapped the paw. The bear growled. The others advanced, lumbering and curious. They weighed maybe a quarter ton each and started to clamber all over the Bronco, rocking it and jouncing it on its squeaky springs, while pressing their wet black noses to the windows.

Remo batted at the obstructing paw again and, bone-white claws extended, it raked the air, narrowly missing his head.

In that interval he got the door shut and the window up.

"Great. Now I'm stuck here."

The bears circled the Bronco for the next hour, testing its sturdiness and making it rock like a cradle. Remo let them have their fun, hoping they would tire soon and leave him alone.

He hoped there would be time to sneak out and try to snag a fish. He was getting hungry, and because his diet was restricted to fish and duck and rice, polar-bear meat was out of the question.

Remo was fishing about the glove compartment for something to use as a line and hook when one of the bears—the big one that had tried to climb up after him before—got his huge front paws on the rear of the vehicle and started pushing.

"You have got to be kidding me," said Remo as the Bronco began creep toward open water on locked tires.

The emergency brake was on, but the ice was slippery. The polar bear had his entire weight against the Bronco, and it was inching forward with a prolonged scratching of chain-wrapped rubber against the ice.

Remo put his foot on the brake. It didn't help much. The bear continued leaning. The Bronco moved forward until he lost his balance. Then he climbed back up and started the comical cycle all over again.

Ahead, the other bears had dropped into the water. Their black bruin eyes regarded Remo with quiet expectation.

"Okay, show's over," he growled, cracking the door. "Get away. Shoo!"

The bear refused to shoo. But it did keep pushing as if he had an intelligence and a single-minded determination to push Remo, vehicle and all, into the frigid Arctic sea. Or wherever he was.

Having no choice, Remo got out, slamming the door behind him like an angry motorist who had been rear-ended.

"What the ding-dong hell are you doing!" he shouted.

The bear jumped away from the Bronco and retreated a few yards, where he began pawing the ice lazily. He yawned, exposing a fanged mouth like a scarlet cave full of stalactites.

"And stay away!" Remo added for good measure.

It must have been the wrong thing to say to a polar bear, because without warning, the bruin started to gallop at him like an express train.

He was fast. Remo, annoyed, was faster. He took a run at the bear, jumped off the ice and nailed it on the tip of the nose with a furious snap kick.

Remo bounced off and landed on his feet. The bear recoiled as if shot. Shaking its head, it came again.

"You don't learn, do you?" Remo snapped. And let fly again.

This time there was a loud snap as the polar bear's spinal column broke under the expert kick. Remo landed on his feet, the bear lay down dead and the Bronco teetered over the edge of the ice pack and into the cold gray water.

"Damn it! Damn it! Damn it!" Remo shouted, scaring the other bears away. "Damn that Chiun!"

Because there was nothing else to take his frustration out on, he walked over and gave the dead polar bear a splintering kick in the ribs.

He felt better, but it hardly improved the situation any.

Standing by himself, he felt the cold of the Arctic Circle take hold of him with crushing, energy-sapping fingers. His rib cartilage began crackling with each breath. The air going into his lungs became like cold fire. Remo began drawing it in slowly, letting his mouth and air passages warm it before it could reach the delicate tissues of his lungs.

"What would Shang do in this situation?" Remo wondered.

The wind picked up. It blew soft waves of heat off the polar bear's dead hulk.

Snapping his fingers, Remo got down on hands and knees and crawled under the warm body of the dead polar bear, figuring it would get him to morning even though technically it was still daylight.

THAT NIGHT, he walked the polar wastes in his dreams.

The snow and ice lay like a trackless expanse as far as the eye could see. The sun hung low to the horizon as if it were slowly dying. A wind howled, creating spiral vortices like sparkling diamond galaxies.

After a time Remo came upon footprints in the snow. He followed them because he recognized them. Prints left by Korean sandals.

As he walked, leaving no footprints himself, Remo thought to himself how interesting it was that in three thousand years, sandal prints had not changed.

Remo didn't ask himself how in this timeless place of snow and wind he knew he was in the polar wastes of three thousand years gone by. He just knew.

Remo found the owner of the sandal prints shivering in an ice cave.

Squatting in snow, the man seemed to be clothed in snow. His limbs peeped out from a white covering that swathed his body. He was looking down at his naked brown feet.

As Remo approached, he looked up. "I will not fight you, ghost-face," he said.

"Good," said Remo.

"It is not for your benefit that I spare you the challenge, but for the future of the House, which was young when I lived."

"Suit yourself," said Remo.

"I have two things of great import to tell you."

"Shoot," said Remo.

"First be careful whom you love. I loved badly and the line suffered. You must love wisely or love not at all."

Remo said nothing.

"The second thing I must tell you is very important."

"Yeah . . ."

"You must wake up."

"Why?"

"Because you will freeze to death if you do not follow my example."

"What example is that?"

But the Korean only bowed his head and reached back to flip a fragment of the whiteness that covered his bare limbs over his intensely black hair.

Remo saw the fragment had a furred snout, black nose and inexpressibly sad eyes.

HAROLD W. SMITH was lurking on the net.

As the international infobahn crept across the face of the globe like an alien nervous system, a new lexicon evolved to capture the uncharted reality of what some called cyberspace. People posted notes on the net, flamed one another in anger and, in an effort to impart feeling to what had formerly been known as cold type, created symbols known as emoticons—like smilies and frownies—the better to make electronic conversation convey exact shades of meaning only spoken words could.

One coinage of the electronic age was *lurker*. A lurker was someone who browsed the nets and bulletin boards anonymously but never posted messages. Lurkers just lurked and watched, unsuspected.

Harold Smith might be said to be the first lurker in the history of the Internet.

Back when the net was limited to a small handful of computers in government and educational hands, Harold Smith lurked, unknown and unsuspected, watching the message traffic and growing aware that the day was coming when the average American would own a home computer and do the same.

Harold Smith feared that day. Not that he thought it would be entirely a bad thing. If it involved the average American citizen, it would offer a mixture of good and bad.

No, the information explosion was feared by Harold Smith because of the enormous drain it would place on CURE resources. CURE operated on several levels. Wiretapping and other illegal information gathering was part of its intelligence-gathering outreach. So were human intelligence plants. CURE had agents in everything from the National Security Agency to the Department of Agriculture. All reported by mail or telephone or dead drop—or most recently, by E-mail. None knew they worked for Harold W. Smith, although many thought they worked for the CIA.

Data constantly flowed into Harold Smith's mainframes. Data that had to be stored, scanned, evaluated and disposed of. Most were erased as not mission specific. Some were filed for future action or investigation. A few were acted upon.

The proliferation of home computers and electronic exchanges of all kinds meant an entire domain of accessible data had come into existence for Harold Smith to patrol.

Thus, he lurked, unsuspected. He had recently created an electronic-mail address that couldn't be traced back to Folcroft Sanitarium or himself. Through this, an increasingly large number of field contacts reported to him.

Early on Smith had written programs whose sole function was to troll the net for events or people. Global searches were executed on all incoming data so that buzzwords captured pertinent data for review.

But not all the buzzwords in the universe could patrol the net in search of CURE-critical events. Only a discerning mind could perform that function.

So Harold W. Smith lurked.

He skipped the news groups. They were the electronic equivalent of graffiti, Smith had long ago discovered. Most might as well have been scrawled in crayon on sheets of brown wrapping paper.

But all sorts of news traveled the fiber-optic route these days. Especially local news that never went national.

Smith was scanning these. He had a particular and unusual way of dealing with vast blocks of trivia that might contain a kernel of importance. It was an adaptation of the primary speed-reading method whereby the reader ran his eye down the middle of the page at a constant speed and absorbed the gist of the text semi-subconsciously.

Smith found speed-reading useless for absorbing important documents, but for trolling the net it was more than adequate.

Certain key words jumped out at him whenever he did this. His eyes saw everything, but his alert brain only picked up on the key words. In a way Smith functioned like a human data processor when he did this.

It was while scanning a continuous scroll of random news reports that Smith's eyes alighted on a word that caused him to instinctively reach for the scroll-lock key.

The screen froze the amber blocks of text on the buried screen.

It had happened so fast Smith's brain hadn't quite registered the word that caused the reflex action to kick in.

He stared at the word now. It appeared on the screen as "Sunonjo."

Smith blinked his tired gray eyes.

"Sunonjo?" he muttered, tapping a hotkey. In response, a window text opened up in the center of the screen.

"Sunonjo: no exact match."

Knowing that reporters were notorious for factual and spelling errors, Smith tried several variations, including "Sinanjo" and "Sunanju," but each time no match appeared.

Giving up, Smith deactivated the encyclopedia program and turned his attention to the main text.

It was a brief news item datelined Yuma, Arizona. Smith read it carefully.

Arizona Virus (AP)

A new form of hantavirus may mean the end to an obscure group of Indians who have survived in the southwest corner of Arizona for centuries. The Sunonjo tribe have dwelt peacefully in the Sonoran Desert, coexisting with Navajo, Hopi and white man alike. Tribal legends say they have never known war. Now a virulent new hantavirus has emerged, which has begun to lay waste to the peace-loving tribe.

Smith laid his blinking amber cursor against the word *hantavirus*.

Instantly a window opened up.

Hantavirus: A genus of airborne viruses, believed to originate in rodent droppings. First recognized during the Korean War, and named for the Hantaan River, where it was encountered by U.S. Army doctors. Symptoms include coughing and chills, which rapidly progress to a pneumonialike filling of the lungs, and coma. Death often comes within forty hours, if untreated.

"Odd," said Smith.

He finished reading the news extract, found it unimportant except for the coincidence of the name Sunonjo and moved on.

An hour or so later, eyes fatiguing, Smith logged off the net, frowning.

It had been an frivolous expenditure of time, he decided.

Somewhere the truth of Remo Williams's ancestry lurked unsuspected. But wherever it was, it was not to be found on the net. Of that Dr. Harold W. Smith was absolutely positive.

WHEN REMO WOKE UP, his limbs were stiff.

The polar bear atop him had grown cold and seemed to have picked up an extra ton of dead weight.

Remo crawled out and got to work immediately.

He started at the neck, where the warm white fur lay smooth and flat against the bear's skin, and dug his cold-stiffened blue fingers deep into the thick skin.

With one fingernail that was always kept clipped an eighth-inch longer than the others, Remo began scoring the blubbery skin. His nails—like those of all Sinanju Masters—had achieved a combination of strength and sharpness that ordinary people who abused their bodies by consuming beef fat and dairy products, tobacco and alcohol, could never imagine. Many years of prescribed diet and exercise had given Remo's fingernails the cutting power of a straight razor.

Still, even a straight razor had its limitations. As he felt the body heat being sucked out of his lean body by the relentlessly contractive Arctic cold, Remo kept at it until the skin at the back of the polar bear's neck parted like a ghastly pink grin, exposing meat and vertebrae.

Then, selecting a spot over the spine, he climbed atop the behemoth and, working on his knees, began ripping the life-preserving pelt back to the tail. The exuding polar-bear warmth kept his muscles from going too stiff.

When he was done, Remo peeled both sides down to the ice and tried to figure a way to roll the skeletal mass of exposed raw meat and bones off its skin. His muscles felt like iron lumps.

The cold continued to suck energy and warmth from his body at a ferocious rate. An internal awareness of his body's state told Remo he was low on calories and to try to move the monster would leave him weak and exhausted on the remorseless ice with a life expectancy of maybe twenty minutes.

So Remo crawled into the body, squeezing between the thick, yellowish fat and the raw meat and ribs, knowing that the blubber would insulate him from the cold.

To conserve energy, he went back to sleep.

This time he did not dream.

10

The captain of the Canadian Coast Guard cutter *Margaret Trudeau* was skeptical to say the least.

But he saw that the ancient Asian was frantic. It could not be acting. His state was agitated in the extreme.

As the cutter cut through the Arctic sea, the old man paced the afterdeck frantically while searchlights blazed across the cold, unforgiving waters of Cumberland Sound.

It was broad daylight now, but there was a chance the searchlights would be seen by the person they were searching for and he would find a way to signal them.

"Would you mind explaining it all one more time?" Captain Service asked.

"Yes, I would mind," the old man snapped.

"It would help us find your friend."

"He is not my friend. He is a fool whom I cannot leave alone for a single moment."

"You landed in Pangnirtung, a perfectly inhospitable place, where you and your traveling companion rented a vehicle. That much I have clear in my mind. And you went for a ride without benefit of guide or map. Why?"

"Remo is very impetuous."

"No. No. What were you doing in this region? What was your purpose?"

"Vacation."

"You and he were vacationing above the Arctic Circle?"

"It is summer, is it not?"

"Yes. But it hardly constitutes the summer of the lower latitudes."

The old man flapped his scarlet sleeves like a flustered bird trying to take off. "We were driving and ran out of fuel. I went in search of a gas station and when I came back, the vehicle was gone and so was Remo."

"Your *friend* sent you across pack ice for gas?"

"I know it is idiotic. But I could not trust him not to become lost."

"I understand you parked at the edge of the sea. A very dangerous place."

"How was I to know the idiot would park upon a shelf of ice that would fall into the sea?"

"Actually it didn't fall. It simply broke off and drifted away. It happens all the time during these summer months."

The old Asian made a snappish gesture with one flapping sleeve. "With Remo and the vehicle upon it. No doubt he was asleep and entirely oblivious to all!"

"Please calm down. He could not have drifted very far in so short a time. I am confident we will find him."

"In this merciless cold? It will sap him of all vitality."

Captain Service said nothing to that. There was no gainsaying it. If the foolish American who had parked at the edge of Cumberland Sound only to drift off on an ice pack was not soon found, he would certainly perish by the time he reached Davis Strait.

"We will find him," Service promised.

But as he returned to the bridge, he saw by his watch that the chances had become very slim indeed. This cold tended to suck the life from a man like some ferocious, icy Dracula.

LITTLE MORE THAN an hour later the first mate called out. "Captain, I spy something unusual."

Captain Service went directly to the bow and raised his binoculars.

"See that growler, sir? There's a polar bear just starboard of the peak."

"Skinned," the captain said, nodding.

"We might take a look."

Captain Service barked out orders, and the cutter changed course. Soon, under the prod of its churning screws, it warped alongside the looming iceberg and was made fast.

First off the cutter—before anyone could stop him—was the frail old Asian named Chiun. Bounding across the pack ice, he suddenly didn't look very frail at all. The crew was hard put to keep up with him, in fact.

His squeakily plaintive voice echoed off the blue berg. "Remo! Remo, are you here?"

The dead and rent polar bear quivered in answer.

And a bluish face popped out from behind a flap of blood-spotted bear hide.

"Chiun!" a voice croaked.

"Look what you have put me through!"

The blue American's face became angry. "Me put *you* through? You're the one who marooned me on a freaking ice pack!"

The old Asian shrieked in reply, "Do not dare blame your miserable failures upon me! After all I have done for you!"

"I was asleep in the back seat one moment, and the next I'm playing Nanook of the North. With no sign of you anywhere."

"Was it my idea to come to this awful place of ice and bitter cold?"

"Yes!"

"Liar."

Captain Service and a complement of men trudged up as the argument grew shrill.

"Hah!" cried Chiun, pointing angrily toward the Canadians. "Tell your false tale of woe to these brave sailors who have risked all to succor you."

"It was his idea," Remo said, pointing back to Chiun. "He thinks this is the moon."

"You flipped the fickle coin that brought us here," Chiun countered.

"You flipped a coin?" Captain Service said, dumbfounded.

"Yeah," said the blue-faced Remo. "It was either here or Africa."

"Why would anyone go to Africa on vacation?" asked Captain Service in a stumped voice.

"Search me," said Remo, crawling out and letting his body shiver.

"Why are you shivering?" Chiun demanded.

"Because I'm freezing, damn it!"

"Bring an oilskin for this man," Service ordered.

Chiun narrowed his eyes to thin slits. "Do not bother. Let him wear the pelt of his handiwork."

"I'm cold, not desperate. I'll take the oilskin."

To the astonishment of all, the tiny Asian stepped up to the dead polar bear and, with quick swipes of his long fingernails, stripped the dead brute of a section of pristine hide.

Remo pulled this over his shoulders. "Man, I thought I'd never live through the night."

Chiun looked around unhappily. "Where is the vehicle? I do not see it."

"Thanks for your consideration," Remo said bitterly, cocking a thumb over his shoulder. "But that moronic polar bear pushed it into the water."

"Then you must pay for it."

"There is also a fine for killing this bear without a proper license," said Captain Service. "I assume you do not possess the proper license?"

"License, my ass!" Remo exploded. "That bear jumped me! It was self-defense."

"He is quite the complainer for one who has been rescued," Captain Service remarked to Chiun.

Chiun rolled his eyes. "His carping has been incessant during all the years I have known the wretch. And he is forever falling into ridiculous predicaments such as this."

"He does appear to be the hard-luck sort," the captain agreed.

"Can we just be on our way?" Remo grumbled. "I feel like an idiot standing here in a polar-bear skin."

"Embrace the feeling," Chiun squeaked.

WHEN THEY PULLED into port, Remo said, "We're blowing this Popsicle stand, and I don't want to hear different."

"After you have paid the lawful fine," reminded Captain Service.

Wearily Remo handed over his gold card.

"As well as all expenses incurred during your rescue," Captain Service added.

"Don't you rescue people as part of your duties?" Remo asked.

"We rescue *Canadians* as part of our duties. Americans have to pay."

"Don't you people have universal health coverage up here?"

"We do. But what does that have to do with your situation?"

Remo pointed an accusing finger at the Master of Sinanju. "Because after twenty years of associating with this old reprobate, I have to be out of my mind to keep following him wherever he goes. Therefore, I plead insanity."

"Insanity is a plea normally made in a court of law."

Remo offered his wrists for cuffing. "Haul me before a magistrate, and I'll so plead."

"Sorry," said the captain of the Canadian Coast Guard cutter as he ran a credit check on Remo.

"I can hardly wait to get home," Remo told Chiun pointedly.

"You can hardly stand," countered Chiun. "And you are not going home."

"Where am I going then?"

"Africa."

"I am not going to Africa."

"Or we can put off Africa and its soothing heat and go directly to Hesperia."

"Where's Hesperia?"

"Where we are going if we do not go to Africa."

"On second thought," said Remo, "how bad can Africa be?"

THE STEWARDESSES on the Air Ghana flight wanted to know if inasmuch as they were flying into war-torn Stomique, Remo wouldn't like to have sex one last time.

"I don't intend to die in Africa," Remo told them.

"Once you are dead, it will be too late to change your mind," a second stewardess smilingly argued.

"I am not changing my mind," Remo assured her.

"Are we not the most beautiful black women you have seen?" asked a third in a pouty voice.

Remo conceded the point. They were as elegantly slim as high-fashion models.

"And are we not alone in this great big aircraft, just you and the four of us, and is it not a flight of seven boring hours?"

"You're forgetting my chaperon," said Remo, jerking his thumb over his shoulder to the Master of Sinanju, seated six rows back over the starboard wing.

"If he is your chaperon, why do you not sit together?"

"We're having a tiff."

"You should not be angry with him. He looks very sweet."

"He tried to feed me to the polar bears a while back. Before that, he almost got me drowned. And I had to move the Sphinx all by myself."

"Then you should not care that your cruel chaperon disapproves your sleeping with four beautiful flight attendants."

"Did you know we were all Miss Ghana?" another stewardess wondered.

"I only sleep with Miss Universes, and even then only one per year."

The four ex-Miss Ghanas looked perplexed. They repaired to the galley, huddled briefly and when they came out again they wore fierce expressions.

"We have discussed this," one announced sternly, "and have concluded that you are a vicious racist for not sleeping with us."

"Yes. An obvious vicious racist."

"I am not a racist," Remo said wearily.

"A definite racist. One who refuses to sit with his yellow chaperon or sleep with gorgeous, willing and eager black women."

Remo got up. "All right, all right," he said.

The stewardesses brightened. "You are weakening?"

"No. I surrender absolutely."

The four ex-Miss Ghanas hurried to unbutton their blouses, uniforms and step out of their panty hose.

"Not that," said Remo. "I'm going to sit with my chaperon."

"Homo," they hooted after him. "Girlie boy."

After he took the seat beside the Master of Sinanju and a frosty silence hung in the air, Remo said, "I met Master Lu."

"Goody for you."

"He hinted that I was Korean."

"You are not good enough, brave enough or wise enough to be Korean," Chiun sniffed.

"These dreams I'm having are just that. Dreams."

Chiun made a snorting sound of derision.

"A person can't meet himself. It's impossible," Remo continued.

"You are impossible."

"You should talk."

The frosty silence returned.

"You know, Lu looked kinda familiar. Around the eyes."

"You have seen Lu's eyes before?" Chiun asked.

"Yeah," admitted Remo. "But I can't place them."

"Look in the mirror."

"I am not Korean."

"Then do not look in the mirror if you fear the truth."

"Don't worry. I won't."

"Coward," sniffed Chiun.

"Sticks and stones break mirrors, but not my resolve to avoid looking into the mirror," Remo said firmly.

A little while later, Remo pretended he had to use the men's room.

When he returned to his seat, Chiun asked, "Well?"

"Well what?"

"Do not take me for an idiot. You looked in the bathroom mirror. What did you see?"

"Coincidence."

"You will never grow up," Chiun said unhappily.

"What are you talking about?"

"You will never achieve Reigning Master status. I should have known better than to train a white. I have been burdened with shepherding a pupil longer than any Master since Yung. I long for the peace and joy of retirement."

"Since when?"

"Since I have been burdened by your insufferable whiteness," Chiun said, turning his face to the window and the marching stratocumulus clouds beyond.

"You ache for retirement the way I yearn for roast duckling. Not at all."

"I have trained a pupil who spurns duckling, the most sublime of fowl," Chiun lamented, shaking his head until the cloudy wisps over each ear shook with sorrow.

Angrily Remo changed seats again.

As soon as he did, the four stewardesses drew straws. The winner approached him.

"Leave me alone," Remo snapped. "I'm going to take a nap."

"Before I go, would you like something warm to cover you?"

"Fine," said Remo.

And the stewardess draped her lush, dark body across Remo Williams's lean, vaguely bluish one.

Remo was so beat he just went to sleep with the contentedly purring stewardess atop him. It beat being laid out flat under a polar bear.

EVERYWHERE WAS BLACKNESS. Without form or shape or size. The ground was as black as the sky. There was no horizon and no light. All was ink.

"You are not worthy," a disembodied voice said coldly.

Standing in the breathable ink, Remo said nothing.

"I am Ko," the voice rang out.

Remo tried to fix the voice. It seemed to be everywhere. And since everywhere was blackness, it might as well be nowhere.

"And this is my sword!" the voice of Ko boomed.

As if covered in black silk that had slipped off, the point of a sword appeared in the darkness surrounding Remo.

He recognized the wide, flaring point. It was the Sword of Sinanju, forged centuries ago by Master Ko as a headman's sword. It had been lost to the Chinese until he and Chiun had recovered it years ago in Beijing.

"I find you guilty of the crime of unworthiness and sentence you to lose your head," the voice behind the sword said.

Remo said nothing. The sword lifted high and drew back. When the blade started for him, it might as well have been delivered by a Federal Express carrier.

Remo dodged it easily. On the back swing, he moved in for the Master wielding it.

Somehow he miscalculated and went flying past.

Dropping to a defensive crouch, Remo felt a lock of his hair fly away as the double-edged blade swept back and forth like a great scythe.

Slithering away and up again, Remo assumed a defensive position. One foot tucked against his calf, hands floating before his breastbone.

Masters of Sinanju in the days of Ko were pre-Wang, he knew. They hadn't known of the sun source. They were good, but their techniques were those the *ninja* later copied.

Ko was wearing black silk, Remo understood, and the sword suddenly vanished beneath what was probably a cloak.

"I don't kill that easy," Remo said. Stepping around in the dark, he knew the blade—which, uncloaked, exceeded seven feet in length—could slip out of the silk cape and seek his vitals from any unexpected angle.

"You will die before you become the head of the House."

"Bigot!" Remo taunted.

"Ghost-face."

"Chicken."

"What is wrong with chicken?" the disembodied voice wanted to know.

"Chickens are frightened by any low thunder," Remo countered.

"I am a rooster, not a hen, ghost-face."

And seeing a glint of steel in the darkness, Remo kicked up and high.

His foot connected and the Sword of Sinanju jumped high, cartwheeled in slow motion, and Remo faded back to get out of its way.

A slickness brushed the back of Remo's hand, and instinctively he snared it, yanking hard.

The blade pinned the black cloak against the blacker ground, and Master Ko slipped out of his concealing garment.

Remo got a momentary glimpse of him then. He wore black and a black hood. He shucked this off and, looking at Remo with a grudging respect, bowed in his direction.

Then he snapped up his cloak, and it swallowed him utterly and forever.

Exhausted, Remo slept on.

11

Mahout Feroze Anin, Supreme Warlord of lower Stomique on the Horn of Africa, plugged one ear with a thin brown finger and pressed the satellite cell-phone receiver more closely to his other ear to keep out the steady *thoom* of mortars and the insistent rattle of small-arms fire.

"I challenge all of America to a fight," he raged.

"Over what?" asked the American ambassador.

"Over..." Anin made a face. His lean face, so open beneath his high, shining forehead, dripped sweat. It was the face that had graced the covers of *Time, Newsweek, People* and other great international magazines so often only a few years ago, but now was scarcely to be found in the newspapers of the surviving Stomique capital, Nogongog.

It was called the surviving capital because of all the cities in Stomique, both upper and lower, it was the only one not yet in abject ruins.

This was not how Anin had expected things to turn out when the UN peacekeeping force first stormed ashore in their effort to restore democracy to Stomique. Back then Anin had known exactly what to do. He hastily purchased a Western suit and tie, sought out a CNN microphone and welcomed the Americans with open arms and a beaming smile that soon radiated from news magazines all over the globe. He was certain that this magnificent PR gesture would put him in the good graces of Washington, and after a suitable period, they would install him as the new president of Stomique, his warlord days forever behind him.

But they had not. Instead, they had insisted that he surrender his cached weapons.

"But I am pro-American!" Mahout Feroze Anin had complained to the American ambassador in those early days of the UN occupation.

"Excellent. Have your weapons fieldstripped and hand them over to the chief UN observer."

But Anin hadn't done that. Instead, he'd gone underground. And the UN had come after him. So naturally he'd fought back. When his technicals had ambushed a Belgian UN peacekeeping unit, Mahout Feroze Anin's smiling pro-American face was plastered on Wanted posters all over Nogongog, and the U.S. Rangers were sent in. Mahout Feroze Anin had been forced to take up the sword and the gun and send his followers after the treacherous Rangers, who obviously didn't know an ally when one offered his empty hand.

It had proved to be a smart move. In the short run.

The Rangers had been chased out of Nogongog, and Mahout Feroze Anin had elevated himself to Supreme Warlord of lower Stomique, victorious over the world's last superpower.

The trouble was, after the short run came the long run.

Stomique fell back into internecine feuding. No sooner had Anin liquidated his most deadly rival warlords than others sprang up to take their place. Instead of two enemies, he had four. And when he had the four butchered, there were suddenly eight. All weaker than those who had come before, but just as vexing.

Eventually, the UN relief supplies ceased to flow into Stomique. And when that happened, there was no more food for Anin to seize, some to feed his followers, the rest to be converted into gold bullion.

As Stomique fell more and more into ruin, Anin was forced to pay his followers in shiny ingots until his gold stocks began to dwindle.

Now, three years after the Americans had left, Mahout Feroze Anin realized there was no percentage in being Supreme Warlord over a smaller and smaller corner of lower Stomique if in the end there was no country left and, in consequence, no place to hide.

So it was time to play his last card.

"Why are you calling, General Anin?" the American ambassador asked in a cool voice.

"Our fight has not yet been decided."

"You won."

"I do not agree. Tell your President I am prepared to give him the rematch he secretly covets."

"The U.S.," the ambassador said patiently, "has no interest in a rematch."

"Cowards! You run away at the merest casualties."

"We entered to feed your people, disarm all warring factions and restore peace, and your particular faction turned it into a shooting gallery. Fine. Now it's your private shooting gallery. Best of luck with it."

"I will not be trifled with in this unseemly manner. It is an insult."

Anin cringed from the sudden *thoom* and *crump* that came through the French colonial windows of his office.

"Is that mortar fire I hear in the background?" the ambassador asked pointedly.

"Firecrackers. We are celebrating our glorious triumph over the cowardly U.S."

"Three years later?"

"It is a victory that will reverberate down the ages," Anin said in a grandiose voice from the well of his bulletproof steel desk. "Unless you move swiftly to reengage on the field of honor."

"What do you know about honor? You called yourself a patriot of Stomique while you pillaged the relief food that poured in to feed your own people."

"My people do not need food. For their bellies are full of victory. Hah. How do *your* citizens feel?"

"Stomique is last year's news. They're already onto something else."

Mahout Feroze Anin made his voice wheedling. "Do you not desire to occupy your luxurious ambassadorial residence once again?"

"Absolutely. When there's a stable country surrounding it. In the meanwhile, Washington will do just fine."

Anin pounded the floor in anger. "There will never be stability while I am Supreme Warlord. You must know this. You will have to dislodge me if you wish to enjoy stability again."

"Do I detect you angling for something?"

Anin took a deep breath and threw down his cards. "I will agree to surrender to the despised U.S. in return for guaranteed safe passage to an exile country of my choosing—provided, of course, a lifetime stipend comes with it."

"Sorry. We have no vital interests in Stomique."

"Did I mention my nuclear reacting? I will soon be in possession of many kilograms of enriched helium. Weapons grade, of course."

"Nice try," said the U.S. ambassador just before the line went click in Mahout Feroze Anin's ear.

"Idiot!" said Warlord Anin, throwing the receiver against his official presidential portrait, puncturing the black velvet.

The tapping of shod feet came from outside the heavy mahogany double doors of the presidential office. They were not the heavy clump of boots, so it couldn't be his personal guard or the rebels. Since almost no one else owned shoes in post-UN-occupied Stomique, Anin knew it had to be a relative.

"Father! Father! The enemy approaches!" came a husky voice.

Anin looked up from under the desk. It was his eldest daughter, Persephone, her dark face a sheen of sweat.

"How did you get past my personal guards?" Anin demanded.

Persephone looked perplexed. "What guards? There is no one here."

Anin leaped for the door and looked out. The corridor was bereft of guards.

"Who guards my gold?" he demanded hotly, wiping his high balding forehead.

"Eurydice and Omphale."

Anin nodded. "Excellent. If a man cannot trust his daughters, who can he trust?"

Persephone took hold of his chest, which rattled from clusters of medals he had awarded himself for every engagement in his military career from shooting rival foes in the back to surviving a six-year drought. "Father, we must flee. The rebels have secured their hold on the main roads and are now advancing on your palace."

"I will not leave my gold behind."

"But who will carry it?"

"You and your wonderful and loyal sisters, Persephone. Of course."

"We are not strong enough. The gold will slow us down."

Anin ripped his daughter's hands from him and turned away in disgust. "Bah! I curse the day I had daughters instead of strapping warrior sons. Sons would never fail me as you three have."

Persephone sank to her knees, taking Warlord Anin's legs in her tapered brown fingers and pressing her strong cheeks to his knees. "I do not want to die, father. You must save me."

"Your sisters, they have good weapons?"

"Oh, the best. Soviet-made Kalashnikovs. Not those shoddy Chinese ones."

"And the basement vault door, it will withstand mortar and grenade attacks?"

"Just as you decreed it should."

"Then go to the basement vault and shut yourself in until I come for you and the gold."

"How long will that be, Father?"

"Until I have vanquished the rebels."

"You cannot fight them single-handed."

Anin shook a defiant fist like mahogany. "And I will not. The Americans will fight them for us."

Persephone stood up. "But the Americans are our enemies."

"In the past, yes. In the future, absolutely. But for this crisis, I will inveigle them into siding with me. For they are fools who are easily hoodwinked. Now, go shut yourself in. Be certain you have food and water to sustain you, for it may be two or three days.''

"You expect to defeat the rebels in so short a time?"

"Yes," said Mahout Feroze Anin, guiding his flesh and blood into the secret trapdoor in the downstairs kitchen and into the underground vault room.

Pushing the ponderous door shut, he waved farewell to his smiling and tearful daughters, who blew him kisses and swore undying love.

With the door closed, Anin activated the time lock, after first setting it for the year 1999.

By that time, he reasoned, the revolution should have settled down. The heat would be off, and Mahout Feroze Anin could reclaim his gold unchallenged.

And bury his long-dead and useless daughters, as well. He cursed their mothers, all of whom had promised him a male heir and every one of which were ceremoniously beheaded when they failed so simple a task.

Throwing a lever that caused a thick wall of rough boards to drop into place before the great stainless-steel door, Anin went to the trapdoor in the floor—which he had kept secret even from his trustworthy offspring—and slipped down into his cool, loamy burrow.

From here it was a simple matter to walk the three or four miles to the secret boat house on the water, from which he would escape to a safe haven.

What safe haven, he didn't know, but Africa was full of safe havens for brave and cunning men like Mahout Feroze Anin. Perhaps there would be a place for him in Rwanda, he thought as he walked along. There was always someone to be slain or relief food to be pilfered.

As he moved through the insect-ridden tunnel, he wondered if Rwanda was accessible by boat. He had no idea. During his brief regime, Anin had the official Stomique map of Africa redrawn so that it appeared to occupy eighty-six percent of the continent.

It seemed only fitting that the unconquered and unconquerable defier of the United States of America should govern a nation as vast as his ego.

THE LANDING at Nogongog Inter-African Airport was smooth, considering the cratered condition of the single runway.

The plane didn't come to a full stop. Engines spooling down, it trundled past the terminal and the door was flung open by stewardesses in flak jackets.

A speeding truck with a set of bullet-pocked air-stairs scooted out from a hangar and ran parallel to the open door.

"I demand this craft halt and I be allowed to leave it with the dignity befitting my station," Chiun told the stewardess in charge.

"It would be suicide to stop," the stewardess said.

"Come on, Little Father," said Remo, hanging in the door frame. "Shake a leg."

The stewardess tried to pull Remo back in with her gold-painted nails. "No, please do not go. It would be suicide."

"Why are you okay with him getting off and not me?" Remo wondered, indicating the Master of Sinanju.

"He is old and will die soon. You are full of youth and brimming with sperm."

"Sperm?"

"Your sperm is important to us."

"Check with me on the ride back," said Remo, jumping off and onto the rattly top step of the speeding air-stairs.

The Master of Sinanju floated off and joined him. There were no other passengers.

The truck careered toward the terminal and came to a brief stop at the gaping hole where the jetway ramp used to be before a mortar barrage had taken it out. It still smoked a little in the brassy midday sun.

Remo and Chiun stepped across the gap and entered the refugee-choked terminal. On the tarmac the jet screamed back into the sky with tracers chasing it.

There were no taxicabs waiting outside, but there was a line of scarred and bullet-pocked camels.

Chiun walked up to the man who seemed to be in charge of the camels and began conversing with him in fluent Swahili.

"I am not riding any camel," Remo called over.

Chiun continued his haggling. Hot words were exchanged, and the argument might have gone on two or three hours except one camel expectorated on the Master of Sinanju's sandals.

Emitting an offended scream, Chiun began walking in circles, alternately pointing at the offending camel, at the offending camel's owner and at the offending camel again, his squeaky voice escalating into fulsome shrieks.

Chiun came back leading the offending camel by a thick rope. "We have a steed," he announced.

"No, *you* have a spitting camel."

The camel obligingly backed up Remo's statement by spitting rudely in the dust of Nogongog.

"He cannot spit on those perched atop him," Chiun declared.

"No sale. And don't think I didn't see what you did, because I did."

"I have gotten redress for an insult."

"My left foot. You saw that camel was spitting to beat the band. You moved your sandal closer to take a shot in the foot."

"Ridiculous. It was an insult."

"Even if you didn't move your foot into spitting range, you could have moved it away in plenty of time."

"I gave the camel drover a choice. Loan me the offending beast without charge or wipe my sandal clean with his beard."

"You don't have to tell me how it turned out," Remo said, glumly, eyeing the camel. The camel eyed him back. His rubbery mouth masticated something dark and malodorous with ominous relish, and Remo took three hasty steps back and one to the right.

The saliva made a greenish splash off to his left. The camel resumed his patient masticating.

"I'm not riding that spitball maker!"

"Of course," said Chiun. "You must bargain for your own camel."

"I don't ride camels. They smell, they're unsanitary and they're rude."

"Then you may walk," said the Master of Sinanju, motioning for the camel to kneel. To Remo's surprise, it did, getting down on all four knobby knees.

When Chiun was comfortably balanced atop its hump, he made a clucking sound, and the camel rose with a strange grace to his feet.

The camel started off. Remo followed.

He soon found there was no happy place to walk near a moving camel. If he led, the camel tried to taste the back of his T- shirt. Walking on either side invited expectoration.

And walking in the rear subjected Remo to camel gas or puddinglike droppings.

The city seemed to be victim to the immediate aftermath of revolution. There was looting. Dark, frightened faces peered from bullet-broken windows. Fires had blackened many buildings.

They were only challenged once when a Stomique technical came rattling up a dirt road to block their path.

It was a pickup truck, a .35-caliber machine gun bolted to the bed. The perforated muzzle swung in Remo's direction, and something was said in harsh Swahili.

Remo lifted his hands to show he was unarmed, walking up to the muzzle as if it were no more threatening than a water pipe. He offered his wallet. An eager hand reached out to snatch it. Remo pulled it back before questing fingers grazed it.

The red-bereted Stomiqui soldier screeched something angry and brought his thumbs down on the machine gun's trips.

The bullets began knocking out of the barrel.

The first shell exploded a full second and a half after Remo had given the cold muzzle a casual bat with one hand.

The weapon spun on its steel tripod so fast that when the first bullet emerged from the flaming barrel it had swung a full 180 degrees.

The machine gunner screamed surprise as his belly was ripped apart by the very bullets he himself had unleashed.

There were other rebels in the truck. They stuck their heads out of the cab to see what had happened, and Remo showed them how vulnerable their eardrums were. He clapped their ears between his hands, producing a thunder that never ended.

The two ran off with their eardrums permanently ringing.

"Okay," Remo said as they resumed their stroll through the remains of Nogongog. "What brings us to this hellhole?"

"We have come for the gold," said Chiun, searching the neighborhood from the high vantage of his ungainly perch.

"What gold?"

"Do you not see that there is a rebellion?"

"It looks more like an earthquake with small-arms fire for punctuation."

"This sorry nation is in revolt. Ruling heads are about to be separated from ruling shoulders. Allegiances are soon to change. And where there is revolution, there is sure to be gold and treasure destined to change hands."

"I take it we're after the gold and treasure?"

"No. *You* are."

"It's mine to keep?"

Chiun nodded. "If you can seize it without losing your life."

"Is mere gold worth my life?"

"Ordinarily, perhaps."

"Do I have any say in this?"

Chiun shook his head firmly. "None."

THEY CAME UPON the presidential palace in what had been the southern outskirts of the city before the jungle had begun to overrun it. Two things were noteworthy about it. It looked like a giant frosted cake standing at the jungle edge. And it was the only building in all Stomique that had not been scorched and broken by rebellious residents.

The Master of Sinanju brought his ungainly steed to a halt outside the palace gates.

"I don't see any guards," Remo said.

"A good sign."

"Couldn't that mean the gold is already gone?"

"If you are unfortunate, that is possible," Chiun admitted.

"I don't care if I grab off any gold or not. I'm on an unlimited expense account."

"If you do not seize this gold, you will be reduced to pillaging Fort Knox."

"I don't think they have gold in Fort Knox anymore, Little Father."

"Then you will have to strain the very gold dust from the ocean to accomplish your task."

"That could take years."

"Especially if you strain this gold with your teeth."

"Be back in a minute or two," said Remo, hopping the twenty-foot fence from a standing position. There was no warning. Remo didn't even flex his knees visibly.

When his feet hit the ground on the other side, they did so with no more noise that an autumn leaf touching grass.

Remo advanced, his entire body keying up. His eyes scanned the ground for faint depressions that would tell of buried land mines. None. Motion-vibration detectors were either off line or untended.

No one took a shot at him as he crossed to the veranda and stepped into the great French colonial villa.

Remo pushed open one of the double entrance doors and heard a distinct click.

Instinctively he grabbed the hand grenade that dropped off its spoon that had been held to the door with bungee cord.

Pivoting on one foot, Remo relaxed his fingers when he felt the grenade's mass tug at the top of his throw.

The steel egg flew nearly fifty yards and let go in midair. Hot steel went in all directions, breaking windows and setting tiny fires in the dry grass.

One fragment arced toward Remo, its velocity nearly spent.

Casually he broke a spindle off the veranda and used it to bat the grenade fragment away.

Then he entered.

The place echoed with no sounds. Remo shut his eyes. He sensed no living beings—unless the mice skittering in the partitions counted. They didn't.

Remo swept up the great staircase that looked as if it had come out of *Gone with the Wind* and found the presidential office.

The room was empty. Every room was empty. He opened every door to make sure. He encountered no more boobytraps until he tried a cleverly concealed trapdoor in the downstairs kitchen.

It was a solid piece of carpentry, invisible except for the faint imprint of human oil left by four fingers on the floor where the last person to go down had braced himself while dropping the trap shut after him.

Remo got down on one knee and looked for a catch or keyhole. He found none. So he punched a finger into the hard wood and curled it.

When he retracted his arm, the trap came up, something mechanical coughed and an ironwood spear with a barbed point ripped through the spot where he would have been had he opened the trapdoor normally.

It impaled the ice dispenser of an imported avocado Hotpoint refrigerator. Ice cubes clattered out.

Remo let the trap clank back and, ignoring the wooden steps that might be booby-trapped, dropped into the space.

There was a concrete conduit that smelled of heavy air, and Remo padded along it to a room at the other end.

There was no door, only a bead curtain, and Remo passed through it without rattling the beads. There was an open trapdoor in the center of the floor, showing a tunnel. There was no gold in the room. In fact, there wasn't anything in the room expect the square hole in the center of the concrete floor.

Anyone else would have turned back, but the faint hum of electricity reached Remo's sensitive ears and made the hairs on his bare forearms lift slightly in warning.

The south wall. It was faced with crude planks, resembling barn-board. Remo attacked the boards and exposed a dirt wall. But the wall looked wrong. The dirt was too dry. This deep in the humid ground, it should have been moist and busy with insects and rootlets.

Plunging a finger in, Remo felt a hard surface behind the dirt that was plastered to it like dried mud.

The catch was actually a small hole near the floor. Remo poked his fingers into it, there was a click and he jumped straight back and down the convenient hole in case it was wired to blow.

It was. Clods of dirt and wood shards went flying. Some showered down into the hole.

When the concussion waves abated, Remo climbed up and took stock.

The explosion had revealed the ponderous face of a time vault that would have done credit to Chase Manhattan Bank.

Remo approached. The mechanism was locked. There was a digital window that silently counted down the days, hours, minutes and seconds to April 28, 1999.

"Oh, great," said Remo in the echoing, post-blast silence.

Making a fist, Remo drove it into the door. The steel rang like a bell.

And deep behind the door, someone rapped in response.

Remo hit the door again. Harder this time. He got another response. There seemed to be more than one person inside, because the return rap was a confused tattoo of overlapping sound.

Feeling around the thick edge of the door, Remo sought weak points. When he had something, he dug his fingers into the flange.

He yanked. The door groaned slightly. Remo moved in, finding another place. He yanked again. Each time, the door groaned slightly. And as he moved his hands around the dial of the door, the hard, thick steel began to look frilly.

Three times around the dial Remo worked, each time making the steel looser and looser.

When the safe door resembled some bizarre, giant frilly flower, Remo had the edges of the two great hinges partially exposed. After that it was easy. He just hammered at it with the edge of one hand until the steel, vibrating higher and higher, succumbed to Sinanju-induced stress fatigue.

The door toppled out and hit the floor with a ringing clang.

Remo peered into the space beyond.

Three dark faces stared back. They were pretty faces, and the eyes in those pretty faces were almond shaped and exotically beautiful.

Until they went wide at the sight of his unfamiliar white face.

Then they lit up their Kalashnikovs.

12

Three screaming bullet tracks converged on the same point, where the white intruder stood.

They collided and began ricocheting wildly, bouncing off steel, burying themselves in planks and bringing screams from the three African women who had unleashed them.

"Where is he, the white one?" asked Persephone, blinking dully into the hanging gun smoke.

"I do not know," said Eurydice, yanking out a clip and inserting another into the receiver.

"Maybe we have shot him to tiny white slivers of flesh," suggested Omphale.

But when they stepped out of the vault to see, there wasn't a solitary drop of blood on the concrete floor to show that a man had stood there a moment before.

"We have missed...." Eurydice hissed venomously.

"How could we miss? These are Russian-made Kalashnikovs, not shoddy Chinese rip-offs."

"That's 'knockoffs,' foolish one," said Persephone.

A commotion from the vault brought them swinging around.

It was the white man. He was opening the apple crates that filled the vault. The amazing thing was that they were nailed shut by ten-inch nails driven by pneumatic nail guns.

Yet the white was lifting each lid with no more effort than a child peering into a cookie jar. Except the nails screeched. They screeched like tortured Stomiqui dissidents. It brought nostalgic smiles to the three sisters' fine-boned faces.

Persephone screeched, too. "Get away from our father's crates!"

"He lock you up in this vault?" asked the white, not looking up from his investigations.

"*Oui*. And we are sworn to protect his property with our very lives."

The white pulled out a can of piña colada mix.

"I don't think he left you enough food," he said.

"Get away or we will blow you to Chicken McNuggets, white meat," Omphale boasted.

"You tried that already. Remember?"

"*Oui*. So why are you not dead?"

"It's not my time."

"You are protected by Shango?" asked Eurydice.

"Who's Shango?" asked the white, reading the label on a tin of imported Bulgarian caviar and making a face.

"Shango is our god. After our father, who is more than a god to us, having given us life."

"Guess he felt he could take it away any time he pleased, too," the white said with casual disinterest.

Persephone demanded, "Why do you say such a blasphemous thing?"

"You've got around three weeks' supply of food here."

"That is none of your damn business, stringy chicken meat."

"Maybe not, but it's yours if you thought it was going to last you till 1999."

"What does he mean?" Eurydice asked Omphale.

"*Oui*, what do you mean?" Persephone asked the white who was now hovering dangerously near the gold.

"Check the time clock."

"Do this thing," Persephone told Eurydice.

"Do this thing," Eurydice told Omphale.

"Why do I have to do this if Persephone told you to do it?" Omphale grumbled.

"Because you are the youngest," sneered Eurydice.

"Someday I will be older than both of you and we will see who bosses who about like a Filipina maid. I was not named after a Greek goddess to be a slave."

Omphale looked at the time-clock display. It was still counting down. It had counted down nearly a day and, according to the digital display, it was a long way from opening by itself.

"It says 1999," she said.

"Liar!" Persephone screeched.

"See for yourself."

Persephone rushed to the display. "You changed it," she accused the white.

"If I could change it," the white countered, "wouldn't I have changed it so I could just throw the handle and open the door instead of ripping it apart?"

"This is a reasonable point," Omphale whispered.

Everyone agreed it was reasonable point. Then realization dawned on their dusky faces.

"You have saved our lives!" Persephone cried.

"You're welcome. Where's the gold?"

"It is our father's gold. You cannot have it."

"Is that the same father who locked you in to starve to death slowly?"

"*Oui . . .*"

"Don't see that you owe him much." The white ripped open another crate. "You sure have a lot of apples in these boxes."

"They are apple crates," said Persephone.

"We like apples," added Eurydice.

"*Oui*," Omphale said. "They are very exotic fruit."

The white lifted a deep red apple out of the crate he was inspecting. "Waxy, too," he said.

"The wax is to keep it fresh," Eurydice said. "So that they do not spoil in the baking heat."

"*Oui*," Persephone added. "Apples are very delicate."

The white tossed the apple into the air. It returned to his palm with the meaty smack of a cannonball. "Heavy, too."

"These are magic apples. They were picked to sustain us many weeks."

"All the way to 1999?"

The three sisters wavered in their defiance. Their AK-47 rifle muzzles wavered, too.

"Should we shoot him?" Omphale hissed.

"He saved our lives," Eurydice countered.

"What good is being alive if we have no country, no father and no wealth?" Persephone persisted.

"*Oui*. Without wealth, life is not worth living."

"Let us kill him and enjoy life," Persephone urged.

"*Oui*, let's," agreed Omphale.

And the three AK-47 muzzles lifted toward the white who was puzzling over the waxy apples that were too heavy for fruit.

Three simultaneous bursts ripped toward him. He was already behind a stack of crates when the bullets arrived in the space where he had been.

The crates shook under the thudding lash of lead, and splinters flew everywhere.

One grazed Persephone in the arm, and she dropped her weapon screaming, "I am hit! I am hit! I am bleeding to death!"

"Good," said Omphale, who redirected her fire at her sister's heaving chest. "Let me put you of your misery."

The muzzle erupted.

"Aiiee!" shrieked Persephone, crumpling to the dirt floor.

The white was suddenly among them, and the first hint of being disarmed came when their fingers began stinging the way they did when their father used to take an admonishing riding crop to them.

The rifles went down the hole in the floor.

The two surviving sisters dropped to their knees and began begging for their lives.

"You can have your useless lives. I don't want them," said the white, returning to the crates. He picked up an apple and balanced it on one thumb. He set it spinning and dug the opposite thumbnail into the waxy flesh. Skin skimmed off like red wood shavings under the action of a high-speed lathe.

The meat exposed was not white, like the pulp of an apple should be, but yellowish and metallic. Gold.

"Bingo!" said the white.

"You worship Bingo?" said Eurydice.

"Today, definitely."

"Bingo is more mighty than Shango?" asked Omphale.

"Shango," said the white confidently, "has nothing on my man Bingo."

"If you do not want our lives, we offer our bodies."

"Bingo has forbidden me from taking the bodies of beautiful women," said the white while he hammered the crate lids back on with no more tools than his hard fist. "I can only have ugly ones. It's the price I pay for having my magical powers."

"Then take us with you and keep us until we are old and ugly like the women the great Bingo has decreed that you enjoy."

"Who said I enjoy them?"

"You cannot leave us here to be tortured and killed by the enemies of our treacherous father, who slew our mothers for no reason."

"Your father the warlord who stole all that UN relief food that was supposed to feed his people?"

"Pah! They are beggars of no value," Omphale answered.

"You eat the food he stole?" the white countered.

Omphale scrunched up her face. "It was not very good. Mealy and wormy."

"Then you gotta pay for your meal."

"We will be your love slaves. Bingo will never know."

"Bingo sees all, hears all, knows all. But tell you what. Help me carry this gold out, and we'll see if we can get you to the airport."

"We will do as you say because we respect your god and your mighty manly powers," Eurydice announced.

Remo carried three crates of gold on either shoulder without stooping a micron. Eurydice and Omphale each bent under the weight of one crate apiece.

That way they got every crate up to the veranda. When Eurydice dropped the last crate onto the stacks and fell panting across it, Remo whistled.

The gates parted and the Master of Sinanju padded up, eyes shining.

"Who are these?" he asked, indicating the panting women with a curt nod of his bearded chin.

"The warlord's black-hearted daughters."

"You have been abusing them?"

"If you call honest work abuse, yeah."

Chiun examined the crates with interest. "There is much gold here. You have done well."

"You should have seen what I had to go through to do this."

"You should have seen what I had to do to win my first gold."

"Tell me about it some other time," Remo said. "So, how are we going to get this stuff to the airport? This is camel-flattening gold if I ever saw it."

"*We* are not."

"Huh?" said Remo.

"*They* are," said Chiun as an armored column came up the dusty road.

The half-tracks and Soviet-era T-55 tanks deployed all over the compound and a man sporting a red beret and eight gold stars on each shoulder jumped off a half track and advanced confidently.

"I am Major Domo General Supreme Jean-Renoir Bazinda," he announced.

"I could tell by the sixteen stars," Remo said dryly.

"You are all war criminals and must be shot."

"Do you have a Federal Express office in this city?" inquired the Master of Sinanju in an even tone.

"Your diplomats will not save you in revolutionary Stomique."

"I will require the gold of my son to be packed well for shipping to an American address I will provide," Chiun continued.

And Major Domo General Supreme Bazinda threw his head back and laughed at the tiny little Asian who dared to threaten the only sixteen-star general on the entire African continent.

As he laughed, he waved for his soldiers to come and stand these interlopers before the villa wall for proper shooting.

Instead, someone handed Bazinda a human head.

The head plopped wetly onto one palm, and instinctively Bazinda grabbed it to keep it from falling into the dirt.

He saw that it was the head of his second-in-command, Colonel Avenger Barang. There was a very serious expression on the colonel's face. When he realized what he was holding, Bazinda's face mirrored it almost exactly. Except for the tendril of blood just starting from one corner of Barang's slack mouth.

Bazinda looked up to see the old Asian. His thin fingers were slipping back into the sleeves of his kimono, which closed over the long, sharp nails. Making the connection, Bazinda shuddered.

"If there is not a Federal Express office in Nogongog, I will decree that one be established for your every need," he announced loftily, handing the head to his startled third-in-command, Super Sergeant Mobondo.

"And whistle us up a plane, will you?" asked the white boy with the thick wrists. "We're anxious to be on our way."

"You will not stay for the celebration feast?"

"What's for dinner?" asked Eurydice.

"Oui," Omphale chorused, "we have not eaten well in nearly a day. Only old tinned caviar."

"Are these harlots with you?" Bazinda asked.

"No," said Remo.

"In that case," Bazinda said, stepping up to pinch Eurydice on her fleshy arm, "you are *both* for dinner."

Eurydice and Omphale fell to the ground and beseeched Lord Bingo to intervene on their behalf.

In the end it cost Remo a case of golden apples to take the daughters of Mahout Feroze Anin off the revolutionary menu. He regretted it almost immediately.

"I am your slave," Omphale said, falling to her knees before Remo.

"I need a slave like a fish needs a wheel," said Remo.

"Then I am your love slave."

"You know what Bingo says about love slaves," said Remo.

"Then what will we be?" asked a tearful Eurydice.

"You can be our personal stewardesses on the flight out of here," Remo decided.

ON THE AIR GHANA FLIGHT leaving Nogongog, Omphale and Eurydice wanted to know if Remo was someone famous.

Before he could answer, the Master of Sinanju said, "This is being investigated even as we speak."

"Why?"

"Because this poor man's parentage is uncertain. He is seeking his father."

"I am not," said Remo.

"There are those who believe he is the long-lost son of Montel Williams," whispered Chiun.

"Who is Montel Williams?" asked a hovering stewardess.

"Some talk-show guy," said Remo.

"Is he famous?" asked Eurydice.

"He's bald," said Remo. "I'm not."

"And rich," added Chiun.

"I am not Montel Williams's son. Montel Williams is black. I'm white."

"Perhaps," Chiun allowed.

"I'm obviously white."

"You have a nice tan," the stewardess said.

Omphale shot her a look full of daggers. Eurydice tried to intimidate her with a nail file clenched in a tight fist.

"You would too if you were were being dragged all the way around the planet by him," said Remo, indicating Chiun.

"Is it true that you will inherit Montel Williams's millions when he dies?" asked Omphale.

"Montel Williams can keep his money," snapped Remo.

"Others," Chiun inserted, "believe him to be the illegitimate offspring of Clarence Williams the Third."

Remo's brows knit together. "Clarence Williams the Third is black, too. How can I be the son of Clarence Williams the Third?"

"If San Fermin, a Christian saint, can be a Moor, you can be the son of Clarence Williams the Third," said Chiun.

Remo looked skeptical. "I don't believe San Fermin was a Moor. He probably had a deep tan."

"And Jesus was black," Chiun added.

"Jesus was *not* black."

"He was not white."

"Stuff it," said Remo, turning away.

"Master Pak met Jesus," Chiun said casually.

Remo looked interested again. "That so? What did he say about him?"

"He called him a long tallow with a short wick."

Remo looked blank.

"That means that same thing as all hat and no cattle."

Remo grunted. "That shows how much Pak knew."

Chiun shrugged unconcernedly. "It has been barely two thousand years. The House is far older."

"Back to Clarence Williams the Third," said Eurydice. "Will you inherit his lands and title when he dies?"

"No."

"Could you be the son of Billy Dee Williams?" asked the still-hovering stewardess.

"He's black too," Remo answered wearily.

"You say that like there is something wrong with it."

Remo threw up his hands. "I didn't mean it that way. Look, can we just change the subject?"

The three women were only too willing to oblige.

"Are you married?" asked Omphale.

"Or at least separated from your wife?" Eurydice asked.

"I don't have a wife," Remo growled.

The stewardess clucked in sympathy. "Any of us would be willing to marry you to save you from unhappy bachelorhood," she offered.

Remo folded his bare arms. "My bachelorhood is not unhappy."

"Then why are you so cranky?"

"I am not cranky," Remo shouted, storming off to the back of the cabin to sit by himself.

"He is not getting any, is he?" Omphale whispered to the Master of Sinanju.

Chiun shook his aged head sadly. "No sensible woman would have him."

"Why not?"

"It is not obvious? He is incurably cranky."

This made perfect sense to the Air Ghana stewardess, who nevertheless made sure Remo did not lack drinks, food or female companionship all the way across the Asian subcontinent.

"I don't need anything, unless it's information on where that old reprobate is taking me next," Remo snarled.

"I will ask," said the stewardess.

But it was Omphale who came back with the answer, along with a welter of scratches on her face. They were flecked with bits of gold, and remembering the stewardess's nails were gold painted, Remo figured there had been a cat fight over who would carry word to the back of the plane.

Another clue was the fact that Omphale was wearing the stewardess's green uniform, which was very snug in the hips and rather loose at the chest.

Omphale smiled triumphantly. "You are going to Nihon, the old man has told me."

"That's big help," Remo said glumly. "Where the heck is Nihon?"

"It is the same as Japon."

"You mean Japan?"

"In French, the name is Japon."

"I wish countries would just pick one name and stick with them a few centuries," Remo complained.

"I have always thought this," Omphale said agreeably. "Is there anything I can get you now that I am your personal serf stewardess?"

"Yeah. A parachute."

To Remo's surprise, Omphale came back with a big fat one. Remo used it for a pillow and soon nodded off.

THE SKY WAS the color of lead and oysters. Remo found himself on the terraced side of a red hill. The terraces were paddies, and falling raindrops made them pucker and rill.

Standing bareheaded in the rain was a Master wearing green silk decorated with gold trim. He was ancient but carried himself with ramrod erectness as he approched Remo.

"I am Yong. No Master lived longer than I."

"Good for you," said Remo.

"I slew the last dragon and for the rest of my days drank dragon-bone soup. My days were very long because of dragon-bone soup."

Remo snapped his fingers. "Right. Chiun told me about you. He said you ate every bone so no succeeding Master had any."

"And for my greed I dwell in perpetual rain."

"At least there's rice."

Yong looked Remo up and down critically. "Where is your kimono?"

"Out of fashion."

"Your nails are too short. How can you fight?"

"Oh, I get by."

"The Masters who came after me were wrong. I saved a piece of the dragon's spine." Yong opened his fist. "I give it to you."

Remo took the piece of bone. It was gray and porous. "What am I supposed to do with it?"

"It is powerful medicine. You will know when the time comes."

And Yong walked back into the rain, which increased its tempo upon the beaten ground until the red mud ran.

13

They said it was impossible for an American.

For a Japanese it was exceedingly difficult. This was well-known.

For a Korean it was unacceptable even if it were possible. Koreans were not Japanese, no matter what airs they took on. Chinese couldn't do it. Not the best Chinese man who was ever born. Not even if he trained until the end of time.

But for an American it was utterly, absolutely unthinkable.

Yet Wade Pupule had done it. He had become sumo.

Becoming sumo, of course, was only the beginning. A first step. And as difficult as it might seem, it was in fact the easiest step.

For Wade, born on Oahu, Hawaii, an American by nationality but of Hawaiian parentage, it was just a matter of reaching his goal weight, which in this case was a well-rounded 350 pounds.

This was accomplished by eating prodigious quantities of fermented bean paste and a thick stew flavored with raw sugar called *chanko-nabe*, washed down with Sapporo beer.

And beef. Whole sides of steer—which was criticized severely. Not even Kobe beef, raised in Japan—which every Japanese knew was vastly superior to Hawaiian beef and especially Texas beef. Every Japanese, that is, who had never sampled any beef other than Kobe beef.

But the real secret of Wade Pupule's success was a simple one: his mother's meat loaf. It couldn't have been more fattening if it was deep-fried in liquid lard.

When Wade petitioned one of the great sumo stables for acceptance, he sent a grainy photograph that concealed his Hawaiianness and was granted an audience.

"But you are not Japanese," the stable master sputtered upon meeting him. They had just exchanged bows. Wade had gotten down on hands and knees, prostrating himself in a full bow. The sumo stable master had barely nodded his head.

"So sue me," Wade shot back angrily.

To his surprise, the stable master allowed his face to acquire a faint smile of surprise. "Ah, last name Sosumi. You are half-Japanese, no?"

"Yes," Wade lied, immediately adopting the Japanese name of Sosumi. And he was in.

They laughed when Wade Sosumi entered the Jifubuki Sumo Academy. They called him Wahini Boy and Pearl Harbor and Beef Brain. They made him shower last and eat after everyone else was through, even though he had cooked the very food he was forced by his lowly rank to eat cold. They hit him in the head with glass bottles to show their contempt for the Hawaiian-American who would be sumo. And to show his humility, Sosumi was forced to say *"Domo arigato"* in thanks.

After a while they were calling him Beef Blast because that was the way it seemed when his 350 pounds of solid body fat collided with the shuddering bulk of his worthy opponents. He began to best true sumo in the ring. Japanese sumo. It was unthinkable.

When Sosumi had worked his way up to *ozeki*—champion—they began calling him Beef Blast-san.

Still, they insisted it was impossible for a *gaijin* to become *yokozuna*—a grand champion. Culturally impossible, that is. Because in the tournaments there was no one greater or stronger or more agile than Sosumi, a.k.a. Beef Blast-san.

But he had done it, winning the prestigious Emperor's Cup. Japan was rocked. Internally it was a scandal of the highest order. But because the Japanese had been so long vilified as xenophobic, they dared not deny Beef Blast-san what he had rightfully earned in the circle of sumo.

Sosumi Beef Blast-san had fame, women and, most important in Japan, a large house with a spectacular view of Mount Fuji's snowcap—which one certainly required when one weighed 350 pounds.

But having achieved the pinnacle of success in his chosen field, Sosumi still ate his mother's meat loaf every Saturday to keep his strength up. It was overnighted from Honolulu in a heat-retaining box the size of a small safe.

Wade was thinking that hundred-pound meat loafs just didn't get him through the week the way they used to as he wolfed *chanko-nabe* from a bamboo wok the size of a garbage-can lid while straddling a ceramic throne designed for his special needs when the tiny little man appeared before him.

"You a priest?" Sosumi asked.

"No," said the little man, who wore a scarlet-and-lavender silken kimono. It was not Japanese. Too gaudy. Maybe Chinese.

"Because if you are, I'm no Buddhist. Though I'm sometimes mistaken for him on the street." Sosumi chuckled. His big Buddha belly shook.

Not a wrinkle moved on the old man's papery face—and that was a lot of wrinkles.

"I am no priest," he repeated.

"What, then?"

"I offer you a challenge."

"I'm king of the hill, pal. I don't need any challenges."

"You will fight my son."

"How much does he weigh?"

"Nine stone."

"Give that to me in pounds. I don't know from stones."

"He weighs 155 pounds."

"Never heard of a sumo that skinny."

"He is not a sumo."

"I kinda figured that. What is he, then—suicidal?"

"No."

"You looking to have him bumped off, I'm not your man. I'm a wrestler. All I'd have to do is sit on a 155-pound guy and every bone would break, his internal organs would liquify and I'd be up on manslaughter charges faster than I could say, 'So sorry san.' Which would be my name if it ever happened."

"My son is not sumo. He is Sinanju."

"Never heard of it. Is it like jujitsu? I've seen jujitsu men do amazing things."

"Such as?"

"Saw one once walk up to a guy and just tap him in the clavicle. The other guy went flying backward like he'd been zapped by a live wire."

"I can do that."

"You a jujitsu man?"

The little old man bowed formally. A ten-degree bow. The smallest, most meager bow. As a grand champion, Sosumi had earned a forty-five degree bow. Minimum. Anything less was an open insult.

"I am Sinanju. I am a Master."

"Just a second," said Sosumi, polishing off his *chanko-nabe* and tossing the empty wok aside. Reaching behind him, he tapped a solid silver handle. From under the rolls of fat spilling over the seat of his ceramic throne came a loud flush.

"Gotta maintain my weight," Sosumi said, standing up and pulling up his cotton britches, which he drew snug with a drawstring. "The Nagoya tournament is this month."

"That is disgusting."

"That's the price I pay to keep my title. In one orifice and out the other. Sometimes I feel like a human shit processor."

"You were bred to battle my kind."

"No, I was bred to battle other sumo."

"That is now. In the past it was different. My kind defeated yours, and you turned your might against others because what else was there for you monsters to do?"

"Hey, I don't appreciate being called a monster. Have you know I'm a god in these parts. I devoted my entire life to sumo. I don't need your crap."

"You obviously possess sufficient crap of your own," the old man said, voice dripping with disdain.

"More than sufficient," said Sosumi, giving the silver handle another bat. "Takes two, sometimes three flushes to do the job. Wonder if they got a Guinness-world-record category for turd size?"

"If they did," said the little man, "you would be both immortal and undefeated."

Sosumi smacked his meaty paws together. "Okay, bring on your boy."

"Tonight at midnight."

"Hope he's insured."

REMO TOSSED AND TURNED on his tatami mat in his suite at the Tokyo Bay Grande Sheraton Hotel.

In his dream he sat facing a Korean of indeterminate age who wore the formal silk kimono and topknot of the unified Shilla Dynasty. He was very lean, as if he ate only straw.

The Korean had kindly eyes, and when he spoke, his voice was like water rippling along the stones of a clear brook.

" 'The bee sucks,' " he said.

"So?" said Remo.

"No. Now it is your turn. I have said the bee sucks. What do you say?"

Remo shrugged. "The bee sucks eggs."

The Korean's kindly eyes grew troubled. "Bees do not suck eggs."

"This isn't word association?"

"No. I have provided the first line of a poem. You must provide the second line."

"Oh. Okay. How's this? 'The turtle ducks.' "

"Why do you introduce turtles into a poem about bees?"

"Because 'ducks' rhymes with 'sucks,' " Remo said.

"Rhyming is for Greeks and children. We do not rhyme. You must try again."

"Try this. 'The flower waits.' "

"What kind of flower awaits?"

"Is that the third line?" Remo asked.

"No!"

"Don't get upset. It was just a question."

"You must specify which flower. 'Flower' means nothing. Would you ask for fruit when you desire pear?"

"'The tulip awaits,' then," Remo said hastily.

"Tulips are not Korean."

Remo sighed. "Why don't you take my turn?"

"Very well. 'The chrysanthemum trembles like a shy maiden.'"

"Nice image. I add, 'The bee stings.'"

"What does this bee sting?"

Remo shrugged carelessly. "Whatever he wants. It's my turn so it's my bee. Your turn now."

"No, you must specify. Why can you not specify? Ung poetry is very specific. Image is all. Meaning is what is gleaned from the image."

"Okay, 'The bee stings you.'"

"Why me?"

"Because you're annoying me with this dippy Ung stuff."

"What means 'dippy?'"

"Silly. Stupid. Take your pick."

And the Korean drew himself to his feet. His face became a thunderhead. "But I am Master Ung. To insult the purity of my poems is to challenge me. Prepare yourself, ghost-face."

Remo backed off fast. "Look, I'm sorry. I didn't mean to offend you. Tell you what. I'll take the next three lines. How's that?"

"No, you will stand quietly while I recite the next three thousand lines."

Remo's face fell. "Three thousand lines?"

"Because I am angry," Ung said in an injured tone, "I can recite only a short Ung poem."

And in his dream, Remo groaned while Master Ung said, "Chrysanthemum petals fall from a celadon sky" three thousand times, varying in the intonation each time but leaning toward angry nine falls out of ten.

A STEELY VOICE BROKE the endless rain of petals.

"It is time to face the wrestler."

Remo shot up out of bed, bathed in sweat.

The Master of Sinanju stood like a stern idol by his tatami sleeping mat. His face was in shadow and unreadable.

"Christ, Chiun—what time is it?" Remo asked.

"Midnight approaches."

"Midnight! Feels like I just closed my eyes."

"You may sleep again after you have faced the most fearsome foe you have ever faced."

"I don't want to face any foe, fearsome or otherwise."

Chiun clapped his hands peremptorily. "You have your duty to the House."

Remo pulled the sheets over his head. "Make me."

Something that felt like a red-hot needle touched Remo's elbow. It connected with his humerus. He snapped up again.

"Ow! What did you do?" Remo demanded, rubbing his elbow.

"I merely grazed what you whites call your funny bone."

"It doesn't feel very funny to me," said Remo, willing the pain up his arm and into his central nervous system, where it diffused and left his body tingling mildly.

Chiun turned abruptly. "Come. Your foe awaits."

On the way through the darkness of the seacoast south of Tokyo, Remo tried to keep the fishy smells wafting into the cab from clogging his lungs.

"I had another freaking dream," he volunteered.

"They are the only kind you have been having of late," Chiun said with no touch of interest in his voice.

"Don't you want to hear about it?"

"No."

"I dreamed of Ung."

"Goody for you."

"We had a poetry face-off."

"I assume Ung won."

"He buried me in chrysanthemum petals."

Chiun flicked a speck off his silken lap. "There was no Master greater than Ung. Unless it was Wang. Or possibly myself."

"Says you," said Remo, rubbing his still-tingling elbow.

By the beach there were squid drying in lines strung between bamboo poles, their triangular heads flat as tapeworms. The breeze coming in from the Pacific made their tangled tentacles wriggle fitfully. They reminded Remo of the Greek octopuses drying in the sun, but for some reason their flat, dead eyes made him shiver deep inside.

"Why do squid suddenly make me feel creepy?"

"Because squid *are* creepy."

"I hate octopi, but I've eaten squid in the past and they never bothered me before."

"The octopus is harmless. But the squid is a fearsome creature, for they grow to great size."

"Everywhere we go lately, I see tentacles."

"Did I ever tell you how the sumo came to be?" Chiun asked suddenly.

"Not that I can remember."

"Good."

"That's it? Good?"

"Yes."

"Why is it good that you never got around to telling me how the sumo came to be?"

"Because it is."

Remo eyed Chiun. "Well, aren't you going to tell me now?"

Chiun's almond eyes grew heavy and hooded. "Beg me."

"I am not going to beg you to tell me about the sumo," Remo scoffed.

"Good."

"Not if we both end up on a deserted isle, just the two of us, a sick monkey and a coconut palm for entertainment, will I ask you how the sumo came to be."

"I accede to your wishes."

Remo returned to staring out the cab window. "Fine. Good."

Silence filled the car. Patterns of light and shadow cast by passing street lamps whipped through the cab's interior, making their stiff faces come and go by turns.

"So why'd you bring it up?" Remo asked after a long time.

Chiun began to hum. It was a contented hum. But as Remo listened, it grew more and more to sound like an I-know-something-you-don't-know hum. But he couldn't be sure, so he kept quiet during the rest of the cab ride.

"Is it important that I know how the sumo came to be?"

"I do not know," Chiun said vaguely.

"Am I going to meet any sumo?"

"You might. You might not."

Remo folded his lean arms defiantly. "Well, I pity the sumo I meet in the bad mood I'm in right now. He gives me any lip, and I'll roll him around the block for exercise."

"Sumos do not give lip," said Chiun.

"Good for them," said Remo.

"They are very polite. They give hip."

"Hip?"

Chiun nodded. "Hip."

"Hip, hip, hurray for the sumo," Remo said sourly.

THE CAB LET THEM OFF before a great Japanese-style house on a low hillock, and the Master of Sinanju led Remo through a gate into a walled courtyard where stunted bonsai trees crouched in perpetual agony. In the center of the courtyard lay a circular clay spot. A shinto-style roof protected the clay from the elements.

Warm amber light came from the closed screen of the house that faced the roofed courtyard.

"What's this?" Remo asked, enjoying the faint scent of cherries in the night air.

"The ring in which you will fight your fearsome foe."

"What foe?" asked Remo, looking around warily.

And suddenly something as large as a baby elephant appeared on the other side of the screen, cutting off almost all trace of the warm amber light.

"That looks like a sumo's shadow to me," Remo said.

The screen slid aside and out stepped a great pink hulk, naked except for a cotton loincloth, his head shaved all around a ponytaillike topknot. He resembled nothing so much as an overweight baby who had outgrown his Pampers.

"Quick," urged Remo, "tell me how the sumo came to be."

"It is too late. I must instruct you in the rules of sumo."

"Shoot."

"You face your foe in the clay circle. There is no hitting with the closed fist or below the belt."

"Got it."

"You must not inflict harm or mortal injury on your foe."

"Does Baby Huey know this?"

"You may ask him after the bout."

"Great."

"The winner is decided when one opponent is forced out of the circle or if any part of the body touches clay but the soles of the naked feet."

"My feet aren't naked," Remo stated.

"You will remove your shoes and your shirt."

Stripping to the waist, Remo stepped out of his shoes, complaining, "I'm going through a lot of shoes lately."

"Sandals wear better."

"I'll stick with shoes."

Chiun extracted a small vial of glass from one sleeve and, as the giant sumo wrestler waited patiently as a mute Buddha, he shook the vial around the ring of clay.

"What are you doing?" Remo asked, one eye on the inscrutable face of the sumo wrestler.

"Blessing the ring with salt."

"I thought that looked like one of the salt shakers from the hotel restaurant."

"They will not miss it." Finishing, Chiun said, "You may enter and face your worthy opponent."

Remo stepped into the circle, feeling the cool, moist clay against the bare soles of his feet.

The great sumo regarded him with a dour face. He bowed from the waist. The merest of bows. Ten degrees.

Remo bowed equally in return, saying, "I'll try to make this quick."

"Suit yourself, skinny," rumbled the sumo.

"You speak English?"

"So sue me."

"Huh?"

"Private joke. It's my stage name. I'm as American as you, chopstick legs. Born on Oahu. Raised on MTV. Destined to stomp your gourd."

"Says you."

And with a speed that surprised even Remo, the giant lunged, sweeping his great flabby arms around in a bear hug.

Remo ducked under the scissors of flesh and aimed two stiffened fingers for a nerve cluster under one sweaty armpit.

The fingers sunk in up to the second knuckle and came out again. Remo wove to one side so the falling sumo didn't land on him.

Except that the sumo didn't fall. He laughed again and took Remo's shoulders in each hand. Remo felt himself lifted off his feet and, when he landed outside the ring, he rolled and snapped to his feet unharmed.

He found himself facing the Master of Sinanju.

"Does that mean I lose?" Remo asked.

"You wish. I neglected to say two falls out of three."

"Good," said Remo, jumping back into the ring.

The sumo lifted one foot and slammed it down. The other came down a moment later. He assumed a crouching defensive posture.

"Get set for a ride, skinny."

"Any time you're ready, fat boy."

From outside the ring, the voice of the Master of Sinanju floated out. "In the time of the early Chrysanthemum Throne, a shogun of Japan, jealous of the spreading fame of Sinanju and unable to secure the secrets of the House, sought to create an invincible army that would protect him from a rival shogun. These warriors were called sumo."

"I never heard that," said Sosumi.

"History is written by the victorious," Chiun countered.

Remo circled his foe warily. The sumo held his ground as if daring Remo to strike first.

"This shogun discovered that no weapon, no samurai or *ninja,* was proof against Sinanju," intoned Chiun.

A hand as broad as a seat cushion swatted at Remo. Remo evaded it easily. Still, the speed of the sumo was greater than he imagined possible.

"The shogun knew that there was no speed equal to Sinanju. No blow faster than Sinanju. And no skill greater than Sinanju. So he consulted his advisers for a defense against Sinanju."

Remo feinted for the blubbery, rolling stomach and came around with an open-handed spank to the kidneys.

"He discovered an armor that was proof against the blows and strikes of Sinanju."

With a meaty smack, Remo's hand bounced harmlessly off—and the sumo laughed boisterously.

"This was called fat," said Chiun.

Remo tried for the solar plexus. He stepped in, using the hard heels of his hands, machine-gunning the rolls of fat that lay there.

"Fat, the shogun discovered, was proof against the blows that could otherwise paralyze nerves and break bones."

The sumo's stomach muscles rolled like pink waves. He laughed from deep within his gargantuan belly. A red mark like a rash bloomed where Remo had struck, but otherwise no harm had been done.

"For fat gave before the hand of Sinanju, accepting and resisting like water."

"I can see that, damn it," Remo said in frustration.

"Big surprise, huh, skinny?" The sumo laughed. "You thought a big guy like me would be a pushover for your slick kung fu moves. Not so easy, huh?"

"Get stuffed."

"How do you think I got to where I am?"

"Fat, dumb and happy?"

"*Yokozuna*. That means 'grand champion.' I'm the first American to pull it off."

The Master of Sinanju resumed his tale. "The shogun surrounded himself with giant men who shook the earth with their tread. Word was sent out to the countryside. The Master of Sinanju of those days was challenged to assassinate the shogun, if he dared."

Remo eyed the ankles like fleshy tree stumps. "What do the rules say about tripping?"

"Tripping is forbidden," Chiun said.

The sumo grinned like a Mack truck. "You gotta grab me about the waist and try to muscle me out of the ring," he said. "Too bad you don't have the wingspan for it."

"Master Yowin came to Japan to meet this challenge," Chiun continued from the shadows. "By night he stole into the sleeping chamber of the shogun, but a wall of living flesh blocked him. Blows were struck and landed forcefully. But the sumo wall stood resolute. And in the safety of his bed, the shogun laughed heartily and long."

Stepping back, Remo coiled his muscles tightly. He drew in a deep breath and sprang.

Both hands slammed into the sumo's great chest. He staggered back. Staggered one step, then two—but five feet from the periphery of the ring of clay, he recovered and flung his bulk forward like a cannonball with pumping legs.

Remo backpedaled, staying one tantalizing step ahead of the sumo. When he felt the bite of gravel under his right heel, he leaped high over the Sumo's head, pivoted and gave the sweaty pink back a hard push.

Sosumi leaned like a sequoia in a hurricane—his upper body tipped out of the ring, but his feet stood firm, like immobile roots. Body nearly perpendicular to his legs, he grunted explosively as he fought the natural tendency of his great bulk to topple.

Remo watched in helpless frustration as he slowly righted himself and turned to face him again.

"I'm going to kick your ass for that," Sosumi warned.

"Can I kick him?" Remo asked Chiun.

"You cannot kick him below the waist or above the neck, nor may you land an injurious blow."

"That means my feet are tied," Remo growled.

"It means only what I have said," Chiun intoned. "Nothing more, and not a breath less."

"It means your ass is sassafras." Sosumi grinned, lifting his meaty paws before Remo's face.

Watching those giant hands, Remo stepped back and planted his bare feet in the moist clay, digging his toes in.

"Rules say whoever touches clay with anything but his feet, loses, right?" said Remo.

"Yes," said Chiun.

"Then get ready to lose, tubby," Remo told the looming sumo.

Sosumi lunged without warning. Remo was ready, exploding off his feet and launching a double kick so sudden and violent Sosumi felt Remo's left foot bouncing off his right hand and the right foot rebounding from his left hand as one jarring impact.

The sumo staggered back a half step—no more. His eyes held a stunned light. But he quickly blinked it away. "Hah!" he laughed. "If that's your best shot—"

"You lose," announced Chiun.

"What are you talking about?"

"You have touched clay. You have lost this round."

Frantically Sosumi looked around. He was still in the ring. His knees were clean. He looked behind him, and his nearly naked cheeks were clean. "Where? Where did I touch clay? Show me."

"Look upon your unwitting palms, sumo," said Chiun.

Sosumi unclenched his fists. And the angry lines of his face collapsed in shock. They were brownish gray. "No fair. You wiped your feet off on my hands!"

Remo grinned. "And now I'm going to wipe the ground with your stupid face."

The sumo stamped his feet like a toddler throwing a tantrum and, shaking the house walls with his roaring, he crashed around the ring as if trying to get up a head of steam.

"We're even, blubber butt," Remo said as they circled one another like belligerent binary stars.

"The shogun slept peacefully for many weeks," Chiun said, resuming his tale.

The sumo grunted like a mad bull, eyes turning fierce.

"Not so cocky now?" taunted Remo.

The sumo said nothing. He was all business now. He dropped into his grunting crouch and wriggled his pudgy fingers at Remo in a come-on gesture.

Remo began circling, looking for an opening. Hitting below the belt was out. Punching was out. Not that any punch less than a death blow would fell the big behemoth. Couldn't do him. Couldn't kick at the vulnerable ankles and bring him down like a big tree. The power of a Sinanju Master lay in his ability to deal swift and sudden death. But in this arena, Remo's best moves were forbidden.

Chiun's remote voice resumed speaking.

"Long nights the Master of Sinanju slept under the stars, fretting over this new foe that seemed invincible to all of his wiles and skills."

Remo ducked between the sumo's legs suddenly, catching the man unaware. Coming up on the other side, he tried something simple. He grabbed the fat ankles and pushed hard. The sumo stood his ground. Bent over, Remo redoubled his effort. Little by little the sumo's feet began to slide along the moist clay. He refused to budge. He simply held his stance.

The sumo's feet scraped an inch of clay. Then two. Three.

Remo got him to the edge of the clay when abruptly the sumo reached between his dimpled knees and grabbed for Remo's wrists. Remo evaded a hand as big as a TV screen by fading back.

And Sosumi calmly lumbered back from the edge of the ring.

"This could take all night," Remo grumbled.

From the shadows Chiun intoned, "You are Sinanju. He is only sumo. It is too bad you did not beg me to tell you how the Sumo came to be."

"Aren't you telling me now?"

"If I had told you before, the bout would not be even, and you would not now be frantic with worry that you are going to disgrace me against this fat tub of entrails."

"Hey, I resent that," Sosumi said in a hurt voice.

"If the diaper fits," Remo said.

The sumo wriggled his fingers again, mocking Remo's impotence.

Remo called over to Chiun. "I'm open to broad hints."

And the Master of Sinanju resumed his tale where he had left off. "Master Yowin thought long and he thought hard. And in time he realized if to strike fat was to be foiled, he must therefore strike not-fat."

"There isn't any such place on this blimp's body," Remo complained.

"Tell it to my momma," Sosumi said.

Remo called out, "How about another broad hint?"

"It is up to you not to disgrace me or the House," Chiun said.

"Can I stick him in the eyes?"

"You stick me in the eyes, runt," Sosumi growled, "and I'll wrench your head off, plant my mouth on your exposed windpipe and inflate your dead body like a puffer fish."

"You cannot strike him in the eyes," Chiun called out. "But you are getting warm."

"Warm?" Remo wondered, searching the sumo's broad, fleshy face.

A knowing grin coming over his face, Remo began weaving his hands in the air with casual menace.

Sosumi blinked. "You better not be thinking what I think you're thinking," he growled.

"Come on, let's go. I don't have all night," Remo said.

"Sticking me in the eyes is against the rules."

Remo continued weaving.

"This time I'm going to nail your big fat butt to the ground," Remo warned. "No outside-the-ring stuff this time."

Perspiration began forming on the sumo's high, furrowed forehead. It drooled down. His topknot, coated with linseed oil, began to droop.

Lifting one fist, Remo popped two fingers. And drove them forward at high speed.

Sosumi saw the forked fingers coming at him like pink arrows and did the only thing possible. He clapped both hands over his eyes protectively.

And so never saw the flat heel of a hand that bopped him on the cartilage tip of his broad nose.

The resulting howl would have done justice to a wounded elephant.

And the sound Sosumi a.k.a. Beef Blast-san made as he fell into the clay was like a big wet smack of a whale's kiss.

"So much for Baby Huey," said Remo as the big sumo lay there quivering. He turned to the Master of

Sinanju, who offered him a forty-five-degree bow. Remo returned it equally.

"Is that how Master Yowin did it?" Remo asked.

"No," said Chiun as they walked from the courtyard. "Yowin used his killing nails to gouge out their eyes. For what good is a wall of protective flesh if it is stamping about in circles and bumping into one another howling that it is blind while the Master of Sinanju steals up on the waking shogun in time to slice open his unprotected throat?"

And Remo laughed.

14

Remo found that by pretending to sleep all the way from Tokyo to Honolulu, the geisha-style flight attendants of the JAL flight kept their hands to themselves.

It was hard not to sleep. He felt like he had circumnavigated the planet at a dead run.

When the plane landed in Honolulu, they bowed him out of the cabin, and when Remo neglected to bow back, ambulances had to be summoned when it was discovered that the flight attendants had all repaired to the gallery and tried to sever their wrist arteries with knives.

Since all the cutlery available to them were butter-knives, there were no deaths and only minor stitches were needed.

Remo and Chiun were entirely oblivious to this. Hawaiian girls had accosted them in the terminal, cooing "Aloha" and decorating their necks with sweet-smelling leis of pink carnations mixed with white-and-yellow ginger flowers.

When Remo said "Thanks" in a deliberately uninterested voice, they tried to anoint his face with kisses. When he evaded their lips, they removed their own leis and showed him their bountiful breasts.

That caught Remo's attention. The fact that these

weren't technically stewardesses probably softened his attitude somewhat.

That and the fact he couldn't immediately recall if he had ever slept with a Hawaiian girl or not.

"How long are we staying in Hawaii?" he asked Chiun.

The Master of Sinanju passed among the grass skirts and bare breasts, and although he seemed to keep his hands to himself, the Hawaiian girls began grabbing at and covering their grass-covered bottoms as if spanked by unseen paddles.

"Hussies," he hissed. "Begone! And bother us no more."

"Hey!" Remo complained, watching six gorgeous pairs of breasts bounce out of his life. "What happened to me siring a son?"

"You have no intention of impregnating those flaunting ones," Chiun sniffed, moving on.

Reluctantly Remo followed. "How do you know?" he asked.

"You would only have held back your sperm."

"Maybe. But I seem to recall you were the one who taught me how."

They walked out of the terminal into the heavily moist and jasmine-scented air of Honolulu.

"So you didn't answer my question. How long are we going to be in Honolulu?"

"Ten, possibly twenty minutes."

Remo frowned. "That's not very long."

"It is long enough," said Chiun, gesturing for a cab. He was ignored. When Remo inserted two fingers into his mouth and whistled, a cab pulled up with alacrity.

"Long enough for what?" Remo asked dubiously, holding open the door for Chiun.

"Long enough to acquire a vessel worthy of conveying us to our destination."

Remo got in. The cab got going. "Which is what?"

"Which is a boat."

"I meant the destination, not the vessel. And where are we going that can be reached by boat?"

"When you have conveyed us there, you will know."

"Do you mean 'convey' as in 'get there by cab,' or 'convey' as in 'boat?'"

"You ask too many questions," said the Master of Sinanju, lapsing into silence.

Near the waterfront the Master of Sinanju left Remo to contemplate the blue Pacific, but as he waited, his attention was drawn to a bus-stop billboard advertising one of the summer's films.

It showed a green-faced man with roots and leaves growing from his mottled skin. The film was titled *The Return of Muck Man*. It wasn't the swampy face that caught Remo's eye, but his deep, soulful mud brown eyes.

Something about them held Remo spellbound. The eyes seemed to be looking at him. When Remo moved to the right, the eyes seemed to follow him. The same thing happened when he drifted left.

Chiun returned minutes later, saying, "I have found a worthy vessel."

Remo seemed not to hear.

"What are you looking at?" Chiun asked.

Without shifting his gaze, Remo said, "That face on that billboard seems to be looking right at me."

"Perhaps it is your long-lost father."

"Not funny, Chiun."

"He does have your complexion."

"Something about those eyes strikes me funny." And Remo started to approach the billboard.

Chiun clapped his hands abruptly. "Enough. Come."

Remo snapped out of his pensive mood. Chiun led him to the end of a wharf, and Remo found himself gazing out over the sparkling blue Pacific.

"So where is it?" he asked.

"You are looking out when you should be looking down."

Remo looked down and saw the rowboat. Its oars were tucked in at the gunwales. It could seat two people comfortably and a third in a dire emergency.

"Who's rowing?"

"He who boards last, of course," said the Master of Sinanju, stepping off the wharf. He floated to his seat in the stern with the ease of a feather landing.

"Figures," said Remo, climbing a ladder to take his position at the oars. "Where to?" he said sourly.

"Row south. And take care that you do not bump any larger craft."

Remo took up the oars. "Bump? If we hit anything bigger than a Coke bottle, we're going under."

"Save your breath for rowing," Chiun admonished, rearranging the splendid folds of his kimono skirts.

As they beat out of Mamala Bay, the sun began to dip in the sky once more, and Remo realized he had lost track of the days since they had left the U.S.A.

"How long does this go on?" he asked an unperturbed Chiun.

"Until we reach our destination, of course."

"No, I mean how long does this marathon go on?"

"It is not a marathon. That is something else. These are your *athloi*."

"How long do *they* go on?"

"Until *you* reach *your* destination."

After Remo had rowed many hours, with the Master of Sinanju frequently looking up the night sky, Chiun lifted his hand sternly.

"Cease rowing!"

"A pleasure," said Remo, stowing the oars.

"We are here."

Remo looked around. The Pacific in all directions was as black as ink. The sky was a litter of bright stars around the misty arm of the Milky Way.

"How do you know this is the right place?"

"What star is that?" Chiun asked, indicating an especially bright bluish white one directly overhead.

"Vega."

Chiun made a disgusted face. "Pah. And that?" he asked, pointing to another.

"Altair."

"Again you are wrong."

Remo craned his head, trying to fix the positions of the stars. There were the two brightest in the early-July sky, and they straddled the Milky Way.

"That's Altair and that's Vega," he insisted.

"Only to a white," retorted Chiun unhappily. "They are known to my people as Kyon-u the Herder and Chik-nyo the Weaver. They were lovers, who having neglected their duties, were exiled to opposite sides of the Silvery River, by Kyon-u's father, the king. It is said that the seventh day of the seventh moon always begins with a light sprinkling of rain, signifying the beginning of another year of bitter separation for Kyon-u and Chik-nyo."

Remo looked down. "So what do we—or should I say I—do now?"

"*We* wait."

"In the middle of the freaking ocean?"

"Unless you would rather row in stately circles."

"On the other hand," Remo said quickly, "waiting can be very restful."

Chiun smoothed his silken lap. "If you wish to sleep, you may."

"I'm tired but I'm not that tired."

Chiun looked up. "You are certain?"

"I've been sleeping too much as it is. And I'm sick of these dreams I've been having."

"Dreams cannot harm you," Chin said thinly.

"I said I'm not tired. I just need to rest."

The Master of Sinanju said nothing. His unwinking eyes came to rest on Remo's own. He stared. Remo stared back. After a while Remo looked away. When he looked back at the Master of Sinanju, the Master of Sinanju was still regarding him like a stern old owl.

"What are you staring at?" Remo asked peevishly.

"You."

"Cut it out, will you?"

"I have nothing but darkness surrounding me," Chiun intoned. "I will stare where I will."

"It's making me uneasy."

"Then do not look back," said Chiun, looking hard and unflinchingly at his pupil.

Remo averted his eyes again. Every time his gaze wandered back to the Master of Sinanju sitting at the stern, Chiun's hazel eyes were fixed and unblinking upon him.

After a while Remo closed his eyes.

He never felt himself drop off. He just did. There was no transition from wakefulness to slumber. But he dreamed.

A SPLASHING BROUGHT HIM out of sleep. Remo sat up on his hard wooden seat of the rowboat. "Where am I?" he asked.

"Beneath the Silvery River."

"No, I meant what's making this splashing? Sharks?"

Chiun shook his aged head coldly. "These are the children of Sa Mangsang."

Remo looked over the side. Luminous shapes glided in the water, just beneath the surface. They resembled circling torpedoes with flexible tails. A few wallowed on the surface, slashing it with birdlike beaks. Several disconnected circular eyes stared skyward.

"What are those things?"

"Squid."

Remo looked more closely. He recognized them now. The flexible tails of the circling squid were their bundled and trailing tentacles. They were an eerie sight.

"What's got them so riled up?" he asked Chiun.

"They are feeding."

"Any danger they'll bite the boat?"

"Yes."

"I hate squid."

"Squid cannot harm you. Not squid so small."

"Small! They're easily five feet long."

"They are small for squid. In the deeper parts of the Pacific, some grow large enough to pull down whales to their doom and eat them."

Remo said nothing. On every side, for nearly a quarter mile around, the long phosphorescent shapes sped, wallowed and slashed. Occasionally a whipping tentacle would lift and slap the water.

Remo felt a preternatural chill run through him.

Chiun spoke up. "Do you remember my telling you of Sa Mangsang?"

"What Master was he?"

"Sa Mangsang was no Master of Sinanju. He was—and is—the dragon of the abyss. In Korean, 'Sa Mangsang' means 'Dream Thing.' In Japanese, he is known as Tako-Ika, Octopus Squid. To the Vikings, he was Kraken. To the Arabs, Khadhulu. To the Moovians, he was Ru-Taki-Nuhu, the enemy of life."

"Wait a minute. Are we talking about the lost continent of Moo here?"

"We are."

Remo's strong features grew grim. Years ago he and Chiun had discovered an island outpost of an ancient continent that had sunk during a Pacific upheaval, leaving only its highest hill, which poked above the sea like an island. The continent was called Moo. It was an ancient client state of Sinanju five thousand years ago. One of its beliefs was in Ru-Taki-Nuhu, the Heaven Propper, a giant octopus that had fallen from the sky to sleep beneath the waves, awaiting the end of the world, during which it would drink up the oceans. Remo and Chiun had briefly lived with the survivors of Moo until even the island was swallowed by the Pacific.

"I remember," Remo said quietly. "The people of Moo thought Ru-Taki-Nuhu held up the sky with his tentacles."

Chiun held a fist over the side. A finger coiled out and down. "Ru-Taki-Nuhu, known to Sinanju as Sa Mangsang, sleeps below us."

"Good for him. Not that I believe in him, that is."

"These squid are his offspring and acolytes. They guard his resting place, dreaming of the hour their lord will awaken to consume them, as he will consume all earthly life.''

"Why don't we just be on our way?" Remo said suddenly.

"Because you are going to awaken Sa Mangsang."

"And have him drink up the ocean? No, thanks."

"You must awaken Sa Mangsang so that he sees you. Then you must make a certain sign with your fingers. Like this." Chiun made an arcane gesture by separating his two middle fingers.

"I don't think my fingers bend that way."

"You will make this sign, and once Sa Mangsang has seen it, he will know you for Sinanju. Then and only then you must return him to slumber."

"With what? I don't exactly carry sleeping pills on me."

"You would do well to remember that the Greeks had another name for Sa Mangsang."

"What's that?"

"Hydra."

Remo made a thoughtful face in the murk. "Hydra. Hydra. I've heard of the Hydra."

Chiun pressed his hands together firmly. "Enough! It is time for you to awaken Sa Mangsang from his ancient sleep."

Remo folded his arms. "No way I'm jumping into a sea full of unhappy squid," he said defiantly.

Chiun's eyes narrowed in the darkness. "I will not insist that you jump, if you are afraid to," he said, voice as thin as his unreadable eyes.

Remo looked at his master's stern eyes. "You don't exactly say that like you mean it."

"I mean it exactly. I will not insist that you to jump into these evil waters."

"Good," said Remo. "Because I'm not jumping."

And taking the rowboat's creaking oarlocks in both hands, Remo held on.

Chiun took hold of his gunwales and began rocking on his seat. The boat began rocking in sympathy.

Remo tried rocking in counterbalance. Chiun redoubled his rocking. Having established the rhythm first, he had the advantage. Remo tried to find the rhythm in the hope of setting up a counterrhythm. But during the precious seconds in which he was searching, he only aided Chiun in destabilizing the tiny craft. The boat took on water on the port side, then in the bow.

Quickly it began swamping.

"If you don't stop," Remo warned, "we're both going in."

And they did. The boat tipped precariously one way, and letting go of the oarlocks, Remo threw his weight to the other side desperately.

With the end result that the rowboat capsized completely.

Remo plunged into the cold water, automatically charging his lungs with oxygen. Though caught by surprise, his body did the natural thing and took in as much air as possible.

Orienting himself, Remo looked up. The sea above was choked with feeding, darting squid. When he saw the Master of Sinanju's feet dangling in the water, his skirts floating high like the mantle of a jellyfish, the upturned boat beside him, Remo started up to help.

Abruptly the boat righted itself, and the skirt collapsed like an umbrella. The feet of the Master of Sinanju vanished completely.

Remo broke the surface at the boat's stern. He looked up.

In front of him the face of Chiun hovered. Above his head the flat part of an oar hovered, too.

The other end of the oar was firm in the Master of Sinanju's bony fists as he sat in the rowboat's stern.

"You letting me back aboard?" Remo asked.

"After you have troubled Sa Mangsang's sleep as a warning to him that he should remain steadfast in slumber so long as the House of Sinanju exists in the world."

"What if I don't come back?"

"It will not matter, because Sa Mangsang will then drink up the entire ocean and with it this fragile craft and its very sad occupant. So do not fail."

"I don't believe in Sa Mangsang."

"You will soon change your mind, as did I when my Master brought me to this place, as did the Master before him and all Masters before him going back through the mighty ages."

Remo hesitated. But the scattered squid were returning to the vicinity of the rowboat, and so Remo took in a deeper breath, held it and willed his body to sink feetfirst.

THE LIGHT OF THE MOON and stars barely penetrated deeper down in the water. But Remo, with his Sinanju training, could adjust to the lack of ambient light. Compensating for the increasing pressure, Remo worked his way down gradually. He might need his full strength for the swim back to the surface—even if he encountered nothing.

The seafloor was relatively shallow here. A depth of hardly more than an eighth of a mile, not so deep that he couldn't prevent nitrogen narcosis—the bends—upon ascent.

Letting his eyes grow accustomed to his surroundings, Remo at first saw only diatoms floating past. Then the seafloor began to resolve itself.

It was jagged, geometric and encrusted with staghorn coral and other marine life. There were volcanic cones. Thermal vents belched an unnatural subterranean heat.

Then Remo saw the pyramid.

It was not a true pyramid, like the Great Pyramid of Giza. It didn't rise up from the ocean floor to a point. It wasn't four sided, but three sided. The angles weren't true. It was strange. Remo, who hadn't done well in geometry in school, nevertheless realized the angles were incorrect.

Whoever had built the pyramid hadn't used solid geometry correctly. The base of the pyramid was off kilter, and the sides weren't aligned or true.

Yet the pyramid reared up to a flat summit that waved with fanlike hands. Kelp. They seemed to beckon with feathery fingers.

Remo swam to the pyramid, searching its sides. It wasn't made from blocks, he soon discovered. He wiped sea scum from different places, trying to find the joints where giant blocks would have fit together. There were none that he could find. It might have been carved from a solid chunk of matter.

The material under the scum was smooth and hard. Underwater and in this low light, it was difficult to figure out what the material was. If not blocks of stone, then what?

Turning, Remo zoomed up to the flat base to rest. It was big enough to park a sedan on. And as he kicked away the scummy residue and the waving kelp, he uncovered a long rectangular slot in the cap.

Getting down on hands and knees, Remo tried to peer into the slot but could see nothing. He stood up and walked back a few paces, pondering his next move.

And it was while Remo stood waiting in the near-absolute darkness of the Pacific Ocean that a sinuous length of rubbery matter quested up, out, to curl toward his chest from behind.

Remo felt the cold suction power of a hundred pads attach themselves to his skin, and before he could respond, the thing withdrew, dragging him into the great pyramid with it.

His last thought was a plaintive, *Chiun, what did you get me into?*

REMO CAUGHT the sides of the slot with both hands.

The tentacle—it felt like a slime-coated rubber hose—squeezed reflexively. Remo heard his own rib-cage cartilage crackle. An eruption of bubbles was forced from his mouth. The tentacles squeezed anew.

Suspended with his palms flat on the cold material on either side of the slot, his elbows bent, Remo forced his lungs to retain their energizing air.

The tentacle around his chest began to grope for better purchase. Through his T-shirt Remo could feel the cold suckers grow warm, as if blood and vitality were flowing through the being in the pyramid after a long hibernation.

As he struggled to keep from being dragged into the slot, some of the suckers let go. Remo strained upward, but relief was momentary. The suckers were simply seeking better adhesion.

The more Remo struggled, the more the tentacle groped and adjusted itself with a casual assurance. A thick length under one arm lifted free, and the warming pads reattached themselves lower down along his ribs.

Other tentacles snaked up to find his ankles. Remo kicked, but the tentacles simply waved loosely with his feet.

Remo looked down. Below, an eye stared up at him with a sleepy, near-human regard. It looked old—older than time itself. There was inhuman confidence in that stare, and a dreadful patience.

A kick like an electric wire ran through Remo's solar plexus. Fear was something he had been taught long ago to master. Not banish, but master and direct. Fear was a good thing, Chiun had assured him many years before. It could spur a man to do the impossible, or convince him to flee a danger that anger or pride or other foolish and destructive emotions might compel him to fight. And in fighting, perish.

Remo looked down at the terrible hooded eye that was so human yet so inimical to all things human, and a fear washed over him that was unlike any fear he had ever before known.

He wanted to escape but could not. He wanted to fight back but was helpless. Above all, he wanted nothing to do with the titanic entity Chiun called Sa Mangsang. No matter what punishment Chiun was prepared to inflict, no matter if Chiun shunned him till the end of time, Remo wanted no combat with Sa Mangsang. The eye glaring up at him looked hungry, and deep in the pit of his stomach—believed by Koreans to be the seat of the soul—Remo felt less like a man than like *food*.

Food for Sa Mangsang.

Even that knowledge wasn't enough to get him free. The fear was too great, too overpowering.

Remo let go. And the tentacles of Sa Mangsang drew him into the darkness of the great pyramid of greenish blue mineral.

Darkness swallowed him. He could barely see the brooding head that looked old and intelligent, but managed to pick out the single sleepy eye. But that was all. Remo could no longer see his hands in front of his face.

So he closed his eyes.

The fear evaporated. It should have increased, but it went away. The primordial fear that solitary eye stabbed into his belly faded. Remo saw nothing, heard nothing and felt only the gristly arms with their wet, slickly cold skin and warm suckers.

A roiling in the water warned him of grasping tentacles. Remo lifted his arms ahead of the wave pressure. Tentacle tips grazed his wrists. He would need his hands free if he was to breathe oxygen ever again.

His arms vertical, Remo snapped his legs up suddenly. The loose tendrils around his ankles drew taut. They yanked back with a stubborn anger.

Then Remo peeled his T-shirt off his chest with a violent rip. The tentacle constricting his chest slid up with it, squeezing into a small loop around the loose cloth.

Bending, he jacknifed his body. Hands like spear heads, he slashed at the enmeshed tentacles. They parted. He kicked free.

Deep in the the dark water, a deep howl arose. It froze the blood in Remo's veins.

Still kicking, he made for the rectangular slot that meant escape. A boiling knot of tentacle came rushing up after him. Uncoiling, they twisted and grasped.

Fighting furiously, Remo kicked at every cold touch. Tentacles recoiled. Others coiled up toward his upper body.

Remo slashed with the edges of his hands, water resistance muffling his blows, but where they encountered tentacles, the tough flesh parted like stretched rubber.

Soon the water around him was full of disconnected tentacles, floating and curling, reaching and hungry.

But still fresh slick tentacles quested up for his warm form.

How many arms does this thing have anyway? Remo wondered angrily, kicking at a slick tip creeping for one ankle.

Arching his spine, twisting, Remo stayed ahead of the feelers.

Suddenly he could see the answer to his question.

A tentacle stump lifted lazily in his direction. Black blood was clouding the water at the severed end, so it was hard to see clearly what was happening.

But as Remo watched, the black blood flow squeezed off and the stump began to regenerate before his eyes.

There was no question. The thing had been a stump. Now it lengthened, slimmed to a tip and was whole once more.

Remo spun in place. Another stump was closing off its tendril of flowing blood. And like a rubber telescope, it grew whole again.

Remo held still while the two tentacles converged. He could feel the eye of Sa Mangsang looking up at him.

Tentacles were reaching out for his thick wrists, and Remo closed his eyes again. The seeking eddies were a better gauge of their proximity than underwater sight.

When he felt the fine hairs of his wrists stir, Remo lashed out with both hands and brought the tentacle tips together so fast they wrapped around one another like two slashing whips.

Remo chopped at the wriggling knot. Another cloud of blood spurted, and Remo swam under it.

Below, Sa Mangsang watched with a titanic, dispassionate patience.

Now Remo could see two eyes, one on either side of the bloated sac that was its head. He counted eight arms. Just like an ordinary octopus.

But this was no ordinary octopus.

For one thing, it was a mottled greenish blue-gray. It had squid properties. A fin on the horny head that waved lazily. And while it seemed to squat far beneath Remo, it still loomed gigantic in its brooding, alien coldness.

It sat on a dais in the shape of a gigantic starfish, but as Remo looked, the arms of the starfish lifted and fell with a slow agony. It was alive!

Around the throne, clinging to the inner pyramid walls, other starfish adhered like a pox. Their sizes varied. Some had been skeletonized. Others were missing triangular arms.

Remo got the awful feeling the starfish served Sa Mangsang as both slaves and food.

Among the starfish squatted whitish-brown polyps of brain coral, like satellite brains.

The orbs of Sa Mangsang sought Remo's gaze, and he hastily closed his own lids. Too late. A searing stab of fear lanced deep into him.

And all around him the water roiled and purled with regathering sucker-lined arms.

Remo twisted, kicked, fought, but there were too many to fight now. Coils like wet tires wound around his chest and hips. Wrists were captured. His right ankle escaped a groping tip, but his knee was pinioned a second later. His other ankle was soon captured.

And then inexorably Sa Mangsang began to drag Remo down into his lair. Remo punched at the fat rope of gristle across his naked chest. His fist bounced off. And Sa Mangsang squeezed half a lungful of precious air from Remo's chest.

Remo kicked downward, and his body leaped up briefly. The tentacles pulled anew. When he felt an ugly warm nearness, he knew he was being drawn toward Sa Mangsang's great head.

I'm screwed now, Remo thought to himself. Why the hell did Chiun do this to me?

He didn't want to open his eyes. He was afraid to. Still, as the nearness of Sa Mangsang made his skin crawl more so than the touch of his inescapable, multiarmed grip, Remo opened his eyes.

He was down on the level of the great head. It loomed above him, a great bladder with eyes. Orbs so far apart on either side of the blue-green bag of skin, they might have belonged to two different creatures.

That was how vast Sa Mangsang sat on his throne, surrounded by brain coral and slave starfish.

The head lifted, exposing a mouth like the curved beak of a parrot, but upside down. The heavy half was at the bottom. And when it dropped, great inward-curving teeth showed in a round, pulsing hole, bringing the teeth together to form an angry flower.

Remo twisted, but to no avail. The tentacle drew him in toward the gnashing circle of teeth designed to rip flesh into chunks.

Seeing what fate awaited him, all fear drained from Remo Williams's limp body. Before, he could only guess his fate. Now, with it contracting and expanding before him, he lost his fear. Only a sad surrender suffused his body. He was down to his last dribbles of oxygen anyway.

And he remembered the sign Chiun had told him to make with his fingers.

Twisting them apart, he managed to approximate the sign.

The short siphon off to one side of Sa Mangsang's mouth blew out an angry rush of water. The hooded eyes seemed to darken in anger. But nothing else happened.

The tentacles drew him closer.

In the last moments before he was to be ripped apart like so much human chum, the voice of the Master of Sinanju came into Remo's head.

"You would do well to remember that Sa Mangsang is also known as Hydra."

Hydra, Hydra, Remo thought. What do I know about the Hydra?

And a second voice came into his head. A voice he knew almost as well as Chiun.

Sister Mary Margaret's voice.

"The Hydra was the fearsome beast, some say a great serpent, some say a dragon, which possessed nine heads. Each time Hercules chopped off a head, another grew back. But Hercules knew the Hydra had an Achilles' heel. And that was its immortal ninth head."

But this thing has only one head, Remo thought. Eight tentacles but one head.

The truth struck Remo in the last ebbing moments of life.

Relaxing, he let the tentacles draw him closer and closer. He closed his eyes. He would not need them for what he had to do. Maybe vision would be a hindrance.

When the water before him was as warm as a sleeping body next to his, Remo drew his hands together. The entwining tentacles reacted spasmodically. They tightened.

And Remo kicked out with both feet at the great monster's brooding head.

A bubbling scream washed over him.

Remo's eyes snapped open.

Sa Mangsang was changing color! Furious bands of red and orange were washing over his aquamarine skull. The tentacles, including the loops at his ankles, were alive with moving bands of angry colors, like neon racing through glass tubes.

Then, like great curtains, the hooded lids began to descend over the sleepy orbs.

Tentacles relaxed, let go and fell away as if in death.

Remo kicked upward as hard as he could. He had no time to waste. The air was almost exhausted from his lungs. And the rectangular slot above beckoned.

As he arrowed up toward the opening and away from the great arms of Sa Mangsang, Remo looked down.

Retracted tentacles curling into tight, perfectly spaced coils about his throne, Sa Mangsang had turned the color of bone. His great orbs were closed. He slept. He might have been dead. He might have been dead a million years.

But he only slept.

Kicking upward with all his ebbing strength, Remo Williams could only think of two things he wanted most in life—oxygen and sleep.

But as he fought to reach the world of men and breathable air, he felt the last bubble of carbon dioxide escape his lips and the entire world began to darken around him....

REMO SNAPPED AWAKE at the bow of the rowboat. He looked around dazedly. "Where the hell am I?"

"With me," said Chiun, folding his hands in his lap.

"But I—" Remo swallowed hard. "A minute ago, I—"

"—escaped Sa Mangsang?"

"Yeah. Did you pull me out of the water?"

"No. *You* did that."

"I don't remember it."

"Unless you think it was a dream...."

"Dream. Yeah. It was a dream. I fell asleep. I thought I was awake, but I was really asleep. I woke up in my dream but I was still dreaming. I never had that happen to me before."

"If you were dreaming," Chiun asked suddenly, "then why are your clothes wet?"

Remo looked down. His chinos were soaked. His feet were bare. And his T-shirt was missing. "You threw water on me," Remo accused.

"Why would I do that?"

"And you stole my shirt."

"To match your dream?"

"Exactly."

"If it was a dream, how would I know you had lost your shirt to Sa Mangsang's tentacles?"

Remo thought hard. "Maybe I talked in my sleep. Yeah, that's it. I talked in my sleep."

"Possibly."

"What other explanation was there? There's no way an octopus could grow as huge as the nightmare I saw in my dream."

"The Sa Mangsang of your dreams was very large?"

"Titanic."

"And how big were its awesome suckers?"

"Who cares? Big."

Coolly Chiun said, "Show me how big, my son."

Remo brought his hands together and made a circle by touching forefingers and thumbs together.

"That big," he insisted.

"That is very large."

"You know it."

"As large as the angry red marks on your naked chest?"

Remo looked down.

Marching across his pale wet chest were livid scarlet circles such as would be left by the sucker pads of a gargantuan octopus.

"You have nothing to say now?" Chiun inquired coolly.

And looking at the luminous squid who slashed the waters all around them, feeding on tiny surface fish, Remo did something rare for a full Master of Sinanju.

He trembled from head to foot.

15

Dr. Harold W. Smith was following his enforcement arm.

The audit trail was very clear. Boston to Madrid. Madrid to Athens. Athens to Cairo and Canada, with many stops in between.

Remo and Chiun were bouncing around the world like two hyperactive rubber balls. But what did it mean?

Since they were not on assignment, there was no immediate cause for alarm. But Remo and Chiun, since joining CURE, never raced around without a clear purpose in mind.

They took no vacations as such. Remo had no known relatives to visit. No friends, past present or future. He had only Chiun. And the Master of Sinanju had his village.

But they weren't going to North Korea, it seemed.

They had bypassed it in favor of Tokyo. Now they were in Honolulu, according to the audit trail of credit-card expenditures and airline reservations. Smith, who had Remo's many credit cards under fictitious names on his data base, had access to the credit-card companies' minute-by-minute computerized credit-check records. The minute Remo booked a flight, it appeared on the airline's worldwide computerized reservation system and could be called up on Smith's Folcroft office computer screen instantly.

Smith wondered if they were on some kind of extended vacation. But that seemed unlikely. They were in the air more than on the ground in most cases. Thus, they could not be sight-seeing, he concluded.

A check of world trouble spots showed no correlation between their travels and global events.

Perhaps this was some old business of the House of Sinanju, Smith reasoned. Yes, that must be it. Something from Chiun's past had called them to trot all over the globe.

He hoped it was nothing serious, that it would not impact on their availability. Smith had long ago realized his two agents were for all practical purposes virtually uncontrollable.

As it was, he had no missions for Remo. As long as Remo wasn't needed, Smith would force himself not to worry about their activities.

But just to be sure, he popped four extrastrength Tums before leaving his office for lunch. It never hurt to anticipate stomach upsets. And where Remo and Chiun were concerned, upsetting news invariably followed.

SMITH DROVE his aging station wagon to nearby Port Chester, and its post office. In the early days of CURE, letters from field informants and others filled the mailbox every week. In these days of E-mail, Smith received fewer and fewer tips through the mail. One trip a week was usually enough. Rarely did a letter from the field lead to a mission for Remo and Chiun.

Old habits die hard. Smith got in line before going to his box. That way he could scan the foyer unobtrusively. There were no suspicious people hanging about. That was one of the reasons Smith picked up his own mail. Post-office boxes were very safe and extremely anonymous. The federal government didn't tolerate loiterers lying in wait at mail boxes for boxholders.

Smith grudgingly bought a one-cent stamp—the lowest denomination he could purchase—and then went to the bank of boxes. Inserting a brass key shiny from long use, he opened the box.

Inside was a sheaf of mail. He took it, shut the box and left the foyer, clutching the envelopes protectively.

Behind the wheel of his station wagon, Smith examined each one to be sure it was addressed to him. Although he had maintained the box for some thirty years now, sometimes Smith still received other people's mail.

The fourth letter in the stack brought a chill to Harold Smith's age-curved spine. Written in flowing blue ink, it was addressed to Mr. Conrad MacCleary.

There was no return address. Only an Oklahoma postmark. Smith tore open the envelope and read the folded note inside with startled eyes.

Our Lady of Perpetual Care
Home for the Infirm

My Dear Mr. MacCleary,

I trust you are well.

As promised so very long ago, I am writing to inform you of the imminent passing of Sister Mary Margaret Morrow. She has been in declining health for several years now, yet has clung to this earth most wonderfully. But the nurses do not believe that she will survive the month of July.

If it still is your wish to attend the funeral, I cannot say with certainty when this will be, but you should know that Sister Mary Margaret's time is very short. In this case, you would do well to contact me by telephone so I might better advise you.

Yours in Christ,
Sister Novella

Harold Smith read with eyes that skated over the ink script uncomprehendingly. He read the short note again. And for the third time.

"She's alive," he breathed.

Smith thought back. Conrad MacCleary had been his right hand in the creation of CURE. Grizzled, hard drinking and indomitably patriotic, he had executed the frame that had brought Remo Williams to CURE in the first place.

Harold Smith had engineered it all. Masterminded the plan. But Smith couldn't go into the field. As head of CURE, he wasn't expendable. MacCleary was.

From stealing Remo's police badge, to rigging the electric chair to deliver a nonlethal charge, to visiting Remo on death row disguised as a Capuchin monk in order to slip him the pill that suppressed his life signs so he could be pronounced dead after the mock execution, MacCleary had done it all, leaving no fingerprints and no witnesses.

Except apparently Sister Mary Margaret, the one person who had shaped Remo Williams's young life.

Smith remembered the conversation that had taken place so long ago.

"What about the nun?" MacCleary had asked.

"Is she a problem?"

"She was like a mother to Williams. Even after the plastic surgery, she would be able to recognize his eyes or his voice."

"Where is she now?"

"Still holding down the fort at St. Theresa's."

"It's to be burned," Smith ordered. "To the ground. There must be no record of any Remo Williams."

"Got it," McCleary said. "But what about the sister?"

"No one must be allowed to place the program at risk. The nation depends on it."

"Understood," MacCleary replied.

That was all. That was the way they worked. Smith did not have to say that Sister Mary Margaret, despite her good works in life, had to die. Just as Remo Williams had had to die. Just as so many who threatened CURE over the years had had to die. It was understood. MacCleary was a seasoned agent. He had been one of the finest cold warriors Harold Smith had ever known.

It was true he was a hard-drinking SOB with a tendency to get sloppy drunk and sentimental. But it had never interfered with his duty. In fact, MacCleary had a saying for those occasions when the work got nasty: America Is Worth A Life.

But as Harold W. Smith folded the letter after committing Sister Novella's address and phone number to memory and burning it in the immaculate ashtray of his dashboard, he remembered another fact.

Conrad MacCleary had been a Catholic. Although a lapsed Catholic, obviously he'd not been without sympathy for a nun who had done nothing wrong and perhaps everything right.

Smith crushed the warm gray ashes to powder as he drove back toward Rye and Folcroft, his patrician face was thoughtful.

From beyond the grave, Conrad MacCleary may have provided CURE with the one thing it most needed now. A way to hold on to its enforcement agent.

Smith said a silent thank-you to the memory of his old comrade in arms.

As a precaution, he emptied the ashes into three different trash receptacles along the route so no one could ever resurrect the note.

16

"I'm going to hit the sack," Remo said when the keel of the rowboat finally grated on the sands of Waikiki Beach.

Dawn was peeping over the Pacific. The night wind off the water had abated, leaving only an eerie calm.

"If you slept on the boat, as you claim, why do you need more sleep?" Chiun asked, waiting in the boat for his pupil to drag the craft out of the water by its painter so he could step off onto dry ground, as befitted his station as Reigning Master.

To Chiun's surprise, Remo did no such thing. He started inland, saying with utmost disrespect, "I'm going to find a nice quiet hotel and sleep on a Western bed for a change."

Chiun's facial hair trembled in anger. "You will not sleep on a Western bed. I forbid it!"

"Try and stop me," Remo hurled back.

Suddenly the Master of Sinanju was standing in the darkness before Remo.

Remo took a wary step backward. "Do I have to fight you, too?" he asked wearily.

"It is not yet time."

"What do you mean?"

"If you desire sleep so much, I will allow this. But on the morn we journey to Hesperia."

"Tomorrow we'll see about Hesperia."

"We are going to Hesperia," Chiun insisted.

"I said we'll see!" Remo flared, and stalked off into the night.

The Master of Sinanju watched him go, saying nothing, his face a stiff mask of papyrus. In the moonlight it had the grim aspect of a death mask.

REMO CHECKED into the Waikiki Sheraton and threw himself facedown on a queen-size bed the moment he stepped into his suite. It was against all of Chiun's teachings to sleep on a bed and not a reed mat, but Remo no longer cared. After all that Chiun had put him through, the old Korean could take a flying leap into the Void.

Sleep took Remo within seconds of his face hitting the down pillow.

HE FOUND HIMSELF in a room of gold walls, heaped with treasure. In the center a thick-bodied man sat on a throne of teak chased with silver and gold. He wore a flowing silk robe of the brilliant red hue believed in the Orient to ward off evil demons.

Remo recognized the man on the throne instantly. "Wang?"

"The Great Wang, if you please." And the Great Wang grinned like a cherub. "I see you've made it all the way to the Rite of Attainment. Good for you, Remo Williams. Good for you. I was beginning to wonder about you."

"Maybe you can tell me why I'm having all these dreams about past Masters."

"Chiun didn't tell you?"

"Chiun flat-out denied my dreams mean anything."

"That is so like him. Cloaking a simple ritual in mystery just to milk the moment."

"Simple ritual? Do you know what he's got me doing?"

Wang beamed. His perfect smile made his high forehead fall into doughy rolls of flesh. "Sure. Been through it myself. You chase around till you're ready to drop. When you do, past Masters visit you, look you over and, if they like what they see, dispense wisdom."

"The dreams are part of the Rite?" Remo demanded.

"It was so from the first Master who emerged from the Caves of Mist to those who came just before you."

"So that's who that was."

"Hey. Did you meet Sa Mangsang yet?"

"Yeah. And I hope I never do again. Was it a dream?"

"Is this a dream?"

Remo frowned. "It feels like a dream. I'm asleep. I think. But these dreams are making too much sense to be dreams."

"Have you fought the Minotaur yet?"

"Yeah. It was only Chiun in the dark wearing a bull mask."

"Too bad. In my day we had a real Minotaur. It made for an interesting experience."

"Minotaurs aren't real."

"They say that about dragons now. But I slew a few in my time."

"Hey, I thought Masters were supposed to have a visit from the Great Wang only once in their lifetime."

"They are. That was when you were awake. My appearance signified you had reached full Masterhood. Since you're fast asleep, this doesn't count."

"Oh," said Remo.

"And now you're on the threshold of taking over the House. You know, Chiun should have retired years ago."

"Really?"

"Absolutely. Instead, he's been hogging all the glory long after his time." Wang shook his round head. "Tsk-tsk. Reckless. What if you both fall into the same trap and die? No more House."

"I never thought about it before."

Wang leaned forward conspiratorially. "Did you guess the riddle of the Sphinx?"

"No."

"No? How could you miss that? It was as plain as the nose on your face."

"That's what Chiun said."

"Look, I'll give you a hint." And laying a finger beside his nose like old Saint Nick, the Great Wang pushed his broad nose aside, flattening it. He made his ears stick out, as if pushed forward by a pharaonic headdress.

"You! That was you?"

"The very same," said the Great Wang, letting his nose and ears bounce back. "When a later pharaoh begged me to come help him out, I went back and collected. Made those untrustworthy welchers recarve the entire face to match mine. They were hopping mad when I spurned their gold, but a promise made to the House of Sinanju must be kept. If we let pharaohs go back on their word to us, soon every ragtag emir, caliph and pasha would take advantage."

"You're the Sphinx."

Wang leaned back on his throne. "The *Great* Sphinx. You keep forgetting my honorific. I worked very hard to earn it."

"Sorry."

"Don't tell Chiun I told you, either. Let him think you figured it out for yourself."

"Did Chiun figure it out for himself?"

"Sure. He's very sharp."

"So, do I have to fight you, too?"

Wang grinned broadly. "Do you think you'd win?"

"Well, you *are* the Great Wang."

"And you're the dead night tiger made whole by the Master of Sinanju. The avatar of the prophecy. Shiva incarnate himself."

"I don't believe that Shiva stuff."

"Hey, you're talking to the prophet who first prophesied that."

"Sorry."

"Well, you'll find out. You are allowed to ask me one question, by the way. Got anything interesting?"

"Yeah. When you first discovered the sun source, a ring of fire appeared in the sky and a voice spoke to you. What was it?"

The Great Wang shrugged good-naturedly.

"I've been trying to figure that one out these last two or three thousand years. The fire blinded me and the voice filled my brain. I think it was Sanshin."

"Who?"

"The Mountain Spirit. Don't tell me Chiun never told you about the Mountain Spirit?"

"Maybe he did. I don't pay much attention to the mystic stuff."

"Sanshin is the Mountain Spirit. A good spirit. If it wasn't Sanshin, then it could have been Hanunim, the

Celestial Emperor, or maybe the man in the moon. I know it wasn't Yong-Wang, the Dragon King. He rules over water, and I wasn't anywhere near water. Maybe it's better not to know. The fire came, I understood my brain and my body better than any Master before me and the House was saved.''

"I always wondered about that."

"If you ever find out," the Great Wang said, "look me up when you get to the Void and tell me."

"Mind telling me how long the Rite of Attainment goes on?"

"Sorry. You used up your one question. Next time."

"There's a next time?"

"No. Figure of speech. Listen, before I go, I have a question for you. How come you didn't ask me about your father?"

Remo started. "How would you know about my father?"

Wang wagged a remonstrating finger. "Uh-uh. That was a question. Ask Nonja. Maybe he'll tell you."

And standing up, the Great Wang threw up his arms, making the folds of his red robe lift like wings. When they covered his face completely, the red silk dropped, empty, to drape the teak throne.

And in the empty air, the Great Wang laughed happily.

IN THE MORNING, Remo checked his suite. There was no sign of the Master of Sinanju. So he called Harold W. Smith at Folcroft, knowing that it would be afternoon there.

"Smitty, I need a favor."

"I have news about your past."

"Save it. I'm not interested."

"Do you mind telling me why this change of heart?"

"Yes. Now, about that favor."

"State this favor," Smith said coldly.

"An assignment. Fast."

"I thought you were on strike."

"I'll strike later. I need an assignment yesterday."

"I have nothing for you."

"Make something up. I gotta get away from Chiun."

"Why?"

"He's dragging me to hell and gone and back again. It's called the Rite of Attainment and it's killing me. I gotta get away for a while. He's got me doing these things he calls *athloi.*"

"*Athloi?*"

"I don't know what it means, either, but so far I've run against the bulls of Pamplona, moved the Sphinx, fought the Hydra and the Minotaur—"

"Did you say Minotaur?"

"It was only Chiun in a costume."

"Remo," Smith said, "what you are describing reminds me of the Twelve Labors of Hercules."

"Yeah, that's what I said six or seven *athloi* ago."

"No, I mean literally. To atone for the slaying of his wife Megara and their three sons, done under the influence of madness visited on him by the goddess Hera, Hercules was instructed by the Oracle of Delphi to complete twelve *athloi,* or labors, after which he would become immortal."

"Wait a minute. *Athloi* is Roman, not Korean?"

"Actually the word is Greek."

"You get that off your computers?"

"No, from my classics studies. But I am calling up my data base. Here it is. Scholars disagree on the number and order of these labors, but generally they include besting the Nemean Lion, the Lernaean Hydra, the Erymanthian Boar—''

"You mean 'bear.'"

"It says 'boar.'"

"I tangled with a polar bear. Chiun tried to get me to wear the skin."

"Hercules wore the skin of the defeated Nemean Lion. Did you encounter a lion?"

"Not unless you count the Sphinx. He had me move it. What else?"

"There are defeating the Stymphalian Fowl, cleaning the Augean Stables—''

"I think I got them both in one shot on a Greek isle," Remo muttered.

"Besting the Cretan Bull, capturing the Horses of Diomedes, winning the Apples of the Hesperides, finding the Girdle of Hippolyta, saving the Oxen of Geryon, tricking Cerberus. Conquering Cacus the ox-rustler, Antaeus the wrestler and the Arcadian Hind round out the list," finished Smith.

"What's a hind?"

"An animal with hooves of brass and antlers of gold."

Remo groaned. "Man, I feel like I've been wrestling dinosaurs and I hardly made a dent in that list. You gotta find me an assignment, Smitty. Anything."

"Remo, I may have something that will interest you."

"What's that?"

"Do you remember Sister Mary Margaret Morrow?"

"Yeah. What about her?"

"She is still alive, Remo."

In the hotel suite, Remo was quiet for a long time. When he spoke again, his voice was seared with shock.

"MacCleary swore she was dead. Said she died when the orphanage burned down."

"MacCleary lied. Sister Mary Margaret is in a nursing home maintained by the Catholic Church."

"She would have to be as old as the hills by now," Remo breathed, looking out at Honolulu basking in the midday sun.

Smith cleared his throat. "I suppose you would like to visit her?"

"Try and stop me," Remo growled.

"She is dying. She can do us no harm if you are discreet."

"Why are you doing this?" Remo asked suspiciously.

"Call it a gesture of good faith. I am at a dead end in the search for your progenitors. Sister Mary Margaret may be able to put your mind at rest."

"If she knew anything, she would have told me long ago."

"Did she ever tell you she caught a glimpse of the man who left you on the orphanage doorstep?"

"Who told you that?"

"MacCleary. Back at the beginning. Since she failed to recognize the man, it didn't matter. It was a dead end."

"Tell me where she is."

"Oklahoma City. Our Lady of Perpetual Care Home for the Infirm. Ask for a Sister Novella. Tell her you are a friend of Conrad MacCleary."

Remo grunted. "A nursing home. No wonder I never heard different. She might as well have been in prison."

"You should waste no time, Remo. I am reliably informed she is at death's door."

"Don't sweat it. I can hardly wait to get back to the U.S.A. Chiun has some godforsaken place called Hesperia on my itinerary."

And Remo hung up.

Sneaking out of the hotel, he hailed a cab and got on the first standby flight to the U.S.A., figuring he could reach Oklahoma City from any spot in the country. But once Chiun caught up with him, all bets were off.

He wasn't followed. This made Remo suspicious. He wondered where the Master of Sinanju had disappeared to. It wasn't like the old reprobate to be so easily fooled.

But as he flew to San Francisco, Remo prowled the aisles several times, searching the faces of the other passengers. None of them were Chiun.

The first-class stewardess wondered if the seat next to Remo was empty.

"You're the flight attendant," Remo said. "You should know."

The stewardess took Remo's surly growl as an invitation. "Do you live in San Francisco?" she asked.

"No."

"Visiting? I could show you the town!"

"It's a stopover. I'm going on to Oklahoma City."

"I have a third cousin twice removed in Oklahoma City! I haven't seen her in years. Tell you what, I'll take the rest of the month off and we'll do Oklahoma City together."

Remo made his face sad. "Actually I'm going to a funeral."

"Wonderful! I *love* funerals. So does my cousin. Maybe we can find a date for her, too."

"Are you listening to anything I'm saying?" Remo asked. "I'm going to a funeral and I'd like to be alone with my thoughts."

The stewardess rested a soothing hand on Remo's own. "I understand perfectly. I'll just sit here and give you silent emotional support."

"Get lost," said Remo. Setting his seat back all the way and closing his eyes, he let himself sink into blackness.

A STURDY MAN with a bull neck and merciless black eyes rose up from a plane of darkness all but invisible against a deeper blackness.

"I am Nonja," he said, his voice the croaking of a bullfrog.

"You can call me Remo."

"I mastered the sun source at an early age, but all my life I lived in ignorance."

"The Great Wang said you know about my father."

"I had a son. His name was Kojing."

"I think I heard of him."

"I had to come to this Void before my ignorance was banished," Nonja intoned. "Know this, O white-skin."

"Master Kojing lived in the Choson Kingdom era," said Remo. "That much I remember because Persia and Egypt were no longer clients, and there wasn't much work for the House."

"Master Kojing had a secret. Do you know it?"

"If I did, I forgot it long ago."

"You must try to remember. It is very important."

"Sorry. I give up. Tell me about my father."

Nonja frowned deeply, his dour face falling into fleshy gullies. "Kojing will tell you this. For I must go."

"That's it? I don't have to fight you?"

"No, you do not have to fight me," said Nonja.

"Good," said Remo. "Not that I couldn't take you."

And without warning, Nonja swept Remo off his feet with a sweeping kick to his ankles.

"Hey! What was that about?" asked Remo from the plane of darkness on which he sprawled.

"It was about never dropping your guard. Your Master should be ashamed of you."

"Hey, I just wrestled the Father of All Squid. I'm bushed."

"Be grateful then I did not strike a death blow, big foot."

"Wait! What about my father?"

Master Nonja crossed one ankle before the other. His legs scissored apart at the knees. Dropping into a lotus position before Remo's sprawled form, he dropped into the black plane of the Void and out of sight.

WHEN REMO WOKE UP, the stewardess was still holding his hand lovingly. She smiled dreamily.

"You talked in your sleep."

"Did I make sense?" Remo asked.

"No. You were adorable. I could have listened all night."

"It's day."

"That was an invitation." And the stewardess favored Remo with a blatant wink.

Excusing himself, Remo went to the rest room and locked himself in until he heard the landing gear whining down from their wells and the passengers stir from their seats.

Slipping among the exiting passengers and walking low behind a lady who weighed more than a baby elephant, Remo managed to slip past the sentinel stewardess and off the plane unseen.

Changing planes, he found all flights to Oklahoma City full.

"I'll fly standby," Remo told the redheaded clerk.

She gave him an inviting smile. "Every flight is absolutely, positively filled to capacity until tomorrow. At least."

"I'm in a rush."

The clerk leaned forward. Her lips were almost as red as her hair. "I'd be happy to put you up at my place until tomorrow," she purred. "I have a very comfy sofa bed. It sleeps two. Three if you're adventurous." She winked.

"I have to go out today."

"In that case," the clerk snapped, her face reddening, "you can walk for all I care." She slapped a Closed sign on the counter.

"Damn," muttered Remo. "Since when did Oklahoma City become so popular?"

Going to the gate, he tried to bribe his way onto the flight. One passenger expressed interest, but changed his mind when Remo found he had only thirty dollars and two ancient coins on him.

When a male steward happened by, Remo got an idea. Digging into his wallet, he pulled his Remo Black sky marshal's ID card. It was a little waterlogged around the edges, but still readable.

Accosting the flight attendant, Remo showed his ID and said, "The federal government needs your cooperation."

"Sure. What can I do?"

"We have intelligence out of the Middle East there will be an attempt to skyjack the Oklahoma City flight.

It's booked solid, and I have to get on board without alerting the terrorists.''

"How can I help?"

"I need your uniform."

"Excuse me?"

"I'm going to take your place. It's for the safety of the passengers and crew."

When the man hesitated, Remo told him. "If you're not on the flight, you're not likely to catch a stray round."

The flight attendant squared his shoulders bravely. "If it's for my country, I'll do it."

Five minutes later Remo emerged from the men's room and boarded the flight unchallenged.

It was a smooth flight. He only had to step on the toes of one smitten stewardess to discourage her. And he picked up two hundred dollars in tips and assorted phone numbers and propositions on crumpled napkins from female passengers.

He kept the money. The napkins he threw away.

17

Everywhere he went, Sunny Joe Roam saw death.

They lay sick in their hogans. They sprawled in the hot sun drinking again, drinking heavily to kill the pain and numb the mind to that fact that they were doomed.

They were all doomed, Sunny Joe saw. Even himself, if he stayed. Death hung in the very air. Men shivered unnaturally in the 130-degree heat.

By the time he realized it was too late for them all, Sunny Joe had kicked out the virologist flown in from New York and turned away the Arizona State epidemiologist, saying, "This is Sun On Jo land. Sun On Jo laws apply here, not yours."

"I know that," said the state epidemiologist through his particle-filter mask. "But state law requires the reservation be quarantined. No one in and no one out."

And he solemnly handed over a big red sign.

Sunny Joe had nailed it to the corral fence on the spot.

Walking his horse back after posting the sign, Sunny Joe met Tomi on the dusty road.

"We're all gonna die, aren't we, Sunny Joe?"

"You knew that from the time you were a pup, Tomi."

"No, I mean we're all gonna die soon. And together."

"Would you rather die alone?"

"I'd rather not die at all." Tomi spit into the dust. "Think it's the deer mice, like the paleface medicos say?"

"Does it matter?"

"I'd like to know what killed me, yeah."

"The specialist says it's the mice. The rains made 'em multiply. They carry the virus in their bodies and in their droppings and their urine. He says we make a mistake when we abandon the hogans of those who die. The mice get in and make it their home, and when the mourning period is over, we catch it when we clean out the mice. The more who die, the more will die if we stick to our ways, he said."

"White people been trying to get us to mend our ways as long as I can remember, Sunny Joe."

"Well, even if we all turned apple now, it'd be too damn late. There's no cure. Not for this kind of hanta-virus."

"That what he called it?"

"Yeah. He said the healthy had only one hope. That was to clear out. Get as clear off the reservation as possible. Desert mice are too plentiful. No way to find and trap them all so they can't spread the Sun On Jo Disease."

"You should go, Sunny Joe."

"Can't. I'm the last Sunny Joe. The tribe depends on me. How could I turn my back on my people now?"

"But you're a big man in the white world. You got money, position, fame. We're just Indians. The world will spin just fine without us."

Sunny Joe spit into the dust, killing a tiny pinacate beetle.

"I'm just as Sun On Jo as you, Tomi. Don't you ever breathe different. I said I come home to save my people or to die with them. Now I'm doing it. One or the other, I'm doing it."

Sunny Joe stared off toward Red Ghost Butte. His rugged face was thoughtful.

"It's the end of the Sun On Jos, ain't it, Sunny Joe?" said Tomi.

Bill Roam nodded. "Hell, we been dying a damn long time. Not enough children been born, and too few of 'em female. When the last Sun On Jo squaw passed through the change of life, that was it. I thought I could bring some fresh blood in and keep us going a generation or two longer, but I was a fool. It was all pipe smoke. Without another Sunny Joe to take my place, there is no future."

"What about the prophesy?"

"Which prophesy is that?"

"The one that says Ko Jong Oh will send one of his spirit warriors to help out the tribe when it is most in need."

"Yeah. Forgot about that."

"Well?"

Sunny Joe blew out a long, sad breath. "I think if old Ko Jong Oh was going to do it, old Ko Jong Oh would have done it by now. Don't you, Tomi?"

"Yeah. Guess it was just happy firewater talk."

"Maybe."

Abruptly Sunny Joe put his booted foot into a stirrup and mounted his big chestnut horse. He forked it toward the west.

"Where you going?" Tomi called after him.

"To Red Ghost Butte."

"Nothing up there but the ancient ones."

"That's where Ko Jong Oh dwells. I'm going to talk to him. Maybe he's plumb forgot about his spirit warrior. Maybe it's not too late. Maybe he'll be along directly."

"Good luck, Sunny Joe."

"Hah, Sanshin! Ride!"

And the horse disappeared in a cloud of desert dust that hung in the hot still air like the red breath of death.

As soon as he inhaled it, Tomi began coughing. The trouble was, he just couldn't quite stop.

18

Remo kept glancing in the rearview mirror as he piloted the rental car from Will Rogers International Airport. He was not followed. He was sure of it—not that there was any way the Master of Sinanju could have followed him all the way from Honolulu.

But Remo wasn't taking any chances.

Our Lady of Perpetual Care Home for the Infirm was a rambling, nun-black Victorian building ten years in need of paint, with the sign hanging on rusty chains on the lawn. Remo walked up to the dark front door not knowing what to feel. Would Sister Mary remember him? Would she still be alive?

He rang the bell and waited, focusing on his breathing. His stomach tightened in a way it used to when he was a boy and the world was a frightening place.

The door opened and a middle-aged nun peered out. "Yes?"

"I'm looking for Sister Novella."

The nun regarded him owlishly. "And what is your business?"

"My name is Remo. Williams," he added. The taste of the last name he no longer used was strange on his tongue. "I grew up in the orphanage where Sister Mary Margaret taught a long time ago."

"I see. Well, in that case I am Sister Novella. Come in, Mr. Williams."

Remo stepped in, and the smell of the place hit him with a shock. It was a mixture of antiseptics, candle wax and must. It smelled a little like Folcroft's main patient-care wing but not as clean. The mustiness was winning.

He followed Sister Novella to a genteel sitting room with an old-fashioned tin ceiling. Her black habit swayed as she walked, her hands tucked absently into unseen pockets. Seen from behind, her head encased in a starched wimple, she might have been Sister Mary herself.

"How did you find us, Mr. Williams?" Sister Novella asked after they had taken seats.

Remo leaned forward in his chair. "I knew Conrad MacCleary."

"And how is he?"

"Dead."

"Oh, I am sorry to hear that. Of course, I didn't know him personally. Mr. MacCleary arranged for Sister Mary to join us. It was after the fire, you know. She wasn't young, and when the orphanage—oh, what was its name?"

"St. Theresa's."

"Yes. St. Theresa's. Thank you. When St. Theresa's burned, it seemed to take the heart out of the poor dear. She had no more appetite for teaching. So she came here. First she tended to the sick and, as time passed, she duly became one of them. Mr. MacCleary seemed to take a special interest in her and asked to be informed in the event of her passing."

"Sister Mary. Is she . . . ?"

"Still with us? Yes. But she was given the last rites one week ago."

"I'd like to see her as soon as possible."

"I must warn you, Mr. Williams, she may not know you."

Remo's face seemed to fragment. His shoulders dropped.

"Oh, it's not that," Sister Novella said quickly. "Her hearing is very poor, and she suffers from low vision. Cataracts, you know. You must not expect too much from her."

"I understand."

"Come this way."

They walked down a corridor and into a floral-papered wing of the rambling old house that suddenly revealed the place for what it really was—a nursing home. Old women were visible through half-open doors, lying in beds or propped up in recliners, staring vacantly at televisions with eyes connected to brains that seemed not to quite comprehend the world around them.

Remo suddenly felt a lump rising in his throat. A wave of overpowering sadness flooded through his body. He took a deep breath, charging the mitochondria of his body with reviving oxygen, drawing upon reserves of strength he knew he'd need to come face-to-face with his past.

They came to a paneled door at the far end of a musty corridor. The predominant smell in the air was candle wax.

"Let me look in on her first," whispered Sister Novella. Remo nodded. The sister opened the door just enough to slip in, and it closed after her with a hesitant click.

Remo waited, flexing his thick wrists. His heart seemed to be beating high and hard in his hot, tight throat.

After only a moment the door reopened. "You may come in now."

Remo stepped into a darkened room. The shades were drawn snug. There was only one item of furniture in the room. An oaken bed worn at each pineapple-style post. It was covered with a fringed bedspread that had once been white but was now very yellow.

On the bed, stretched out like a mummy, lay Sister Mary Margaret. Remo thought he was prepared. But the shock of recognition was a kick in his stomach that made his heart jump and pound.

Remo had never seen Sister Mary's uncovered head. Never even knew the color of her hair. But even without her wimple, her hair like iron strands on the dingy pillow, Remo could trace the sweet lines of the womanly face that could be so tender and stern by turns. It was Sister Mary Margaret. But Remo had carried for years a memory of a woman with strength in her face and wisdom in her pale gray eyes.

That face was as twisted as a tree root now. Her head started on the pillow, struggling to see and hear with organs that had long ago failed.

"I have a visitor for you, Sister Mary," Sister Novella called in a rising voice.

The reply was a frail croak. "Eh?"

"I said, you have a visitor."

Weak eyes strained to see in the dim light. "Yes?"

"His name is—"

Remo interrupted, "Why don't I handle it from here? Could we be alone?"

Sister Novella hesitated. "Oh, I don't think I—"

"She practically raised me. There are things I need to say to her. Privately."

Sister Novella nodded. "I understand. I will be in the sitting room when you are done. Please do not tire her."

"I promise," Remo said.

When the door closed, Remo stood in the semidarkness for a long time. Sister Mary seemed to forget she had been spoken to. A chink of light fell upon one searching eye, and it was a like a fat pearl dipped in egg white, cloudy and thick.

Remo knelt at her bedside and took a waxy-smooth hand in his. It was cool to the touch. Her veins pulsed threadily.

"Sister Mary?"

Her voice was whisper thin. "Yes? Who is it?"

"I don't know if you remember me."

"Your voice . . ."

Remo took a deep breath. "My name is Remo. Remo Williams."

And Sister Mary Margaret started. A low sigh escaped her lips. "Yes. Yes. I recognize your voice," she said breathily. She tried to make out his features and, failing, let her head fall back. "Oh, I knew you would make it."

"Sister?"

"I could not be so wrong about you," she said, gazing at the peeling ceiling.

"I came to ask you about myself."

"What could I tell you that Saint Peter cannot?"

Remo frowned. Was she delirious?

"I was left on the doorstep of St. Theresa's. Do you remember?"

A wan smile quirked her contorted face. "Yes. I found you. You weren't even crying. Left in a basket

and you never cried once. I knew you were special
then.''

"They say you saw the man who left me there."

"Oh, that was so long ago."

"I know. I know. But try to remember. You saw a
man. What did he look like?''

"He was very tall and quite lean. Thin, the way you
turned out to be. Rugged. Not in a bad way, but in a
strong way. When you began to become a man, I
thought I saw some of his features in yours."

"Why didn't you tell me?"

"I didn't know his name. No one did. You were left
for reasons no one knew, but they must have been very
good reasons. Why cause you to fret and seek the face
of your father in every man's face you passed in the
street?''

"For a long time," Remo said thickly, "I did that
anyway."

"We called you the Window Boy. Did you know
that? Always waiting to be taken home. So brave and so
sad. But it was not to be. You had to live your own life."

"You never found out who the man was?"

"No."

"Damn," Remo muttered under his breath.

"But I did see him again years later."

Remo paled. "Where?"

"I saw in him a movie theater," Sister Mary said
breathily. "He had grown older but he was the same
man. I was certain of it. He had your deep, serious
eyes.''

"What city was that?"

"I'm not sure I recall. Was it Oklahoma City? Yes,
Oklahoma City."

"Did you speak to him?"

"No. How could I?"

Sister Mary Margaret lay in silence. Her breathing was steady, monotonous, fragile. Under the fringed blanket, her thin, flat chest rose and fell with each breath.

Remo squeezed Sister Mary's cool hand hopefully. "Do you—do you remember anything else? Anything that might help me?"

"Yes. I do."

Eagerly Remo leaned closer to catch every syllable. "Tell me."

"I remember the name of the movie," Sister Mary said in a dreamy voice.

"That's nice," Remo said, patting her hand.

"It was *The Sea is an Only Child*. It wasn't very good. It was in color. I much prefer films that are not in color. Don't you?"

"Sure, Sister Mary," said Remo, squeezing out the tears of disappointment starting from his eyes.

"I remember thinking as I watched the screen how sad it was the way it all turned out. I remember wondering if the man knew."

"Knew what?"

"Knew that you had died."

Remo felt an electric chill rip through his nervous system. When he spoke, his voice was thick with emotion. "You knew?"

"I was very sad for a long time. For a very long time I could not get what had happened out of my mind. I simply could not believe that I had been so wrong about you."

"You weren't. I was framed."

Her cool hand squeezed his. "I knew that. I always felt it. But now that you're here, I know it for certain.

If you had truly gone bad, how could you be here with me?'' She struggled for breath. ''Here in Heaven.''

And Remo swallowed hard. A lump rose in his throat.

''I knew you had died in Christ,'' whispered Sister Mary Margaret.

Remo swallowed again, but the lump wouldn't go away.

''Lately I had not been able to get you out of my mind,'' she said, her voice disconnected from the body that lay so helpless and fragile. ''Isn't that strange?''

''I've been thinking of you lately, too,'' Remo said thickly. ''The things you taught me helped me more than I can tell you.''

''That's good, Remo. That's fine.'' Her free hand, tangled with rosary beads, reached out for his. ''Now run along and play. Sister Mary is feeling very tired today. We'll talk more tomorrow.''

''Goodbye, Sister Mary. I'll never forget you.''

''Goodbye, Remo.''

Remo stood up. He gazed down at the woman who had all but raised him, so shrunken in the dim light. Her breath was slow and measured. Her heartbeat tentative. She had not long.

After a long while Remo turned to the door. A delicate rattle followed him. At first he barely noticed it. It trailed off into a sigh that made Remo's blood run absolutely cold when it penetrated his grief.

In the bed behind him, Sister Mary Margaret, at last at peace, surrendered herself to death.

''SOMETIMES IT HAPPENS this way,'' Sister Novella was saying. ''She had clung and clung to life for so long.

Seeing you must have been the scissors that cut the silver cord."

Remo said nothing. He felt cold inside. His eyes were hot yet dry. They sat in the sitting room of the nursing home, looking at the fading rug.

"You mustn't reproach yourself, Mr. Williams. In a way your coming was a mercy. What had she to live for?"

Remo said nothing. Sister Novella took another sip of tea.

"Did you two have a nice talk?" she asked after a moment.

"I'll never forget her," Remo whispered.

"Will you be staying for the funeral?"

"I can't. I don't think I could."

"You're welcome to come if you change your mind."

Woodenly Remo stood up. "Thanks. I have to go."

Sister Novella followed him to the door. "It was nice of you to stop by," she said as if they were discussing a passing rainstorm, not a human life blown out like a guttering candle.

At the door Sister Novella said, "She never got over the loss of St. Theresa's, you know."

"Yeah," Remo croaked.

"It was perfectly understandable, I suppose. The orphanage was her life's work. She was quite devoted to it. And after all, it was where she was raised."

Remo turned. "What?"

"Sister Mary was an orphan, too. You didn't know?"

"No," Remo said dully.

"Who better to understand the wants and fears of her charges than someone who had been through such a loss herself?"

"I guess you're right. Thanks for telling me that."

"You're quite welcome, Mr. Williams. Go with Christ."

Remo walked out into the Oklahoma sun with eyes that saw and ears that barely heard. He climbed into his rented car and drove around in circles well into the evening.

When he got tired, he pulled into a motel near an elevated highway in a ramshackle part of the city called Bricktown and lay in bed, replaying the scene in the nursing home over and over in his mind while freight whistles blew long and lonesome in the night.

Already it seemed so unreal he wondered if it had been a dream.

One thought kept coming back to haunt him: who was the rugged man who had left him at the orphanage so many years ago?

19

There had been a hard rain, and the pattering drops had made little craters in the Sonoran Desert. The pipe-organ cacti were looking hardy. Cholla blossoms made amber-and-ruby splotches against the sand, which wasn't so much red as gold in the morning light.

Crying River lay quiet under the hot sun. Sunny Joe Roam sent his horse across its golden sand crust, which made brittle sounds like breaking potato chips under each hoof fall.

At the foot of Red Ghost Butte, he dismounted and unsaddled his horse, saying, "Don't know how long I'll be, Sanshin. You take your ease."

The big horse stood immobile.

Roam spanked its flank. "Go on now, you stubborn hay burner."

The horse remained where he was.

"Have it your own way, then." Roam gave him a pat on the muzzle and started up the butte.

The trail was all but invisible if one didn't know the way. Sunny Joe skirted a fuzzy clump of teddy bear cholla and picked his way up. It was no place to ride a horse. Only bighorn rams and fool Indians climbed Red Ghost Butte, Sunny Joe thought ruefully.

The trail snaked, vanishing and resuming.

"Getting too old for this," he said, taking a rest on a red sandstone outcropping.

Sunny Joe Roam reached the cave thirty minutes later, thinking that when he was young and full of vinegar, he used to run up the butte and not pant for air. He panted now. Maybe it was the damned dust.

The cave mouth was sheltered by a shield of woven reed covered with plucked brittle-bush and ocotillo. Sunny Joe reached into the shield and pulled it loose. Setting it to one side, he let the old musty damp smell wash over him. It was not a bad smell. It suggested caves and death and ancient mystery.

He entered. All light faded fifteen feet in. He stepped carefully into the zone of darkness, then began counting his steps, deviating neither left nor right. He had no wish to tread on the feet of his honored ancestors.

When he counted thirty-three paces—it had been forty-seven back when he was a short-legged boy—Sunny Joe stopped and dropped to the dirt floor. He stared into the darkness. The darkness seemed to stare back. But he knew there were no eyes in the darkness, only hollows.

"O Ko Jong Oh, I am come to remind you of your promise to the Sun On Jo people, whom you founded in the days before the white man and the Hopi and the Navajo. Hear me, ancestor spirit. I seek guidance."

From the darkness came only silence.

"I seek your wisdom in the hour of our greatest need, O Ko Jong Oh."

In the darkness something stirred.

Sunny Joe Roam felt his heart leap with fear and joy at once.

"Guide me, Ko Jong Oh, for blinded by bitterness and white ways, I have strayed from the path of Sun On Jo and cannot find the path back to my own heart."

The rustle persisted.

Something warm brushed Sunny Joe's left hand where it rested on the the cave floor. Like the passing of a spirit, it slipped furtively past.

He turned. And into the zone of light the thin tail of a deer mouse skittered. A chill washed over Sunny Joe's tall, lanky form.

Turning back to the unresponsive blackness, he said quietly, "And if it is your wish that I die in the here and now, I will die without complaint, among my honored ancestors, whom I have sorely let down."

20

All night freight trains rattled through Bricktown, their whistles blowing mournfully. But Remo Williams slept through it all.

He was back in the Void and he was not alone.

Remo sensed a presence. But there was nothing but blackness all around him.

In his dream Remo called out, "Anyone here?"

No one answered. But the feeling was strong. Closing his eyes, Remo listened for the gulp and wheeze of heart and lungs, but there were no such sounds. Just a feeling of imminence and menace.

Opening his eyes, Remo saw thin orbs regarding him. They winked out like a black cat closing his eyes in a deep cave.

Remo blinked. Had the eyes been real? They were hazel, the eye color of Sinanju Masters going back who knew how long. Something about the eyes made Remo tense up.

Remo padded toward the patch of blackness where the disembodied eyes had floated. When he reached the spot where he judged they had been, he stopped. The darkness before him seemed palpable.

"Hello?" he said.

In response something struck him in the solar plexus.

Air escaped his lungs in a harsh, explosive gust, and Remo staggered back. A Sinanju blow. Nothing less could do that to him.

Out of the Void came a harsh laugh Remo knew well, because he could never forget it.

Nuihc!

Turning in place slowly, Remo wove a finger web around his personal defensive zone. He stepped left two paces, then right three. Backing up, still turning, he protected himself while scanning the dark for his opponent.

But Nuihc, the renegade Master of Sinanju who had been Chiun's pupil before Remo, craftily kept his distance.

"Come on, you rat bastard," Remo growled. "Come out and fight like a man."

A cold voice said, "You must defeat me, mongrel Master, if you are to return to the world of flesh."

"I never got a good crack at you when you were alive, so we're overdue," Remo said, stepping this way and that, wishing he had something visible to zero in on. Obviously Nuihc was wearing black, his face somehow blackened down to the eyelids. Only when he opened them again would Remo have him dead to rights.

As long as he kept his eyes shut, Nuihc was as blind as Remo. Yet he had struck a perfect blow with his eyes closed. How?

Remo listened. His feet made no sound in the endless black plane of the Void. Nuihc hadn't detected his footfalls. Soft as they were normally, here they were completely soundless.

I get it, Remo thought suddenly. He zeroed in on my voice.

Turning in place, Remo slowly eased himself into a crouching position. And waited.

Time passed. How much there was no way of knowing, no method of measuring. Remo made himself as still as a stone. It might not help here in the Void, but the old Sinanju tricks rarely failed.

All the while time dragged by, Remo watched for the cold slit eyes of Nuihc to open a crack.

The mocking voice broke the silence. "What is wrong, whelp of the West?"

Remo kept still and silent.

Nuihc said after a long time, "Can you not find me?"

Remo kept his silence.

"Have you given up, white?"

Remo said nothing. His head turned this way and that, his body coiled like a tense spring. The voice seemed to be changing position, as Nuihc would have to if he wished to foil Remo's ears.

"I will accept your surrender, if you will not fight me."

The Void seemed to reverberate in the silence that followed.

Just as Remo was about to give up, not three arm lengths to Remo's left two cold almond eyes winked open.

They snapped shut almost as soon as they fell on Remo. But it was enough. Lunging forward on the plane of blackness, Remo drove two fists ahead of him, one aimed for the head and the other for the belly. With his eyes shut, Nuihc was a sitting duck.

Unless he had stepped aside in the instant after he closed his eyes.

Doing so was an old Sinanju night-fighting trick. Nuihc would know that Remo knew it. He might hold his ground. Or he might think three steps ahead as opposed to Remo's two, and step aside, poised to strike when Remo walked into his trap.

There was no way to know.

Until his fists struck solidness, Remo didn't know what to expect.

"Ooof!"

Nuihc was driven back a unit of measure unknown on earth. Remo leaped after him and, spotting the stunned eyes lying on the black plane like dropped marbles, he brought the heel of his left foot square on the spot where Nuihc's larynx should be.

The croak of agony matched the sudden widening of Nuihc's stunned hazel eyes.

"Give?" Remo asked, setting his foot on Nuihc's unprotected chest.

"Urkkk."

"I asked you a question, dog meat," Remo snapped.

"I . . . am . . . yours. . . ." Nuihc gurgled painfully.

"Too bad," Remo growled. "I don't want you." And he began exerting pressure on the chest he could feel but not see. Cartilage crackled as ribs groaned. The hazel eyes went wide till the whites showed all around.

To his surprise, Nuihc sank into the blackness. His eyes, comically round in a mixture of agony and anger, were like startled gems slipping into a pool of viscous tar.

Left standing in the darkness, Remo looked around. He was alone in the emptiness of the Void. Nothing happened for a long time.

Then a sound like a freight train moaning assaulted the great Void.

REMO SNAPPED UPRIGHT with the screeching of steel wheels ripping through his skull. He flung himself out of bed, getting into his clothes on the way out the door.

Frightened faces were popping out of doors up and down the motel facade. And the shriek of steel wheels became an agony of howling metal and screaming voices. The voices were high, shrill, inarticulate. It seemed impossible they were human.

"Train wreck!" a man yelled.

Remo flashed around to the rear of the motel. Beyond was a rail line. And in the dark, noises were piling up. He got there just as the last car had screeched past in a shower of silvery sparks like molten metal. They splashed onto rails that twisted and warped on their ties, rusty spikes straining. They might have been trying to escape what was to come.

Then the roar became a long rumble, and the tracks let go. They sprang like rubber bands, snapping at their welds and sending rusty spikes and railroad ties flying.

Remo ducked a spike flying like shrapnel. It thudded into a brick wall and smoked like a meteorite.

Running along the grading, Remo came upon the back end of the train. His first thought was for the passengers. But as he worked his way past the first teetering cars, he came to a jackknifed string of cattle cars.

After a ghostly silence, a tortured whinnying came from the cars. And through the galvanized steel slats of the sides, he could see frightened black eyes. The smell of fresh dung filled the night air.

Remo climbed a car, found the lock and snapped it with the side of his hand. He rolled the door back, and inside, a muscular knot of horses writhed and kicked at one another. They began surging and leaping out in a torrent of clattering hoofs.

Remo got clear, letting them run where fear took them.

The next car was another cattle car. It lay on its side. The one ahead was piled up against a fir tree in some kind of sunken arboretum. There was blood coming out of one end. The pungent barnyard odor of dung mingled with it.

Remo moved on.

The middle cars were the worst. They had been literally rent asunder by the sudden compression of the crash.

All were cattle cars, Remo saw to his relief. There were no passengers. Human passengers, that is. He kept going. Sad, frightened eyes peered out at him from bent slats, neighing in their distress.

REMO FOUND THE ENGINE piled into a windbreak of red oaks.

It had come to a stop with its front end against two oaks. The headlight shone between them, cutting a funnel of light in the murk that was already busy with moths.

"Hey!" Remo called. "Anybody in there?"

There was no answer from the silent engine, so Remo found the engineer's ladder and climbed it.

He found the engineer at his controls with his neck like a raw tree stump. There was no sign of his head. It wasn't visible in the cabin. In fact, while the windshield had spiderwebbed, no loose glass littered the cabin.

How the engineer had lost his head was a mystery.

The mystery was compounded as Remo walked the twisted tracks back and spotted the engineer's head squatting in the bough of a tree like some otherworldy beehive.

Remo left it where it hung. Someone would discover it soon enough. The horses were struggling from their strewn cars, and since there were no people to save, Remo decided he would do what he could to help the poor dumb brutes reach safety.

By that time others had come onto the scene.

A man in a blue police uniform was the first Remo met.

"My lord, what a mess. Look at all these poor critters." He drew his pistol. "Guess I'll have to shoot those that won't make it. Hate to do it, though."

"Why don't you give me a chance to pull the uninjured ones loose?" Remo asked.

"You got a crane in your back pocket?"

"Tell you what. Shoot the dying. Anything I haven't got loose is yours."

"Suit yourself," said the cop, and he walked back to where the beastly moans were most pitiful.

Remo moved to the nearest cattle car. It leaned drunkenly against a rows of scarred pine trees. He got to the door and wrenched it open.

The horses—there were mustangs mixed with black-and-white Appaloosas—were jammed up against the far side. Eyes wide, frightened and not at all friendly. Some kicked and screamed.

With one exception, their legs were whole. They could walk. All they needed was a ramp.

Looking around to make sure no one saw him, Remo attacked the sliding door. He broke the rails on which it slid and let it drop. It took only a little jockeying to make it a ramp.

Remo went among the horses and began spanking flanks. The horses responded. After they rattled off the ramp, they kept going, which suited Remo perfectly fine. He had a lot of horses to round up.

The one with raw bone sticking down from his severed leg managed to clump out, too. Its eyes were glassy.

At the next car palominos were trying to squeeze out through a ragged hole at one end, oblivious to the hoof-breaking drop to the ground.

Remo got in front of a struggling horse. Confusion was mirrored in its sad eyes. It was stuck, one leg tangled in ripped galvanized slatwork. Other horses were pushing against it from behind and whinnying in fear.

Remo grabbed the side ladder and took hold of the twisted slats. He began yanking out pieces of metal and throwing them away. Once the hole was big enough, the first palomino jumped. He broke his front legs landing and fell over with a defeated moan. But the others landed in soft soil gouged by the derailment and they made it okay.

It took two hours, but Remo managed to save fully sixty horses from police guns.

The breaking of dawn found him watching mounted riders herding the horses into a circle where they would be loaded onto transport trucks once they had completely calmed down. Back at the wreck, they were field dressing the dead carcasses. The air reeked of bowels and blood.

"Nice work," the cop told him. "Don't know how you done it, but it was a right nice job of running horses."

"Thanks."

"Man who owns that herd's gonna want to reward you, I'd wager."

"Tell him it's on the house."

"That's your right, I reckon. Anyway, you done us a good turn."

"How's that?" Remo asked.

The cop grinned. "Why, we'd have plumb exhausted our bullet budget for the month if it weren't for you."

Remo laughed. It stopped suddenly when he saw the Master of Sinanju standing off where the trees were thickest. "Excuse me," said Remo, starting off.

The visage of the Master of Sinanju was stern as Remo approached, thinking he might as well get this over with.

But when he stepped into the trees, Chiun's wrinkled face broke out into a beaming grin. "Very good, Remo. I am pleased to see you take the initiative."

"What are you talking about? And how the hell did you find me?"

"I found you here the same way you found yourself here. Emperor Smith."

"Oh."

"Did you find what you sought?"

"Sister Mary Margaret died last night, Little Father. I was there."

Chiun nodded gravely. "It was good that she did not die alone and forgotten but with one who truly cared for her."

Remo said nothing.

"Did she reveal to you any of the truths you sought?"

"No. But she did say she saw the guy who left me on the orphanage doorstep, but she didn't know him."

"Then you have not discovered your roots?"

"No. Sister Mary did tell me something strange, though."

Chiun cocked his head to one side curiously. "And what is that, Remo?"

"She saw him again. In a movie theatre."

"Ah."

"The strange thing is that it was here in Oklahoma City."

"That is strange?"

"Why would the guy who left me at a Newark orphanage where Sister Mary worked show up years later here, where she'd come to live?"

"I do not know."

Remo looked around. "I think I'll stick around here for a while."

"And if you do not know who this man is or what face he wears, how do you expect to recognize him, my son?"

"I don't know. But I will."

"I do not think so."

"How would you know?"

Chiun shrugged carelessly. "You would be surprised at the things I know and do not know."

"Right. Well, you can forget about the Rite of Attainment and going to Hesperia. Because I'm staying here till I figure this out."

"But you have already gone to Hesperia."

"What do you mean by that?" Remo asked suspiciously.

"To the Greeks, Hesperia was the western lands." Chiun lifted his arms to encompass his surroundings. "This is as far west as one can go from Greece and not go east. Thus, you have come on your own to Hesperia."

"Yeah, well, I'm doing no more labors."

"Labors?"

"Don't play coy with me. Smith told me what *athloi* means. The jig's up."

"But you have already accomplished your next labor."

Chiun gestured toward the derailed train and to the horses beyond. "You have succored the steeds of Diomedes successfully."

Remo planted his hands on his hips angrily. "You can't tell me you were going to drag me to Oklahoma City to round up horses?"

"Not here. I was considering Argentina. But this will do. Congratulations, Remo. You are the first Master of Sinanju to perform a labor without his Master's guidance."

"So?"

Chiun frowned. "So it is a good omen."

"Yeah, well, it's also the end of the Rite of Attainment. I want to sniff around here for a while."

"If that is your wish, I will not stop you."

"Seems I've heard that before."

"But if you would know a hidden thing, I would advise you to consult the Oracle of Delphi."

"Delphi? That's back in Greece."

"All Masters consult the oracle in the course of the Rite of Attainment."

"Not me. I've seen enough of Greece. I'm staying here."

Chiun bowed formally and, to Remo's surprise, said, "I will not stop you."

"I don't trust you when you're so agreeable."

"Would you rather I be disagreeable?"

"I dunno. By the way, I met Nuihc in the Void."

Chiun asked suddenly, "And defeated him?"

"Yeah."

"Very good."

"By the way, I figured out the riddle of the Sphinx. It was the Great Wang."

The Master of Sinanju eyes his pupil doubtfully. "Did you meet Wang, as well?" he asked thinly.

"What does that matter?" Remo said evasively.

"That tattletale! What else did he tell you?"

"He said these dreams are part of the rite. And that Nonja had information about my father. But when I met him, he told me to ask Kojing. Haven't met him yet."

"I see...."

And from one voluminous sleeve, Chiun extracted an object of wood and steely metal.

"What's that?" Remo asked.

"It is a gong."

"Doesn't look like a gong. Gongs are round."

"It is very special gong."

Remo looked closely. The object was a length of varnished teak about as long a human hand. Suspended over it by stiff wire loops was a round bar of steel. From one end of the teak base, Chiun drew a wooden mallet whose handle fit into a long groove under the floating bar.

As Remo watched, Chiun tapped the bar of steel sharply. It rang. Perfect C. The vibration made Remo's sensitive ears ache. The note hung in the air for a full minute. Just as it was about to die, Chiun struck the bar again. The perfect C filled the air.

"What the heck are you doing?" Remo demanded.

"Calling for your long-lost father."

"With a gong?"

"This esteemed gong has been in my family since the days of Master Kojing. Have I ever told you of Kojing, Remo?"

"The name rings a bell. But they all do. Every third Master might have been named after a gong. If it wasn't Wang, it was Ung or Hung or Ting and Tang or Kang. No wonder I can't ever keep them straight."

Chiun started off. He struck the gong again. Its extended shimmering note filled the air.

"Where are you going?" asked Remo.

"I told you. I am in search of your father."

"What makes you think he's going to respond to that thing?"

Chiun struck the gong again. "Who can fail to hear it?"

They walked the early-morning streets, Chiun leading, striking the gong whenever the shimmering note was about to die out. And Remo following, wearing a puzzled expression.

Everywhere they went, faces came to windows and doors opened.

They were stared at, honked at and questioned by the police several times, but nothing more interesting befell them.

By noon the Master of Sinanju returned the wood mallet to its groove and, with a firm thumb, silenced the gong—which by now had begun to drive Remo crazy.

"Your father does not answer. Therefore, he does not dwell here," he announced loftily.

"Says you."

"You have the word of the Reigning Master of Sinanju that he does not."

"And how would you know?"

"You must consult the Oracle of Delphi."

"Not a chance. I'm staying."

"You may call Smith if you prefer."

"Why would I do that?"

"Very well. Be stubborn."

Remo folded his arms. "From now on, 'stubborn' is my middle name."

"You look tired, my son."

"Thanks to you."

"Perhaps you would like to nap."

"Not till I've turned this town upside down."

"If this is your wish," said Chiun. "But I am tired. I may nap."

And the Master of Sinanju yawned sleepily.

Remo regarded him dubiously. In twenty years he had never known the Master of Sinanju to need a nap.

Chiun yawned again.

Remo caught himself starting to yawn, too. He shut his mouth with a click of stubborn teeth.

Eyes narrowing, Chiun yawned so wide his head almost disappeared behind his mouth.

This time Remo couldn't help himself. He yawned, too. And yawned again.

Chiun said, "You see, you are sleepy, too."

"You're up to something, you old fake."

"Yes, I am up to assuring that my House and my line continue past this century. And you are not cooperating."

"Well, you have a hell of a way of doing it. In all the years I've worked with you, I've never been so kicked around as lately. And that includes that time you made me eat rancid kimchi for three solid months."

"It was not rancid. It was the best kimchi you ever tasted."

"It tasted like pickled socks. Just thinking about it, I can still taste the stuff."

"It was necessary. The beef poisons had to be purged from your fat body."

"I almost died."

"If you could not survive kimchi, you cannot survive being a Master in training."

"And what about the time you threw me out of an airplane after sabotaging my parachute?"

"If you cannot survive a minor fall, how could you survive doing the difficult work of the House?"

"And now this Rite of Attainment crap."

"If you cannot survive the rite, you can never be Reigning Master."

"I don't want to be Reigning Master. I never did. I never wanted any of this. I just wanted to lead a normal freaking life. Can't you freaking understand that? I wish the hell I had never met you."

Chiun opened his tiny mouth in shock. He seemed about to speak several times. Each time he checked himself.

"I'm sorry, but that's the way it is," Remo said in a subdued tone. "Now you know."

"I will make you a bargain, Remo Williams," Chiun said in a flinty tone. "Complete the rite, and I will help you find your lost father."

"What about the cave I saw in my vision?"

"It is tradition that when a Master achieves the rite, the Master who trained him retires and goes into seclusion. I will help you as long as the search involves no caves."

Remo hesitated.

"I am required by tradition to guide my pupil through the rite," Chiun added. "If it is your choice not to assume the title of Reigning Master, I cannot compel you to do otherwise.''

''You couldn't anyway.''

''It has never before happened that a pupil declined so sublime an honor, but if you insist upon being an ungrateful white, I will accept the shame and emptiness that follows.''

''What's the catch?''

''There is none,'' Chiun said stiffly. ''If at the end of the rite you prefer to go your own way and abandon the Master who lifted you up from whiteness and go off with the ingrate who abandoned you at birth, I will accept your selfish and inconsiderate decision.''

''Done,'' said Remo.

''Then it is done,'' Chiun said, thin voiced.

''All right,'' Remo said grudgingly. ''What's next?''

''You must capture the Girdle of the Hippolyta, Queen of the Amazons.''

''They don't have amazons anymore.''

''We will consult the Oracle at Delphi for the location of the last surviving amazon, then.''

''Greece is out. I'm not going back to Greece.''

''Then we will consult Emperor Smith and his wise oracles.''

HAROLD W. SMITH was surfing the Internet when the call came in on the blue contact telephone.

''Smitty, Remo. Need your help.''

''What is it?''

''Find us an amazon.''

''What do you mean, an amazon?''

''Chiun caught up with me. Thanks to you. Says I gotta capture the girdle of the amazon queen. He says he'll accept any substitute your computers come up with."

Smith frowned with his entire body. "One moment, please."

Keying in the word *amazon*, Smith tapped the Search key on his keyboard. The search executed in a twinkling, and Smith read the words: Prime Time's Reigning Amazon: The Inside Story.

"I do have a reasonable facsimile," he reported.

"Good."

"But I imagine you'd prefer a second choice," Smith continued.

"No time. I have things to do and I'm in a hurry to get my labors behind me."

"Very well."

"One second, Smitty. Chiun wants to know where you got this name."

"I am currently logged on to Delphi."

Remo's voice got strange. "Delphi?"

"Yes. It is an information service."

Remo grunted and said, "I'm handing the phone over to Chiun. He doesn't want me to know the amazon's name until it's time to grab her girdle."

And when the Master of Sinanju came on the line, Harold Smith whispered the name. Chiun said, "It is an excellent choice. Your oracles are exceedingly farseeing."

"It was entirely random."

"It is wonderfully random," proclaimed the Master of Sinanju, hanging up.

And with that, Harold Smith returned to trolling the net. There was no point in trying to intercede. Remo and Chiun would work things out between them. They always had. Why should this time be any different?

21

Roxanne Roeg-Elephante was suffering. Oh, how she suffered. All her life, she had suffered.

She suffered through a childhood filled with unspeakable abuse, which, once her ratings began to sag, she told America about on talk shows ranging from "Copra Inisfree" to "Vicki Loch."

She suffered the affliction of multiple personalities, which America first heard about on "Nancy Jessica Rapunzel."

She endured a double life as a stand-up comedienne and back seat hooker, which a shocked world first learned about on "Rotunda."

She accused her own sister of attempting to lure her into a satanic cult on "Bil Tuckahoe."

Every time she went on TV to reveal another slice of her sordid and painful past, ratings on her hit TV sit-com "Roxanne" shot up. And America reembraced her.

What no one seemed to notice was that she only went on talk shows to reveal these intimate details during May and November. Both sweeps months.

But now Roxanne Roeg-Elephante was really, truly, pitifully suffering.

"Ooww!" she moaned, bellowing like a wounded cow as the six-inch needle penetrated her broad, naked backside. "That friggin' hurts."

"You asked for it, Roxanne," a cool professional voice said.

"I didn't ask for it to friggin' hurt, you quack!"

"I'm your doctor. I would appreciate a little respect for my profession."

"And *I* would appreciate a little respect for *my* problems."

"Just a minute. I need to recharge this needle."

"Make sure you dip it in alcohol. I don't wanna catch AIDS from one of my alters. I got enough problems trying to get myself knocked up."

As the doctor returned to his black bag, Roxanne grabbed a gold-inlaid hand mirror and lifted it to her face. She examined herself critically. The bags under her eyes were still gone. She didn't know whether to be pleased or annoyed. If the bags never came back, she got her money's worth. On the other hand, if just the tiniest puff showed, she could turn about and sue the bastard plastic surgeon who performed the operation. He had cost her a bundle, and although he'd done a good job, her latest husband had still run off with another woman.

"It's so unfair," she whined.

"What is?" the doctor asked.

"Life. Life is unfair."

"I know what you mean," the doctor said absently as he recharged the needle with perganonal, a powerful female hormone that invariably sent Roxanne's moods swinging like a five-hundred-pound gorilla on a chandelier.

"I so, so want to get preggers. Why can't I get preggers?"

"Because you had your tubes tied ten years ago," the doctor said flatly.

"Is that any frigging reason?"

"Normally, yes."

"Well, I got 'em untied, didn't I?"

"I counseled you the original operation might not be reversible."

"Well, I paid enough to have it done. Now look at me. I got track marks all over my butt just because in a weak moment I let some butcher root around in my guts."

"I'm ready with the second shot."

"Just work around the tattoo."

"Which one?"

"Any one. I don't want track marks on my tattoos. *Vanity Fair*'s gonna photograph them for next month's cover."

"Good Lord," the doctor said.

"What's 'a matter?" asked Roxanne, giving her backside a meaty smack. "Don't you think I got a nice butt?"

"It's...colorful," the doctor admitted, his eyes averting to her creased back. It was no more appetizing. All those pimples and inflamed sebaceous cysts.

Roxanne's mood suddenly darkened. "Says you. Now hurry and shoot me up. I can take it. I used to do heroin."

The needle went in slowly, the plunger discharged the syringe's contents while, lying on her stomach, Roxanne Roeg-Elephante gritted her capped teeth and said, "Life is so unfair. I just want to have children. I need to know true motherhood."

"How *are* your children from your first marriage, by the way?" the doctor asked.

"Grown-up and calling up for money all the time. The ones who still talk to me, that is. Forget them. They don't count on account I had them with a jerk and before I was famous. I want a baby. One that doesn't talk back.''

Closing up his bag, the doctor said, ''I'll leave my bill with your personal assistant.''

''Go ahead. But if those hormones don't work, I'm suing your ass for mispractice.''

''You have a nice day, too, Roxanne,'' the doctor said tightly, exiting the dressing room on the lot of Omniversal Studios in North Hollywood, California.

And lying on her stomach, Roxanne Roeg-Elephante laid her apple red cheek against the pillow, muttering, ''Life is so fucking unfair. I'm practically a billionaire and I can't hardly get what I want.''

''What do you want, Roxanne?'' asked a strange voice coming from her mouth.

Picking up the mirror, Roxanne began talking to it. ''I dunno. But I know I ain't got it yet. What do you want, alter?''

''Sex. Lots of it.''

''Me, too. But Studley isn't here.''

''Too bad,'' said the disembodied voice.

''I wonder if a person with multiple personalities can have sex with herself?'' Roxanne wondered suddenly.

''I'm not having sex with you!''

''Why not, alter?''

''I'm no dyke.''

''Speak for yourself. There ain't nothing I ain't tried—or will try—if I think it will make me happy or someone I hate miserable.''

''Just keep your hands to yourself.''

''Don't worry. I wouldn't touch you with rubber gloves and a toilet plunger. You hardly ever bathe, for Christ's sake.''

REMO HESITATED when he heard the two voices on the other side of the trailer door marked with a big gold star and the name Roxanne.

He hadn't counted on Roxanne having company. The back lot of Omniversal Studios was busy with scurrying golf carts and people in jeans and carrying walkie-talkies all hurrying to someplace they weren't. No one seemed to be standing still.

It had been surprisingly easy to gain access to the Omniversal lot. There was a guard at the gate entrance, but this was southern California. No one entered anywhere or anything on foot. They always drove.

Remo had simply walked onto the lot. Because he wasn't encased in a car, no one noticed him. It had been that simple.

Finding Roxanne was simple, too. The big, warehouselike soundstages were plastered with billboards proclaiming the TV shows being filmed within. Roxanne's billboard was five times larger than anyone else's. That was because it showed her entire body, which she was enormously proud of, having lost over one hundred pounds on a diet product she did commercials for. When a disgruntled ex-staffer had leaked the fact that Roxanne never used the product, the manufacturer had demanded his money back. When Roxanne had gone on "Entertainment Tonight" to complain that the product tasted like talcum powder mixed in sour milk, the sponsor hurriedly offered her six figures to just shut up and never mention the Nutra-Sludge again.

Remo found Roxanne's trailer just as easily. It wasn't quite as large as the soundstage beside it. But it was certainly more ostentatious. It reminded him of a Hindu howdah without the elephant.

As a grip walked by, tapping his earphones as he slapped the nickel-cadmium-battery belt pack and complaining, "My radio just took a dump," Remo tried to look inconspicuous. That wasn't difficult, either. A famous director strolled by in torn jeans, making Remo look by contrast like the height of fashion.

It was starting to look like a piece of cake. Remo just hoped that Roxanne wore a girdle. Taking another look at the big billboard, he couldn't imagine how she could live without one. Even minus a hundred pounds, she was a whale.

The voices inside continued their argument.

"The reason *I* don't bathe is *you* don't bathe," a whiny female voice said.

"Well, I shower," retorted the twangy, corduroy voice that had grated on all of America's ears.

"You stick your fat head under the tap to get your greasy hair wet, stand up and call the water running down your back a shower. That's not a shower."

"Well, it's better than not bathing."

Finally Remo decided to just go for it. He knocked.

"Come in," the twangy Roxanne voice called out.

"But I'm naked," the other voice squeaked.

"So am I and I don't give a fiery fart. Come on, drag your ass in here. I ain't got all day."

"Well, which is it?" Remo asked.

"Get in here!"

The other voice said nothing, so Remo figured it was reasonably safe to enter.

When he pushed in the door, he changed his mind.

Roxanne Roeg-Elephante lay on a triple-wide bed, stark naked and regarding him with vaguely belligerent eyes. "Who the frig are you?"

Remo cocked a thumb over his shoulder. "You're wanted on the set," he told her.

"So damn what?"

"Well, they want to do the next scene."

"Tell them to sit on a cactus and rotate. I'll come when I'm good and ready." And she winked broadly at Remo. "Like always."

Not winking back, Remo asked, "Can I tell them how long you'll be?"

Roxanne looked him up and down critically.

"Oh, I dunno. How long are you good for?"

"Good for what?"

"You know. In the sack."

"My contract has an unbreakable no-pachyderms clause," Remo said quickly.

Roxanne rolled onto her side, exposing a generous breast like a boiled ham with a pimple. She grinned like a fat shark. "I've just been shot full of raging hormones."

"Good for you."

She batted her eyes. "You know I'm rich."

"You're worth less than a billion. I charge two."

"I like rough sex."

"Why didn't you say so?" said Remo, closing the door behind him.

Roxanne scooted around to a sitting position.

"Hah! My last husband was just like you. Not as skinny, though." She took her chewing gum out of her petulant mouth, tucking it behind her left ear. "What do you like? Body slamming? Restraints? What?"

"I'd like to squeeze your neck with both hands."

"Oh, goody. Let's do it."

And Remo, using one hand he promised himself he'd wash later, reached under the gumless ear, intending to squeeze the delicate nerve there that triggered instant unconsciousness.

He squeezed. Roxanne squeezed her eyes shut. Remo squeezed harder. Feeling around in the sweaty rolls of fat, he heard Roxanne's voice say, "This is the best sex I never had. So far. Hope it gets better."

"It does," Remo promised, trying to find the nerve. The trouble was, he couldn't find it or make it work. "Damn that Chiun."

"Who's Chum?"

"You ever been a sumo?"

"No, but I wrestled one to a draw once. He was a wimp."

Remo stepped back. "Look, I have a confession to make."

Roxanne opened one disappointed eye. "What's that?"

"I'm a huge fan."

"Great. I get my best orgasms off people who think I'm my character."

"Maybe you can help me," Remo said.

"If you'll help me. I wanna have a baby."

"I don't do that kind of favor."

"No? So what do you want?"

"Your girdle."

"How'd you know I wear a freaking girdle?" Roxanne said, jerking to her feet. Every square inch of her body jounced and jiggled like Jell-O in a pink leaf sack.

"Rumor."

"Well, I ain't giving up my girdle for anything less than sperm. And that's final."

"Damn," said Remo, looking around the trailer. A thought occured to him. "Where's your friend?"

"What friend?"

"The one you were talking to before I came in."

"Oh, her. That was no friend. Just that bitch alter of mine, Rachel."

"Alter?"

"Yeah, like alter ego? That's what my shrink says I should call my multiple personalities. I've got thirty-six. Hey, maybe you'd like to pork one of them. Now, take Rachael. She's twelve years younger and 140 pounds lighter than me. But she's not very big in the hygiene department. If you catch my drift."

"Do you have a timid alter?" Remo wondered.

"Timid?"

"You know, shy."

"Well, there's Mandy. She's very mousy."

"I'd like to meet Mandy. The mousy type attracts me."

Roxanne shrugged. "Well, if you get one of us pregnant, I guess we'll *all* be pregnant. But I gotta warn you. Mandy is a virgin. You be gentle with her, or I'll briss you with my teeth—if you catch my drift."

"I promise."

And Roxanne closed her eyes. Her round face turned placid. Then, like waves rippling across the ocean, her features began to waver and change. They grew slack. A little drool trickled from one corner of her red mouth.

When her eyes opened, the voice coming out was tiny.

"Hello, I'm Mandy."

"Quick," Remo said urgently. "Where's she keep her girdle?"

"Bottom drawer. But don't tell Rox I told you!"

"Promise," said Remo, going to the bottom drawer.

He almost missed the girdle. It was made of black vinyl and went all the way up to the silver-tasseled breast cups. All it needed was a skull and crossbones painted on it and it could have adorned a pirate ship.

"Thanks," said Remo, starting for the door.

"Aren't you going to make love to me?"

"Next life."

"Rats," said Mandy in a pouty voice as Remo shut the door behind him.

THE MASTER OF SINANJU was waiting for Remo outside the main gate on Lankershim Boulevard.

"Here," said Remo.

Wrinkling up his nose, Chiun took the girdle in two fingers. "It smells."

"It's the girdle of the amazon queen, Roxanne. Address any complaints to her."

"She fought desperately to retain it?"

"Tooth and nail."

"And you vanquished her?"

"She was begging for mercy when I left."

"You have done well," said Chiun, holding the girdle this way and that.

"What are you going to do with that?"

"The girdle of the amazons is supposed to confer great strength upon the wearer."

"I'm not wearing that."

"You have not the chest for it," sniffed Chiun, tossing the garment into the nearest trash receptacle.

"Hey! Do you know what I went through to get that?"

"It does not matter. You have completed another labor. That is all that matters."

As they walked back to their hotel, the Master of Sinanju began to yawn broadly.

Remo caught himself yawning, too.

"You are sleepy?" Chiun inquired.

"No. I'm yawning because you are."

"You look sleepy."

"Okay, I'm sleepy. But I'm not sleeping until we get the rite finished."

"You must sleep to conserve your strength for the ordeal ahead," Chiun stated.

"I've been sleeping more than I've been waking lately."

"Your body craves sleep. We will find a suitable hotel."

AT THE BEVERLY GARLAND hotel, Remo was looking out the window. The San Gabriel Mountains hovered in the near distance. He could see the top of the Omniversal Towers. There was a billboard there. He hadn't noticed it before.

It was another advertisement for *The Return of Muck Man*.

"Every time I see that Muck Man billboard I feel like it's staring at me," Remo said.

"I have told you, it is your father."

"Har-de-har-har-har," said Remo.

"He does have your eyes."

Remo looked closer. "They do look awfully familiar."

Bustling up, Chiun drew the curtains shut with sudden violence, darkening the room.

"It is time for your nap," he announced.

"Hey! I was looking out that window!"

"You may waste your time after you have completed your labors," Chiun said, going to the door. "And do not let me catch you in a Western bed."

The door closed and Remo turned in.

ALMOST AT ONCE he found himself in a valley dotted with flowering plum trees. Swallows alighted and took off from their branches, swooping through the warm air.

Under one plum tree Remo saw a figure he recognized. He walked over to the bald old man seated in a lotus position. He was heavy of body with pale, unmoving eyes like stones in a face like crumpled, translucent parchment.

"Greetings, H'si T'ang-*pongsa*," Remo said, using the Korean honorific for a blind man.

Master H'si T'ang looked up with unseeing eyes. They searched curiously while his flat nose sniffed the air. "Ah, Remo. Welcome."

"Can't you see me?"

"I was blind in life, why should it be different in the Void?"

"Well, I just figured a person's sight would be restored to him."

"Spoken like a true Christian." Master H'si T'ang stood up. "I am the Master who trained your Master. This means you are near the end of your Rite of Attainment. This is good, for it means the House will go on."

"Can you help me? I need to find Kojing. He was supposed to tell me something."

"You seek your father?"

"Yeah. How'd you know?"

"Ask Chiun."

Remo blinked. "Chiun?"

"Yes, Chiun will tell you the name of your father."

"Chiun?"

"Chiun," said Master H'si T'ang, reaching up to pluck a ripe plum. Remo's eyes followed his frail hand as it groped. Fingers like bones coated in beeswax closed around the ripest one and plucked it.

When Remo's eyes went back to the face of H'si T'ang, he was gone. So was the plum.

REMO BURST into the adjoining hotel room, where the Master of Sinanju sat on the narrow balcony watching the sun set.

"I met H'si T'ang."

"How is the Venerable One?"

"Still blind."

"One does not need eyes in the Void."

"I asked him about my father, and he said to ask you."

Remo waited for the Master of Sinanju to answer. But there was only silence.

"Did you hear what I said?"

"What were H'si T'ang's exact words?" Chiun asked thinly.

"Ask Chiun."

"My father was named Chiun. Did you encounter him in the Void?"

Remo's voice fell. All the pent-up energy in his body seemed to dissipate. "Damn," he said.

"I have spoken to Emperor Smith," Chiun said. "His oracles have found another *athloi* for you. We will depart on the morrow."

"I'd like to get going now."

Coming to his feet, Chiun pivoted to face his pupil.

"Then we will depart at once." And he breezed past Remo like a secretive wraith.

Remo followed him with his eyes but said nothing.

ON THE PLANE, Chiun was saying, "Perhaps your father is the illustrious Ted Williams."

"I wouldn't mind that, but I know it isn't."

"Andy Williams, then."

"Not a chance."

"Robin Williams."

"No way."

"Why not? He is fat. And you are showing signs of gaining weight."

"My mother said my name isn't Williams. And what makes you think my father is famous?"

"All who sire Masters of Sinanju are famous. Why should you be any different?"

"Look, let's change the subject, shall we?" Remo suggested.

"Tennessee Williams is another famous Williams."

"Tennessee Wiliams is dead."

"But his greatness lives on in you."

"Cut it out. I'm sick of you ragging on me all the time."

Chiun's voice suddenly grew serious. "Tell me, Remo, why is finding your father so important now? It was not like this when we first met so long ago."

Remo looked out at the passing clouds. "I thought I had put it all behind me after I left the orphanage," he said quietly. "Until that time in Detroit when that hit man popped up using my name."

"A name which he pilfered from the gravestone where you are not buried."

"We know that now. But at first I thought he was my father. For a while there I liked the idea of having a father. Ever since then, I can't get the idea out of my mind."

Chiun said nothing.

"Mind telling me where we are going?" Remo asked suddenly.

"You are going to Hades."

Remo's brow clouded. "Hades is the Roman Hell, isn't it?"

"Yes."

"Then why do our tickets say we're going to Bangor, Maine?"

"Because that is where Emperor Smith assures me Cerberus dwells." And Chiun left his seat to inspect the galley.

"Cerberus?" Remo muttered. His mind went back to his childhood, and once again he could hear the voice of Sister Mary Margaret as if it were yesterday: *Cerberus was the three-headed dog who guarded the gates to the underworld, who barred Hercules's path when he descended into the lower regions to complete one of his final labors.*

Remo folded his arms defiantly. "Great. I'm getting near the end."

The seat-belt sign winked off, and the stewardess came up the aisle. Remo noticed that she was wearing no shoes. When she stopped at his seat and leaned down to whisper in his ears, he understood why.

"Go suck your own toes," he told her.

When the Master of Sinanju returned from his inspection of the galley facilities, Remo told him, "The stewardess invited me to suck her toes."

"Before Rome fell, its women insisted upon being on top."

"There's nothing wrong with being on top."

"If these unwholesome ideas take root, the House will have to look to Persia in the next century for its gold. Do you still possess the coins?"

"Sure."

"Let me see them."

Remo produced the coins, one from each pocket so they wouldn't jingle and give him away.

"What do they tell you, Remo?" asked Chiun.

"Spend it while the currency is still good?"

"You are hopeless."

Remo grinned. "But still on top."

Over a mountainous section of the country, Remo happened to look down and saw in life something he had seen many times in books and magazines.

"That looks like Meteor Crater," he said to Chiun.

The Master of Sinanju looked out, sniffed and said, "I see a great hole surrounded by desolation."

Remo pulled from his wallet a square of paper that had been folded many times. It was sealed in plastic with Scotch tape. He undid the tape and unfolded the paper.

The black grease-pencil sketch featured a sad-eyed young woman with long dark hair, framing a handsome oval face. A police sketch artist had made it, based on Remo's description after his mother's spirit had appeared to him the first time months before. Ever since, Remo had carried it everywhere he went.

"She said my father sometimes lived among the stars and sometimes where the great star fell," Remo said softly.

"I see a hole in the ground. No star."

Remo hit the overhead stewardess-call button. Every stewardess on the plane was suddenly beside him, straightening hair and uniform skirts and moistening lipsticked mouths.

"What state are we over?" he asked the assembled stewardess crew.

"Suck my toes till they're wrinkled, and I'll tell you," offered one.

That particular stewardess was pushed to the rear and all but sat upon by the others.

"Arizona," the rest chorused helpfully.

"Thank you," said Remo, dismissing the flight crew. When they refused to dismiss, he carefully folded the drawing and replaced it in his wallet, taking his time and trying to look absorbed.

They were still there when he looked up.

"Was that your mother?" one asked.

"How'd you know?" Remo asked, genuinely surprised.

"She has your eyes. Anyone could see that."

Hearing that, the Master of Sinanju suddenly flew out of his seat like an angry hen and shooed the stewardesses to the back of the plane.

When he returned to his seat to receive the gratitude of his pupil, Remo had all but fallen asleep in his seat. The Master of Sinanju didn't wake him. But he did sit very close, with one ear cocked to catch any syllables Remo might speak in sleep.

RED POPPIES FILLED a valley where herons swooped. There was a clear, crystalline light that was everywhere but seemed to have no source. It was not sunlight. There was no sun in the vaulting blue sky.

Striding through the poppies, lifting his skirted legs in high, purposeful steps came a small-boned Korean.

"Chiun?" Remo blurted.

But as the figure drew near, Remo saw that it was not Chiun. The man resembled Chiun. He was old, his face seamed and wrinkled and papery, his eyes the same clear, ageless hazel.

The figure walked up to Remo and stopped abruptly. No particle of warmth came over his face as he looked Remo up and down. "You are very tall."

"I'll take that as a compliment."

"I have never seen a man so tall. Or so pale."

"That's how we grow where I come from. Tall and pale."

"Is the blood in your veins as red as mine?"

"Yep," Remo said warily.

"Your blood and my blood. They are the same blood?"

"Same color anyway."

"I cannot fight one of my own blood."

"Glad to hear it," Remo said dryly, not letting his guard down.

"I have something for you."

"Yeah?"

And reaching behind his back, the old Korean grabbed the jeweled hilt of a sword that Remo could have sworn was not there a moment before.

When it came into the clear light, Remo saw that it was the Sword of Sinanju.

"I give custody of this sword to you as a token of recognition that the blood in your veins is the same as the blood flowing through mine."

And the sword suddenly reversed in the old Korean's hands so the jeweled hilt was offered to Remo.

When Remo hesitated, the old Korean urged, "Take it."

"No," said Remo.

"Why not?"

"I haven't earned it yet."

A warm light came into the old Korean's eyes. "That is an excellent answer. But I ask you to hold it for me because it is very heavy and I am very old."

"All right," said Remo, reaching out for the hilt. The moment he laid hands upon it, he knew he had made a mistake. Something coldly sharp pierced the pad of his thumb.

"Ah!" said Remo. "Damn it."

The other's voice turned cold and contemptuous. "You have disgraced the blood in your veins. For you do not know the lesson of Cho."

Remo looked at the blood coming from his thumb. There was a drop of it on the barb in the sword's hilt, which had sprung out the moment he applied pressure.

"That had better not have been poisoned."

"It was not. But it might have been."

"You Cho?"

"No. I am Kojing."

And Master Kojing suddenly turned on his heel and stormed back into the field of red poppies.

"Kojing! Wait! Don't you have something to tell me?"

"Yes. Do not bleed over my poppies."

REMO WOKE UP.

"Damn," he said.

"What is it?" asked Chiun.

"I met Kojing."

"Yes?"

"He handed me the Sword of Sinanju hilt first, and I fell for it."

"I told you the lesson of Cho," Chiun hissed.

"A zillion years ago. I'm lucky to remember last Tuesday the way you're running my tail off."

Frowning, Remo looked out the window at the deeply ridged red mountains of Arizona and said to himself, "I wonder what Kojing was going to tell me?"

"Do not bleed all over the seat," sniffed Chiun.

"What did you say?"

And when he looked at his left hand, Remo saw blood coming out of his thumb. "You stuck me while I was sleeping," Remo accused.

"You have disgraced me before my great-great-great-grandfather."

"That how far back Kojing goes?"

"No, but I am in my end days and cannot spend an entire afternoon repeating the word *great* simply because there is no term in English to describe Kojing's relationship to me."

Remo checked the seatback pouch for something to wipe his hand and, finding nothing suitable, reluctantly hit the call button.

The first stewardess took one look at Remo's hand and offered to kiss it to make it better. Remo declined. The second bit her own hand and offered to become Remo's blood sister. Remo declined that honor, as well.

In the end he let them take turns sucking his thumb, but only after they swore they weren't Anne Rice fans.

22

An unfortunate series of misunderstandings had forced underworld figure Vinnie "Three Dogs" Cerebrini to go underground.

Vinnie had been a soldier in the D'Ambrosia crime family, out of San Francisco. For his capo he had killed many times. No one questioned his loyalty. No one questioned his manhood. No one.

Until the Frank "the Fence" Feely hit.

Vinnie had gotten caught on camera coming out of an Alameda warehouse five minutes after 1:00 a.m. on the night a low-life welcher named Frank Feely died. That was unfortunate, because the established time of death according to the coroner's report was 1:05 in the morning of the twenty-fifth of February. The security camera recorded both date and time. Those were the breaks.

No problem there. The D'Ambrosia family had lawyers.

"Three Dogs," Don Silvio D'Ambrosia had assured him after word went out that he was a wanted man, "you will surrender. And we will get you out this very day."

"But they got me dead-bang."

It was an unfortunate choice of words. But Vinnie didn't know then. No one knew it then.

"We have lawyers, Vincenzo. Turn yourself in. We will go your bail, and the trial will end in a very good acquittal," the capo had promised.

"But what about my dogs? Who will take care of them?"

Don Silvio had slapped him lightly on the cheek. It was an affectionate slap. After all, had not Vinnie Cerebrini killed over thirty men for him? "That is the job of your wife. You should have married a long time ago. Like I been tellin' you."

"I'll get around to it. You know I've been busy. What with whacking this guy and clipping that one, I don't got time for broads like I should."

Another unfortunate remark, but that was life.

"Bring them here. If they are your dogs, I am sure they are good dogs." And Don Silvio leaned across the kitchen table conspiratorially. "They do not piddle on the rug, do they?"

Vinnie made the sign of the cross and said, "On my mother's life, they are housebroke, Don Silvio."

"Then they are welcome in my house."

And so grateful was Vinnie "Three Dogs" that he leaned over and gave his don a very long kiss. Which was noticed.

So Vinnie Cerebrini had turned himself in, made bail and returned to his capo the next day. "The trial date's not till spring."

"Good. In the meantime, you gotta take these curs back."

"Sure. What—they been a problem for you?"

"They alla time sniffing my crotch."

"Yeah. They do that."

"What kinda queer dogs you got, Vinnie? They sniff crotches?"

"Some dogs do that. I'm sorry."

Don Silvio eyed Vinnie dubiously. "They sniff *your* crotch?"

Vinnie shrugged sheepishly. "All the time. Hey, what can I do? I love those dogs like brothers."

"Just get these fairy mutts outta my house. They give me the creeps. And I want you married by year's end. *Capisce?*"

Vinnie "Three Dogs" didn't think much of the conversation, but already the rumors were starting.

The trial went well, as promised. Evidence got suppressed, witnesses skipped town or found themselves inextricably caught up in various civic-improvement projects for which the D'Ambrosia family supplied the concrete.

"We got 'em on the run," his lawyer had confided at the end of week three.

"I just wish we could get that damn security tape quashed," Vinnie hissed back.

The lawyer shrugged. "Hey, it's circumstantial. Purely circumstantial. They can't convict on that alone."

And they hadn't. The tape was shown, and his lawyer knocked it down hard on cross-examination.

"I was taking a leak in that warehouse," Vince said solemnly from the stand. "It was dark. How was I to know the poor stiff was laying there with his mouth open?"

"But you do admit to urinating in the deceased's mouth?" the prosecuter asked when it was his turn to question the accused.

"Listen, if my piss—excuse me, Your Honor—was on that poor guy, I profoundly apologize to the family. I did not know. I swear on my mother's grave."

"But your fingerprints were found in his coat. How do you explain that?"

"Hadda wipe my hands on something. It was the only cloth in the entire joint."

In the end Vinnie pleaded no contest to the reduced charge of abusing a corpse. He was all smiles as he stepped out of the San Francisco courthouse while the press surged and jostled around.

That's when the linguini hit the propeller.

"Mr. Cerebrini, what do you have to say to these new allegations about your personal life?"

"There's ain't no such thing as the Mafia, honey. Don't you fall for that old bull."

"I was referring to the rumors of your homosexuality."

"My which?"

"The victim was gay. Didn't you know that?"

"I didn't do nothin' to the guy," said Vinnie in an injured tone. "All I did was piss in his dead mouth. Is that a crime?"

Another reporter jumped in. "According to the security tape, you left the warehouse with your fly open."

"I told you I was taking a freaking leak. I forgot to zip up. Coulda happened to any poor mook."

"Is it true you are not—and never have been—married?"

"What are you—my godfather? I'll get around to it, okay?"

"Did you ever have relations with the dead man before he died?"

"I never knew the guy. I'm telling you. All I did was whack—I mean piss—on him. I got a weak bladder. It coulda happened to anybody. It just happened to happen to me."

And as the mob lawyer shoved him into the waiting Lincoln, Vinnie "Three Dogs" Cerebrini muttered, "What the fuck kinda rap they trying to hang on me now?"

In the car the phone rang.

"Yeah?" barked Vinnie.

"Three Dogs, I hear you are a free man."

"And I have you to thank, Don Silvio."

"Good. Now, Vinnie. We been together a long time. You can tell me anything and everything. Am I right?"

"Yes, sir."

"These ugly rumors, Vinnie. There is no truth to this?"

"I swear before God, I am no fag."

"You married yet?"

"No," Vinnie said in a small voice.

"Engaged?"

"No."

"And you still got the queer dogs?"

"They are not queer! They happen to be African ridgebacks. They used to be used for running down escaped slaves. They are the biggest, meanest, most masculine dogs ever bred. Ask anyone."

"You like masculine dogs, huh, Vinnie?"

"I didn't mean it like that."

"You like to watch them walking around with their great big balls jigging between their furry butts, am I right?"

"I do not look at them that way."

"They lick your face?"

"Sometimes," Three Dogs admitted.

"You know what else they lick, Three Dogs? Their nethers. Their lower regions. You like tongues to lick you there, too?"

"Never. I swear. My dogs know better than to lick me there. They are moral and honorable dogs."

"Have 'em clipped."

"Shoot my own dogs?"

"No, I mean have their balls clipped. I don't want you looking at those dogs that way no more."

"I fix them dogs, they'll turn into girls."

"You don't fix them dogs, and I'll have *you* clipped. And I don't want no rumors around my family. I take pride in my family. We are family men. Fuck the dogs and find a wife. And another thing. I don't want you peeing on the guys you clip no more. It's unsanitary."

"It's just my way of sending them off. You know. It don't mean nothing."

"The papers are calling you an abuser of corpses. I do not want this word *abuser* to be connected with members of my family."

"It's all circumstantial. It don't mean nothing, Don Silvio."

"From now on you don't whip it out except in front of ceramic or lipstick. *Capisce?*"

"I understand," Vinnie said miserably.

When he got home, the dogs were all over him, sniffing and pawing his best suit.

"Cut that out, you three! You'll get me killed. Down, Numbnuts. Get offa me, Bonehead. You too, Fatface."

When they finally settled down, Vinnie tried to explain the facts of being mob dogs to them. "Now listen, you guys," said Vinnie, getting down on his knees on the floor. "We gotta talk about our futures together."

The dogs began licking his face.

"Don't do this to me! I'm trying to break the news to you gently."

In the end he couldn't do it.

"You guys are men. Just like me. It's not right to lop off a man's balls even if he is a dog."

And so Vinnie "Three Dogs" Cerebrini made the most difficult decision of his life. He chose his dogs over his capo.

Unfortunately it wasn't that hard a choice. The rumors that he was gay were all over San Francisco. If he married triplets, he could never live them down.

Vinnie "Three Dogs" Cerebrini would have sued if he could. After all, it was slander what they were saying about him, the rat bastards. The trouble was you really couldn't sue La Cosa Nostra. Even if you were a soldier in La Cosa Nostra, suing your godfather was just not done.

The slander had gotten so out of control, Vinnie was forced to drop out of sight. Way out of sight.

Bangor, Maine, was as far out of sight of San Francisco as you could get without taking up residence in a cave. Vinnie had bought a tract of land and a mountain of old used tires. He dug the hole himself, and with his own hands and the sledgehammer he had once used to split open the skull of Salvatore "Sonny" Slobone pounded dirt into each tire until they weighed three hundred pounds each.

In the piny Maine woods he built himself the hideaway deluxe of all time. It was impregnable because it was completely underground. The buried sides and roof were made from stacks of earth-reinforced tires. Rifle bullets couldn't penetrate it. Hand grenades detonated harmlessly over it. Katushya rockets only turned the graded topsoil.

There Vinnie settled down with his dogs and his savings and figured the D'Ambrosia family would never find him here.

And for a solid year they hadn't. No one had.

Then one day in July the buried motion-sensor array picked up an intruder. Punching up his security cameras, Vinnie saw a man approaching on foot. He was lean and neat with his hair cut on the short side.

"Oh, man, what is this shit?" Vinnie moaned.

In his gray chinos and T-shirt, the guy looked like a poster boy for AIDS awareness.

"Those cocksucker fucking rumors musta spread like wildfire. Now I got the local fags sniffing around, looking for action."

Vinnie hit the loudspeaker system. "You! Get offa my property. You want people to talk?"

But the guy kept coming.

"I get it. I get it. He's bait. That's it. Don Silvio thinks I'll give him a tumble, and either the fruit whacks me or I contract AIDS offa him. Fuck! Gotta get rid of him."

He called out, "Numbnuts, Fatface, Bonehead—where are you stupid mutts?"

The dry padding of sandpapery paws came rushing out of the playroom, where the three ridgebacks had been sleeping contentedly.

Pushing their eager brown muzzles away from his crotch, Vinnie said, "See the guy on the screen? You gotta get rid of him for me. Got that? He's bad."

And Vinnie pulled down the drop stairs that led to the roof and the only exit from his underground tire fortress.

Not having seen daylight in weeks, the dogs poured out, their big, muscular, toast-colored bodies eager.

Vinnie sat back to watch the guy being torn limb from limb. There were no dogs more ferocious than the African ridgeback, for they had been bred to fight lions and hunt men.

REMO SAW THE DOGS coming for him and decided his search was over. They came out of a hole in an embankment. And knowing that dogs don't normally dwell underground, he figured he had the right patch of dirt.

Howling and yapping, the three dogs galloped toward him like small toast-brown horses.

Remo let the first one pass between his legs. The dog kept on going, snapping at legs that his eyes told him were still in front of him.

The second dog went for his throat, and Remo got him by his floppy ears. Spinning, he sent the canine flying tail first into an evergreen.

The third dog, seeing all this, skidded to a stop. The dark bristly ridge along his smooth back lifted like hackles. He growled.

Remo casually tossed him a dog treat. The dog sniffed it, gobbled it up and Remo tossed another.

By this time the other dogs had gotten themselves organized, and Remo began flinging treats in all directions. The dogs fell upon them with eager, sniffling muzzles.

While they were occupied, Remo opened the hatch in the ground and yelled down. "Vinnie Cerebrini?"

"You get outta my house!" an agitated voice shouted up.

"You Vinnie 'Three Dogs'?" Remo asked.

"I said, you get out my house, gaybo. I don't swing your way."

"I don't know what you're talking about. I'm here to kill you."

"Stay away from me," Vinnie said. "Don't touch me."

And Vinnie lifted a Mak-90 assault rifle.

"Look, you're a bad guy and that thing won't help you much," Remo told him. "Let's just get this over with, okay?"

"Listen, I'll blast you to hell before I let you lay hands on me."

Shrugging, Remo set himself as if about to drop in for a visit.

Vinnie "Three Dogs" Cerebrini opened fire. The Mak-90 emptied itself up at the hovering fruit. Trouble was the fruit had some really smooth moves. He sidestepped every shot. Must have studied ballet, Vinnie decided, yanking the clip out and inserting another.

He was about to bring the weapon up to bear when suddenly the roof started coming down. Dirt showered, then heavy tires started dropping like bombs. They hit, bounced and rolled crazily. Vinnie had to dance out of the way to keep from being run over by the very protection he had labored to create for himself.

Above, the fruit seemed to be stamping and stomping around in controlled, angry circles.

"Oh, man, look at him go. This flaming hornbag must not have gotten laid since Christmas."

So Vinnie began shooting wildly into his own roof.

The trouble was, the very tires that had kept bullets out also absorbed those trying to go the other way. Try as he might, Vinnie could not whack the annoyed fruit.

"You are a dead man," he shouted up during a lull.

"Not yet."

"After you are dead, I'm gonna piss into your dead mouth. I am going to abuse your corpse. I don't care what people say. How you like that?" raged Vinnie, peppering the ceiling above with hot lead. Cold dirt showered down in response.

More roof tires sagged and spilled earth. The air became a cloud of unbreathable dust.

Vinnie was on his fourth clip, surrounded by dirt and rubber with a big patch of New England sky overhead when he felt a hand on his shoulder. The hand felt like a claw bucket. Then the fingers dug in.

Vinnie looked up to see the deadest eyes in the world looking at him as if he was dead meat.

He screamed. And the other hand reached out for the Mak-90.

There was nothing he could do. Vinnie was helpless. As the man brought up the loaded Mak-90 to his head with casual ease to intimidate him into surrendering, Vinnie decided right then and there he would rather be dead than raped by some faggot from the Maine woods.

"I'll show him," Vinnie thought, and pulled the trigger.

REMO STEPPED BACK as the body of Vinnie "Three Dogs" Cerebrini fell facedown onto the dirt floor, wondering why it had been so easy.

As he left the grounds, tossing his last dog treats to the three yellow dogs, he decided the Mak-90 must have had a hair trigger to go off prematurely like that.

Cloudy dirt hung in the afternoon air. It billowed slowly out from the zone of destruction, following him down a path of sticky pine needles.

A quarter mile down the road, Remo came upon the Master of Sinanju atop the largest, ugliest moose Remo had ever seen in his life. The moose had antlers like spreading trees.

"Where'd you get that bag of hair?" Remo asked warily.

"Have a care how you address the awesome Arcadian Hind."

"A *moose?*"

"Hind," corrected Chiun, giving the moose's hindquarters a whack. Obligingly the moose launched itself at Remo, head down, antlers sweeping ahead like plows.

Remo dodged the first pass easily. The moose turned on its clumsy, ungainly legs and came at him again.

This time Remo reached up and grabbed hold of a tree branch. When the antlers were almost into his belly, he snap-rolled up.

The moose clopped past noisily.

The Master of Sinanju piloted him back, coming to a stop under Remo's branch.

"You must come down and defeat him," Chiun insisted.

"I'm not fighting any freaking moose!"

"It is the Hind of Arcadia. You must defeat him as Hercules defeated him."

"If that's the Arcadian Hind, where are its golden horns and brass hooves?" Remo shouted back.

"This is a very old Hind. Sadly, its gold has faded."

"Well, I'm not coming down."

"You cannot stay up there forever," Chiun warned.

"You're right," said Remo, standing up on the tree branch. It bowed under his weight, and when it was at its most springy, Remo launched himself off and into the next tree.

The moose followed.

Jumping from tree to tree, Remo stayed ahead of the galloping moose.

When he reached the edge of the tree line, he doubled back. Doggedly the moose doubled back too.

For a solid hour, Remo played the game. He started to tire, but only because he had been through so much in so short a time.

In the end the moose began to show the worst signs of fatigue and disorientation. Its clumsy legs went wobbly. It stumbled.

"You are abusing this magnificent beast," Chiun complained.

"I'm not the one riding him into the ground," Remo shot back.

The moose's long red tongue was hanging out now. Its sides pulsed like laboring bellows.

When the eyes were distinctly glassy, Remo dropped down from an oak and stood there with his tongue hanging out. He stuck his thumbs in his ears and wriggled his fingers like loose four-point antlers.

Chiun urged the moose into action.

The creature took three steps forward—and its legs gave out completely. They splayed in all directions, and its belly hit the dirt. Chiun found himself standing up, straddling the moose.

"I'd color him defeated," Remo said. "Wouldn't you?"

Angrily Chiun stepped away from his panting steed.

"You are a disgrace to your brethren," he spat at the prostrate moose.

"Some hind," Remo said.

"You cannot find good hinds in this land," Chiun complained, joining Remo. They began walking.

"Is this it?"

"How many *athloi* have you completed?"

Remo made a hasty count using his fingers. "Twelve. Time for you to live up to your end of the bargain."

"We must rest before we go on."

"I won't argue with that."

They found lodgings at a Bangor Holiday Inn, and Remo threw himself on the rug three seconds after he got the bellman to open the door to his room.

Sleep took him instantly.

REMO FOUND HIMSELF wandering through a stand of tall green sorghum that rustled in a sultry breeze.

Somewhere to the west, a drum was beating. It sounded familiar. It wasn't the beating of the hourglass-shaped drums of Korea. Nor was it the tom-tom beating of Africa. It sounded, if anything, like the prelude to an Apache attack in an old Western shoot-'em-up.

Remo followed the beating drum.

On the way he met a tall, handsome man with intensely black hair who wore a white cotton shirt and black leggings tied at the ankles. Remo had never before seen the man but he instantly recognized him.

"You're Chiun."

The young Korean threw back his shoulders proudly and said, "I am Chiun the Elder. And you are the avatar of Shiva who wears the skin of a white tiger."

Remo let that go past without comment. He was in no mood to have an argument with Chiun's father.

"Master H'si T'ang, who completed Chiun's training after you died, told me you knew about my father," Remo said.

One black eyebrow shot up. "I know no such thing. He must have meant my son, young Chiun."

"Chiun denied it."

Chiun the Elder shrugged. It echoed Chiun's own gesture perfectly. It was weird to meet Chiun's father, who had died young, Remo thought. It was like meeting Chiun himself as a young man.

"Do you know where I can find Kojing, then?" Remo asked.

"No. But perhaps the drum beating from the next field is calling for you." Chiun pointed the way.

"Okay, thanks," said Remo, hurrying on.

Gradually the sorghum grew less tall and wild. Remo was deep into a field of waving green plants before he realized the sweet sorghum scent had given way to the smell of fresh corn.

"I didn't know corn grew in Korea," Remo muttered.

As he walked along, he saw that the corn was planted in orderly rows. The drumming was very near now. It seemed to find his heartbeat and make it quicken with anticipation.

Remo cut west through the corn until he found the man in the yellow silk kimono seated between two corn rows with his legs wrapped around a drum. He was beating it with his bare hands.

"Kojing?" Remo asked, for he looked exactly like Master Kojing.

The man looked up, and said, "I am Kojong."

"I'm looking for Kojing."

"But you have found Kojong."

"Right. Right."

"Why do you seek my brother, Kojing?"

"He's supposed to know something important about me."

Kojong ceased his monotonous beating. "All of my brother ancestors know something important. That is why we are here. That is why you are here, brother of my blood."

Noticing an eagle feather sticking out of Kojong's thin white hair, Remo asked, "What are you doing?"

"I am calling up the corn."

"That's nice."

"I eat corn. I do not eat rice."

"Good for you," said Remo, looking around for Kojing.

"My people are corn eaters."

"Uh-huh."

"My people are the people of the Sun."

Remo's head snapped around. "What did you say?"

"I say, my people are the people of the Sun. We do not fight. We are forbidden to kill. That is our way. Our way is different."

"Who are the people of the Sun?" Remo asked, anxious-voiced.

"My people. Your people, as well, white eyes."

"That's what my mother told me. What do you know about my people?"

"Your mother has a message for you, white eyes. You must heed the wind."

Remo cocked an ear to the western wind. It sighed through the corn, making it sway and troubling its golden tassels.

And on the wind Remo heard his mother's worried voice call out, "You must hurry, my son. For he is dying."

"Where are you!" Remo cried out.

"Hurry!"

"Where is he?" Remo shouted. "Just tell me where to find him!" But the wind gave no answer.

But from the fertile soil, Kojong looked up and said, "Chiun knows. Ask Chiun."

"Chiun the Elder?"

"No," said Kojong, his hands returning to the ritual drumming, "Chiun the Younger."

All around him the wind-troubled corn began to waver and roil as if a great spoon was stirring the Void.

And Remo woke up.

HE ENTERED the adjoining hotel room without bothering to knock or turn the doorknob. The door jumped out of his way the second he smacked it with his palm.

"I just had a talk with your father about my father," Remo said angrily.

"Is he well?" said Chiun from his place on the floor.

"He's dead."

"Yes, but is he well?"

"He told me he knew nothing about my father. Then I met Kojong."

"There is no Master by that name," Chiun said thinly.

"Well, I met him and he said to ask *you* about my father."

"What were his exact words?"

"He said to ask Chiun the Younger. That's you."

"But my father is younger than I, having died in his prime years."

"Don't hand me that bull."

"Sit."

"No, I want answers. My mother said my father was someone I knew. Just now her voice told me he's in danger. You know who he is, don't you?"

"If you will sit, I will tell you how to find your father, just as I promised I would."

Fists tensing, Remo scissored to the rug before the Master of Sinanju, his face a thundercloud. Chiun regarded him blandly.

"When your mother first appeared to you, it was not an accident. It was because you looked into the mirror of memory, as I have urged you for years."

"So?"

"Looking into your own reflection summoned up her face in your mind's eye before her spirit found you. You saw there the eyes of your own daughter, and deep from your earliest memories came similar eyes. Those of the woman who bore you. It will be the same with your father, if you only have the courage to examine your own features for his likeness, for all who came before have left their mark upon you."

"You're playing games. I want answers."

"I have been your father in many ways. What kind of father would I be if I hand you this important thing and deny you the boon of discovering it for yourself?"

"Take me to my father, damn it!"

Chiun narrowed his eyes. "Very well. If you insist."

And the Master of Sinanju led Remo out to the streets of Bangor, Maine.

They walked up and down the streets aimlessly for nearly fifteen minutes, with Chiun striking his gong often until Remo was ready to explode.

Just before that happened, Chiun stopped before a vacant lot beside an old brick building. He took up a position and, spreading his arms wide, proclaimed, "Behold Remo, your long-lost father."

Remo looked. There was just Chiun. No one and nothing else.

"You're not my father."

Chiun dropped his arms in exasperation. "Oh, you are so blind. I do not mean me."

And turning, Chiun gestured to a billboard perched atop the brick building.

Remo looked up. It was a movie advertisement.

The film was *The Return of Muck Man.*

Remo started to say something harsh, when his eyes locked with those of the leafy green face on the poster. He froze.

"I know those eyes," he said half to himself.

"They exist in the mirror of your memory, which you refuse to consult."

Striding forward, Remo walked up to the billboard and began reading the credits.

He went as pale as a ghost, and his rotating wrists suddenly grew still. Hands fisting up, he spun on the Master of Sinanju. "You knew! You knew all along. All these years you've known, haven't you?"

Chiun said nothing.

"Haven't you?" Remo raged.

"And if you had looked correctly into the mirror of memory, you would have known, as well," Chiun said evenly.

"Bull!"

The face of the Master of Sinanju flinched, and Remo brushed past him, cold and angry.

Silently Chiun padded after his pupil, who neither heard nor sensed his presence.

There would be no stopping him now. All was in the hands of the unforgiving gods.

23

The flight from Phoenix to Yuma, Arizona, was brief. Less than an hour. Nothing but trackless desert lay below.

They were carried through the early evening air by a nineteen-passenger Beech 1900. There was no stewardess. Remo sat in the front and Chiun several rows behind. A thick silence hung between them. Remo passed the time looking at the drawing of his mother's face thoughtfully.

When Yuma with its lettuce groves appeared, Remo's mind went back to an assignment several years before. Posing as a stuntman, he had infiltrated the making of a war movie about an invasion of the U.S. financed by a Japanese industrialist. There were labor problems, and because the famous American film actor Bartholomew Bronzini was starring, Harold Smith had sent Remo to look into matters. It was all a front. The weapons were real, and the extras were a Japanese paramilitary unit. They had seized the entire town of Yuma, which lay like an island oasis in the Sonoran Desert.

Wholesale executions had been undertaken and televised to the rest of the country. The objective was simple. To hold Yuma until the helpless U.S. military was goaded into nuking one of its own cities. The ma

sponsible had sought revenge for Hiroshima and Na-
gasaki.

It had almost worked. Remo had been nearly killed
when he participated in a stunt involving volunteers
from the Yuma Marine Corps air base. It had been a
massive parachute drop. The Japanese had sabotaged
the chutes. The Marines had all died, leaving Yuma
undefended. Remo woke up in a hospital after it was all
over, only to find that Chiun had saved the day without him. He couldn't remember anything that had
happened to him after he'd bailed out over the desert.

A man Remo had worked with had died during the
occupation, Chiun had said. Only now did Remo know
different. Only now. Five years later.

At the tiny Yuma International Airport, Remo rented
a four-wheel-drive Mazda Navajo and turned to the
Master of Sinanju. "You don't have to come any farther."

"I must come. For I know the way, you do not."

Remo said nothing. They drove out of the city and
into the Sonoran Desert with its undulating dunes and
saguaro cactus, where countless Hollywood movies,
from Westerns to science-fiction extravaganzas, had
been filmed.

Remo drove west. There was only one road west. The
Japanese film had been shot west of the city, among the
dunes. It was blisteringly hot. A red-tailed hawk hung
in the sky, searching.

As they approached an unmarked access road, Chiun
suddenly said, "Take this road."

Remo turned onto the road, and after fifteen more
minutes of driving they reached a low corral-style fence.
Braking, Remo got out.

The gate was closed. There was a red Quarantine sign hung on the fence. Remo noticed that the sign covered another.

Lifting the Quarantine sign, Remo saw the word Reservation burned into the wood. The name above was unreadable except that it began with an *S*.

Brushing sand dust off the burned letters, Remo was able to make out one word: Sun.

"'My people are the people of the Sun,'" Remo muttered. Turning to the Master of Sinanju, he asked, "Know anything about this?"

"I have been here," Chiun said thinly. "When you were thought dead."

Without a word, Remo threw open the gate and they drove in.

They passed three domed Indian huts before they were challenged. An Indian toting a pump shotgun stepped into their headlight beam and fired into the air.

Remo braked and climbed out.

"Can't you read that damn sign, paleface?"

"I'm looking for Sunny Joe Roam."

The shotgun dropped level with Remo's chest, "You ain't answered my question, white eyes."

And Remo moved on the man. The pump gun came out of his clutch and disintegrated in Remo's hands.

The Indian stood looking at the shards of his steel-and-walnut weapon with a slack-jawed expression.

"Where's Sunny Joe Roam?" Remo said tightly.

Woodenly the Indian pointed to the west.

"Yonder. Red Ghost Butte. He went up there two days back. He ain't been back since." The Indian suddenly fell into a fit of coughing. "We think he's dead."

"Dead?"

"The death hogan dust musta got him. He went up there to talk to the spirit of Ko Jong Oh."

"You don't mean Kojong?"

"Forget it. Indian talk." The Indian fell to coughing again. "Damn this plague. Steals all the breath from a man."

"Plague?" Chiun said from the shadows.

The Indian coughed again. "Yeah. They call it the Sun On Jo Disease."

"Sun On Jo?" said Remo. "Not Sinanju?"

"Yeah. I ain't never heard of any Sinanju tribe." Then the Indian got a clear look at the Master of Sinanju. "Hey, don't I know you, old fella?"

"I was here when the Japanese sought to rain death on this land," Chiun said gravely.

"Yeah. You came with Sunny Joe. You're a good guy. But I think you're too late. We're all dying of this damn death dust."

"What's the best way to get to Red Ghost Butte?" Remo asked quickly.

"That jeep of yours will take you as far as Crying River."

"Crying River. Not Laughing Brook?"

"How do you know about Laughing Brook?" the brave asked.

"Never mind," said Remo, jumping for the open car door. "Thanks."

Remo turned to the Master of Sinanju. "You stay here."

Chiun's wispy chin lifted in defiance. "I am coming with you."

"That's your decision."

"Yes, it is."

They got into the Navajo and left the Indian choking on the dust kicked up by their rear wheels.

The road gave out eventually. The Navajo climbed the sand, found traction for a while, then got bogged down. They abandoned it.

The sand crunched softly under their feet. It was the only sound in the night. Red Ghost Butte reared up before them like a grounded ship.

They came to a long depressed wash of sand that had formed a crust and passed over it without breaking the crust. Hoof prints of a horse showed as broken patches in the crust, so they were not surprised to find a horse loitering at the foot of Red Ghost Butte.

The Master of Sinanju went to the horse and, prying open his mouth, examined the inside.

"He has known neither water nor food for two days."

"Must be Sunny Joe's horse," said Remo, looking up. Moonlight washed the eastern face of Red Ghost Butte. Plainly visible on one side was a hole.

"Looks like a cave up there," Remo said.

The Master of Sinanju said nothing. His eyes sought the cave mouth and held it.

"Does it remind you of the cave of your vision?" he asked.

"Can't tell from down here." And Remo started up.

Picking his way through brambles and brush, he ascended until he stood at the entrance to the cave. He seemed to take his time, but in reality he reached the ledge before the mouth cave very quickly.

There Remo hesitated. And in that moment he sensed a presence behind him.

Remo whirled. And there stood Chiun, his face stiff in the moonlight, his hands tucked into the joined sleeves of his kimono.

"What are you doing up here?" Remo asked harshly.

"I have come this far, but I will go no farther. This is your quest. You must see it to its end, no matter how bitter it is for both of us."

"You want me to go in here or not?"

"I offer no opinion," Chuin said, voice and eyes thin.

"Okay," Remo said thickly. And he stepped in.

The moonlight showed red sandstone for several yards. When he passed into the dark portion, he stopped, letting the visual purple in his eyes adjust to the blackness. His heart thumped, but he felt a strange calmness come over his mind.

As his eyes adjusted, Remo began to see low shapes on both sides of the cave and his mouth went dry.

THE MASTER OF SINANJU stood in the moonlight looking into the cave. He watched the back of his pupil recede beyond the wash of pure moonlight and in his heart bid a silent farewell to him. After this night nothing would ever be the same again, he knew.

Then out of the cave came Remo's excited voice. "Chiun, get in here!"

"I will not," Chiun called back.

"You gotta. I need your help."

"For me to enter that cave is to die. Your own mother told you this."

"That's not what she said, and if you don't come in here right now, I'm coming out there to drag you in!"

His face warping with a succession of conflicting emotions, Chiun, Reigning Master of Sinanju, passed grimly into the forbidding cave.

He saw the first sack of bones to his right. It was a mummy. There was another on the opposite side, facing it. Two sad bundles of bones wrapped in faded Indian blankets. Farther along sat two more mummies. They reclined in niches carved out of the porous red sandstone.

At the end of the tunnel of sandstone, whose sides were repositories for the dead, Remo Williams knelt beside a living man, cradling his head on his lap.

"It's Sunny Joe," Remo whispered, pain in his voice. "I think he's dying, Chiun."

But the eyes of the Master of Sinanju were not on his pupil or the dying man, but on the thing in the great arched niche beyond. The niche at the very end of the cave.

It was a mummy like the others. It wasn't dressed in Indian blankets, but in a silken robe whose cut and color and fineness marked it unmistakably as a kimono woven in the village of Sinanju long ago during the Silla period.

Looking up, Remo saw Chiun looking beyond him, transfixed.

"That's the mummy I saw in my vision. It looks just like you."

"It is Kojong," whispered Chiun. "It is the lost Master."

"Never mind him. Help me."

Tearing his eyes from the mummy in faded yellow silk, Chiun knelt beside the dying man.

He was well over six feet tall with a strong, weathered face and deep-set brown eyes. Dust caked his face, and his lips were parchment dry and cracked.

Placing a palm to his mouth and nose, Chiun tested the breathing. Long fingers felt along the spine and throat.

"His *ki* is failing," Chiun said.

Remo looked stricken. "He can't die now. I just found him."

A low cough came from deep within the unconscious man.

Resting an ear against his chest, Chiun listened patiently until a second cough racked the body. Chiun lifted his head. "It is the mouse disease," he said gravely.

"What's that?"

"A malady carried by mice when they are abounding. It fills the lungs with death. If he can be revived, he might be saved." And Chiun began to manipulate the man's spine.

Sunny Joe Roam stirred. His eyes blinked open. "I know you," he said.

"I know you, too," Remo said.

"You're dead. Does that mean I'm dead now?"

"None of us are dead, brother," Chiun said softly. "If you have any strength in your body, draw upon it that you might be saved."

"Water. There's water in Sanshin's canteen."

"Sanshin?" Remo and Chiun said in one voice.

"My horse. Appreciate a swig."

Remo ran down to get it, but when he came back to administer it, Sunny Joe took one tentative sip, then his head lolled to one side in Remo's supporting hand.

"No," Remo moaned.

"He is not dead," Chiun said, stern voiced. "But we must make haste."

Tears streaming from his eyes, Remo said, "You told me he was dead."

"And he that you were dead. But if you would have him live, you must do as I say."

"How do I know you won't let him die just to save your village?"

"Because you know just as I know that this man is of my village. I am pledged to preserve his life. As are you. If you are not a good son to him, then you at least will do this for Sinanju."

Chiun accepted the man's head in his lap.

Remo stood up. "What do you need?"

"Viper wine has always been very efficacious against the mouse disease."

"Any viper do?"

Chiun nodded. "So long as it is poisonous."

Remo went out into the night and down into the desert, his heart a stone. Closing his eyes, he swept the desert with his entire sensitive body. It was night. Snakes would be in their holes.

Remo walked purposefully toward the first tiny heartbeat he heard.

It was a mouse. In his anger, he kicked sand toward it. A second mouse led him on a frantic chase through brambles before he saw it was a rodent.

Remo soon learned to tune out the warm-blooded mice and seek the slower heartbeats of cold-blooded creatures.

He found a red-and-black banded coral snake not long after.

When Remo stuck his hand into the burrow, the coral snake struck. Its fangs snapped on empty air, and Remo grabbed its entire head in his hand, dragging it out into the moonlight. With it coiled around his arms, he resumed his hunt.

A sidewinder undulating along the sand saw Remo approach and tried to slither away. Remo enveloped its head in his free hand and, bearing two twisting, squirming, writhing serpents, he ran back to Red Ghost Butte, scared and hopeful at the same time.

But in his heart there was a cold feeling that he had come this far only to watch his father die.

SUNNY JOE ROAM flickered in and out of consciousness as the Master of Sinanju examined the two snakes. Selecting the coral snake, he milked it by holding the head so the jaws gaped. He held the exposed fangs over a rude cup he had fashioned from sandstone, hooking them to the edge. The clear yellow venom dripped for nearly a minute—an agonizingly slow time for Remo.

Chiun added water and, taking some brambles between his hands, set them alight by the friction of his hands.

The venom was soon bubbling.

"Will it work?" Remo asked anxiously.

"We need ginseng root," Chiun said without emotion.

"Where are we going to get ginseng in a desert?" Remo said bitterly.

Chiun looked up. "You must prepare yourself for whatever may come."

"That's easy for you to say. He's not your father."

Sunny Joe's sun-squint eyes fluttered open. He saw Chiun. "Hey, chief. How's it going?"

"I am well, brother. And you?"

"My time's about up, I reckon."

"Do not say that."

Sunny Joe's eyes found Remo's. "I thought I'd dreamed I saw you. The old chief told me you'd bought it during that parachute drop."

"He told me the same about you," Remo said.

"What about it, chief?"

"I did what I must," Chiun said, not looking up from the boiling venom.

Remo swallowed three times before saying his next words, "I'm not who you think I am."

"No. Who are you?"

From his wallet, Remo took the folded drawing. Unfolding it, he held it before Sunny Joe's pain-wracked eyes.

"Do you recognize her?"

Sunny Joe's eyes seemed to pass over the drawing without recognition. Then they grew sharp. "Where'd you get that?"

"It's a police drawing."

"Yeah?"

"Of my mother."

And Remo held his breath as he waited for a response.

Sunny Joe Roam lay his head back and coughed explosively. "What did you say your name was?"

"Remo."

"That much I remember from before."

"The nuns who raised me said the name on the basket was Remo Williams."

Sunny Joe Roam said nothing. Remo held his breath, waiting for the man's next words. They didn't come. Instead, Chiun said, "It is ready."

Remo watched as Chiun lifted up Sunny Joe Roam's head. With a start Remo saw his eyes were shut.

"He lives yet," Chiun assured him.

Remo subsided. Chiun held the steaming venom before Sunny Joe's nose and the open mouth. Sunny Joe recoiled, coughing. Chiun brought the brew close again.

"This is to prepare you," he said.

When the viper wine had cooled, Chiun poured it down Sunny Joe's throat, stimulating his swallowing reflex with a thumb massage of the Adam's apple.

Sunny Joe looked older than Remo remembered. His tall, lean-limbed body seemed to have wasted away in places.

When the cup was empty, Remo eased the head back onto the low hump of sandstone that served as a pillow. Sunny Joe's eyes were completely closed now.

"What do you think, Little Father?" Remo asked in a shrunken voice.

"I am not your father," Chiun said sternly. Then, after a moment and in a softer tone, he added, "We will know by dawn."

"Is there anything we can do?"

"If we had a dragon bone, we could make dragon-bone soup."

A strange expression crossed Remo's face. "Yong gave me a dragon bone."

"What did you do with it?"

"I put it in my pocket. But it was only a dream." The strange expression on Remo's face got stranger as his

hand came out of one pocket clutching a fragment of
bone.

"Did you plant this on me?" Remo demanded of
Chiun.

Ignoring him, the Master of Sinanju began to scrape
the bone into meal in the sandstone cup.

"I don't know if he heard me," Remo said, voice
cracking.

"He heard you."

"No. I don't think he heard me say my name. I don't
think he knows who I am."

"He knows. All fathers know."

The last of the bone lay in the cup. Chiun climbed to
his feet. Padding over to the mummy encased in yellow
silk, he stood looking down upon it. "I bring greetings
from the House of Sinanju, O ancestor."

Remo joined him. "That's Kojong, isn't it?"

"Let us be certain." And from his sleeve, the Master
of Sinanju drew his tubular gong. He tapped it once.
The high note filled the cave. And from the mummy
came an answering note.

Chiun silenced his gong. But the mummy continued
to ring.

Remo looked down. At its bony feet, covered in dust,
a gong identical to Chiun's reposed.

"Yes," Chiun intoned, his voice filled with emotion. "This is Kojong the Lost."

"He looks a lot like you," Remo said softly.

"I have never told you the story of Kojing and Kojong, Remo."

"No. But Mah-Li told me. Years ago. Master Nonja
had a wife who bore him identical twins. Because the
eldest son was always selected to be trained in Sinanju,

she knew one of the boys would have to be drowned in the bay. Otherwise, there could be a succession problem.''

''In those days,'' said Chiun, his voice dropping into the low cadences he used when speaking of his village, ''times were poor and the babies were sent home to the sea every few years. So the wife of Nonja, who bore him the twins, Kojing and Kojong, hid one of the babies from the sight of their father. Since Nonja was old and his eyes were failing, this was possible. As the boys grew, Kojing entered training. But the canny mother switched the boys every other day, and both received training.

''When at last Nonja died, two Masters stood ready to become Reigning Master. When they presented themselves to the village, none knew what to do. Should Kojing become Master. Or Kojong?

''In the end Kojong announced that he would seek another land where there would be no question of who was Reigning Master. He disappeared from the village, saying that should the House ever reach a time when there was no succeeding Master, the villagers should seek the sons of Kojong and pick of them the one most worthy.''

Chiun's hazel eyes shifted from the dead face of Kojing, so much like his own, and seized Remo's. ''You, Remo Williams.''

''What?''

''I know this man's story. He is the last Sunny Joe. For he is a descendant of Kojong, whom he calls Ko Jong Oh. The eldest son of this tribe is called Sunny Joe after the name of the Great Spirit Magician Sun On Jo—He Who Breathes the Sun.''

"My mother said my people were the people of the Sun. Those were her exact words."

"This man is your father, just as you are the descendant of Kojong."

"He—he say why he left me on the orphanage doorstep?"

"No, I did not speak of you to him."

"Then—then maybe I'll never know...."

"At dawn you will know or you will not. But in the meantime, there is something you must do."

"What's that?"

"Your last *athloi.*"

"I thought I was through. I did my twelve."

"No. There is still what the Greeks in their legends called cleaning Augean Stables. For the Greeks miscounted."

"It can wait."

"No. It cannot. This man is dying, as are the others of his tribe—your tribe, Remo Williams—from the mouse disease that is well-known in my land. You must comb the desert for mice and their droppings. Only by ridding the land of mice can this plague be arrested."

"I want to be with him. In case—in case he dies."

"I have promised you that I would take you to your father if you completed the Rite of Attainment. I have kept my part of the bargain. Now you must keep yours."

"I can't go now," Remo protested.

"You will if you are your father's son."

Remo looked to Sunny Joe Roam and back to the Master of Sinanju. Tears started in his eyes. "You can't make me do this."

Chiun indicated the unconscious man. "With his dying breath, he would ask you to save his people. Your people. You know this."

"Okay. But he'd better be alive when I get back."

"I make no promises," Chiun intoned.

"One more thing. If he comes to, ask him why he abandoned me."

"Are you certain you wish to know this?"

"Yeah. I gotta know."

Chiun nodded silently. He handed Remo the tubular gong of Kojong. "This will help you in your *athloi.*"

And taking the gong, Remo went out into the desert night, his eyes hot and wet.

REMO MOUNTED THE HORSE, Sanshin, lashing it into action. As he rode, he struck the gong. It rang angrily.

Mice jumped out of their desert burrows. The gong's extended note seemed to send them fleeing.

Soon Remo was driving them before him. They were everywhere.

Stripping Sanshin of his saddlebags, Remo used them to catch the rodents. He tore across the desert with his thoughts racing ahead of him like uncatchable ghosts.

He couldn't bring himself to kill. They were only mice. So he carried them to the jeep and locked them inside. Soon they filled the back and front seats, sniffing and clawing at the windows, trying to escape.

When he had cleared the surrounding desert, he entered the deserted hogans he found here and there, driving the mice out with the gong and cleaning the interior with brittle-bush whisks.

In the deepest part of the night, Remo came across a solitary wind-scoured headstone.

It was a simple slab. It stood alone in the desert beside a eroded hump of red sandstone that lay at the end of the depressed crust of sand.

There was a name on the stone. No date, just a name. No stonecutter had carved the name. The letters were too irregular, but they had been carved deep and with great force.

The name was Dawn Starr Roam.

Remo knew instinctively it was the name of his mother.

On that spot, a thousand emotions both cold and hot running through his bones, he broke down and wept bitterly angry tears over what he had never known and only now truly missed.

NEAR DAWN, a light rain fell from the desert sky, and Remo opened his eyes to see Vega and Altair burning faintly on either side of the Milky Way.

He sat up. And in the sand beside him the gong suddenly rang. It was very faint. Nothing seemed to have struck it. Unless it was raindrops.

The faint sound faded. Then it came again. Nothing struck the bar of steel. Unless it was a ghost.

Remo stood up. And to the west he heard the sound of the gong's mate coming across the sands.

"Chiun. He's calling me."

Grabbing the gong, Remo pulled the mallet and struck it in response. Then he took off over the sand, toward Red Ghost Butte. The carrying gong note pierced the still air again, and the gong in Remo's hand answered.

The notes blended into a single sustained cry that didn't subside until Remo reached the cave mouth.

There stood the Master of Sinanju, his face a shell of sorrow and unconcealed pain.

"Don't tell me...." Remo said thickly.

"My sorrow..."

Remo squeezed his eyes tight as fists. "Nooooo."

"...is only as great as your joy," Chiun continued aridly. "For you have gained a father, and I have lost my only son."

Remo's eyes popped. "He's alive!"

Chiun nodded. "He awaits you within."

Remo started in. "Well, c'mon."

"No. It is not for me to do this. I will remain here. For it is the seventh moon and it is my custom to bathe in the bitter tears of Kyon-u and Chik-nyo, whose sufferings I understand only too well."

24

Two days later three men rode into the Sonoran Desert on horseback.

Sunny Joe Roam took the lead. Remo rode on his right. Balanced on an Appaloosa pony, Chiun followed at a respectful distance, his face creased with pain like crumpled paper.

The sky was utterly cloudless, and in the clear desert air objects and people possessed an unnatural clarity, as if cut from glass. Overhead the sun beat down like hot jackhammers.

"I owe you two my life," Sunny Joe said after a while.

"Our blood is the same color," said Chiun.

"More than that, I owe you some answers."

Remo said nothing. It was a subject no one had wanted to address in the two days that old Bill Roam had recuperated from the Sun On Jo Disease.

"For you to understand," Sunny Joe began, "you have to understand who I am. Long, long before the white man came, my ancestor Ko Jong Oh arrived in this desert. He came from the land that comes down to us as Sun On Jo. They say all us redskins are Asians originally. So I always figured he came across the Bering Strait from somewhere in China. Anyway, Ko Jong

Oh settled down here among a tiny group of Indians and married one. We think they were head pounders."

"Head pounders?" Remo said.

"That's what we call the Navajo, on account of they used to bash in the skulls of their enemies. That's to differentiate them from the Hopi, whom we call cliff squatters.

"Now, Ko Jong Oh was a mighty warrior and magician, and he took this tribe under his wing. In gratitude, they took the name Sun On Jo. He taught the Sun On Jos the ways of peace. War and fighting and killing were forbidden. Only Ko Jong Oh and each eldest son descended from him were allowed to fight. And only then to protect the tribe. For it was handed down from the mouth of Ko Jong Oh that if any of his sons brought attention to himself, it would bring down the wrath of the Great Spirit Magician himself, Sun On Jo."

Sunny Joe looked back at Chiun.

"I told you this story that time a few years back, chief."

"And I have told you the legend of my village," Chiun returned coolly. "But you did not believe that our legends were one."

"I'm still on the skeptical side. But we'll get to that."

Sunny Joe resumed his tale. "Every eldest male heir of Ko Jong Oh is taught the way of Sun On Jo. How to track game stealthily, to see farther than the hawk, to become one with the shadows. All the better to protect the tribe. When I was born, disease and poverty had claimed many of the tribespeople. It hit the women especially hard. When I came of age, the Sunny Joe before me, my father, took me up to Red Ghost Butte and before I was invested as his successor, he told me that the tribe was dying in spirit. Too many had left for the cities or were buried under the red sands. There were no women my age. And none had been born in a long time. My father thought it might have had something to do with the atomic fallout over in Utah and New Mexico."

Sunny Joe shrugged. "Doesn't matter now. But if the tribe was to go on, I had to go out into the greater world and find the land of Sun On Jo and beg of the Great Spirit Magician for one of his women to be my bride. Otherwise, the Sun On Jos would not survive the century."

Remo grunted.

"So I packed my bag and piled into my old Studebaker, and since west was the direction from which Ko Jong Oh had come, it made sense that I go west. Well, I didn't get very far until I ran out of money and had to look for work. So I fell into stunt work. It paid, didn't demand all of my time and, between shoots, I could travel. Let me tell you I traveled all over the globe. Sometimes with a production, other times on my own. I was searching for Sun On Jo, studying maps, talking to people. But China had gone Communist, and every way in was blocked.

"I was in Japan during the last days of the occupation when I ran into a Korean who told me of a place called Sinanju way up in North Korea, whose warriors were feared and respected throughout Asia. By that time old Marshal Kim Il-Sung was in charge up there, and as an American I couldn't get there for money, marbles or chalk."

"What year was this?" Remo asked.

"I'm getting to that. About that time the Korean War broke out. I watched it seesaw back and forth a while, and when MacArthur took Pyongyang, I saw my chance. I up and joined the Army. After basic, I shipped out for Korea. I asked for action and I got it. They handed me a BAR and put me right on the line. Chosin Reservoir. MiG Alley. I saw it all. It was a terrible war. But I guess all wars are terrible."

"I did a tour in Nam." said Remo. "Marines."

"If I had been around, I would have knocked that notion out of your skull on day one."

Remo said nothing. Sunny Joe went on.

"I was with General Walker's Eighth Army when we took up positions along the Chongchon River in October 1950. Our orders were to hold a bridgehead north of Sinanju. Mountains to the east. Mountains to the west. I never saw so many mountains outside of Arizona. Or such a bitter winter. We had the North Koreans licked, but there were rumors the Chinese were about to take a hand. While we were digging in, they attacked. Wiped out the entire Eight Cav at Unsan. We knew we were in for it then.

"Me, I just wanted to take a look around Sinanju, but I was stuck where I was. So I hunkered down as we pounded the enemy and they pounded us back, with Migs and Yaks and U.S. Sabre jets screaming over our heads and the winter closing in and the bigwigs chanting 'Home by Christmas.' They just never got around to saying which Christmas. Sound familiar, Remo?"

"Yeah. It does."

"Anyway, by early November my unit, the Nineteenth Infantry, were still trying to hold the bridgehead, when the Chinese swooped down on our battery position with their mortars and small-arms fire, blowing bugles to freeze the blood. We fought practically eyeball to eyeball, dead Chinese stacking up not thirty yards from our gun shields. Before long we were surrounded, Chinese knife men killed some of us in our sleeping bags. It was a grim night, I will tell you. I was sure I was going to die.''

Sunny Joe hung his head at the memory.

''We withdrew under fire, abandoning the bridgehead. The tide was turning, just as it would all war long. Then on the night of November 6, the Chinese forces broke contact and went into full retreat. To this day, no one's ever been able to explain it. They just up and marched into the mountains, never to be heard from again. You won't read about the Battle of Sinanju in too many history books, but for my money it was the worst conflict of the war. They had us cold. But they bugged out.''

Remo looked back to the Master of Sinanju.

''You were not near the village of Sinanju, brother of my ancestors,'' said Chiun. ''But in Sinanju town, a lesser place. And on the night you describe, the Chinese ran because to do otherwise was to die.''

''What do you know about that?'' Sunny Joe asked.

Chiun pulled himself up in the saddle proudly. ''On that night I left my village called Sinanju at the edge of the West Korea Bay, and descended upon the Chinese, driving them back to the Yalu.''

''You and what army?''

''I and no army. Just I.''

''Is he kidding?'' Roam asked Remo.

''No,'' said Remo.

"The noise of battle was keeping the women and children awake at night," Chiun explained. "Besides, I did not like the Chinese in my land. It had too many squatters already."

"What about the Americans?"

"They looted and raped no one, and so I suffered them to live."

Sunny Joe grinned crookedly. "Well, you saved my butt that night. If what you say is true."

"It is true," Chiun sniffed.

"Anyway, during our retreat I finally got to see Sinanju. It was a typical Korean town filled with frightened refugees. I talked to the locals. Nobody had ever heard of Ko Jong Oh. Or Sun On Jo, or any of it. It had to be the second-biggest disappointment of my entire life." Then, glancing at Remo, he amended, "No, make that third."

Remo looked away.

Sunny Joe continued. "Well, the war finally ended and I went home. Landed back in Hollywood. I didn't know what to do with myself. My father had passed on while I was at war, and as I saw it, I had failed to find the land of Sun On Jo. So I fell back into stunt work. TV was coming in, and there were Westerns galore. I doubled for the best of them. Worked my way up to stunt coordinator and eventually did some acting. I played black hats and white hats. Spoke my first line on a 'Rifleman' episode. It wasn't all glory, though. I took a lot of falls and broke a lot of bones.

"Around that time—guess it was a few years before, now that I think about it—I took me a wife. Figured if I made enough money I could return to the reservation with cash in my pockets enough to make up for my failure.

"Then my wife told me she was going to have a papoose. It was the proudest day of my life. I was hoping for a son. You know, a Sunny Joe to carry on after me."

Remo plucked a needle off a saguaro and rolled it between his fingers thoughtfully.

"Well, she did give me a son. A dark-eyed, dark-haired squalling little boy. I near to have burst. But the birth went bad and she sickened. Within a week she was no more."

Remo sucked in a hot breath. When Sunny Joe resumed talking, his voice was twisted. "It broke me up inside. I couldn't sleep. I couldn't eat. I couldn't think. I didn't know what to do. You see, I had made plans, but now they had come apart. I couldn't see starting over. I couldn't see raising a boy without a mother. Not in my line of work. Not with the travel and the hours. There was nothing for me back at the reservation.

"So one night I flew east, picked out a nice Catholic orphanage because my wife had been raised Catholic, laid the boy on the doorstep and walked away with my guts a great big ache and agony."

"That was me," said Remo, his voice dull.

"Now, when I got started, I did my stunt work under a stage name, William S. Rome. Turned 'Roam' to 'Rome,' after the city. Figured it sounded more Continental or something. Didn't want the reservation elders to know it was me. In the back of my head I thought I might go and claim that papoose as my own one fine day. So I gave him a name that no one else would have. I juggled 'Rome' to get 'Remo' and gave him my first name as his last, adding an *S* for 'Sunny Joe.'"

"What did you name the baby?" Remo said softly.

"Truth is, my wife died before we could decide on a name. She wanted to name him after me. But I favored something he could call his own. Hell, if he's still alive, he'd be a grown man by now. He can call himself whatever he wants. He's earned that right."

"So did you not claim that child?" asked Chiun.

"Well, time passed, the work took me here and the work took me there. I got into movies and, when that dried up—and it always did—I went back into TV. Black hats mostly. When detective shows replaced Westerns, I played hoods, and when science fiction took over from detective shows, I played Klingons and Cylons and what have you. Producers realized that with my height and thin frame I looked good in a rubber suit, so I played every kind of monster you could imagine. Pretty soon I was stuck as a central casting creature."

"Were you in *The Sea Is an Only Child?*"

"Yeah. You see that one?"

"No," said Remo, not elaborating.

Sunny Joe shrugged and went on. "One year I was in Italy making Spaghetti Westerns when I read about a Newark cop who had been electrocuted for some two-bit killing. The cop's name was Remo Williams. That told me I had waited too long to claim my only son."

"Didn't sound like you were ever going to," Remo said distantly.

"Maybe I never would have. I won't lie to you. Life had dealt me some pretty sorry hands. I wanted my son to start clean and not end up some Hollywood brat too spoiled for his own good, or worse, a half-breed reservation alcoholic with no culture to call his own."

"That's one way to look at it," Remo said stiffly.

For a long time no one said anything. There was only the soft crunch of hoofs in sand. Remo flung the saguaro needle away. It clipped the stinger off a scuttling scorpion.

Sunny Joe noted this without a flicker of surprise coming to his eroded features. "Well, more time passed," he said, "and I got old. Never did make it big as an actor. Too many broken bones and noses. I saw the tunnel one time too many, and decided to retire among my people, whom I had been supporting. Well, you know what happened. The Japanese came to Yuma and hired me as stunt coordinator. Then all hell broke loose. After the occupation, I started getting offers. It was good work at first, then they revived old Muck Man from back in the seventies and I found myself sweating in rubber suits all over again. Only this time I was a star. Nobody knew my face, but I was a star. I was about ready to pack it in when the death-hogan dust kicked up. So I come back. You know the rest."

Sunny Joe plucked a needle off a saguaro and threw it ahead of him. The tailless scorpion caught it in the head and fell over dying. Remo and Chiun exchanged glances.

"Where'd you learn to ride a horse like that, Remo?" Sunny Joe asked all at once.

"Outer Mongolia."

Sunny Joe Roam grunted. "So what've you been doing with yourself all these years?"

"Government work. Hush-hush stuff."

"Say no more."

They rode a little farther along.

"You haven't asked me why I'm still alive if I was executed back in New Jersey," Remo said.

"I ain't convinced you're that Remo Williams."

They came to the long wash of crusty sand.

"Of course there's one way to find out."

"How's that?" asked Remo.

Sunny Joe pulled up his horse, and Remo and Chiun followed suit.

"There's an old prophesy of Ko Jong Oh. He said one day a man would come from Sun On Jo and he would be known not by his face or dress or language, but by his ability to do what only Sunny Joes could do."

"What's that?"

"To cross Crying River without making it cry."

"Where's Crying River?"

Sunny Joe pointed to the sandy wash. "That's it right there. In the spring it's Laughing Brook. But when the summer heat sets in, it dries right up. We get some rain, and the sand crusts up. You walk across it, and it sounds like potato chips. They didn't have potato chips back in the days of Ko Jong Oh. So they said the sounds were maidens crying."

Sunny Joe piloted this horse forward. Its hooves sank into the breaking crust, making faint crying noises. Forking his mount around, he faced Remo and Chiun across the dead river.

"A true Sunny Joe can walk across Crying River without making the sand cry. I can do it. How about you?"

Remo dismounted. Sunny Joe did the same. They looked at each other squarely and in unison they approached each other.

The sand beneath their feet made no sound. The crust refused to break.

When they at last stood facing one another, neither spoke for a long time.

Sunny Joe's eyes squinted up. "Son..."

Remo swallowed. They lifted their hands hesitatingly, as if measuring each other. Remo offered his hand. Sunny Joe started an embrace. They switched, got tangled up and laughed nervously. Several times they seemed on the verge of embracing in a bear hug.

In the end they stood apart and shook each other's hand firmly, fighting back deep wells of emotion neither man could express articulately, if at all.

When they had exhausted that, Sunny Joe Roam clapped Remo on the back and drew him away from the horses. "Come with me, son. I want to tell you about your mother...."

And standing on the other side of Crying River, the Master of Sinanju watched them walk into the desert together, the hairs of his wispy beard trembling, although there was no wind.

He noticed that Remo didn't look back....

25

That night, under a thousand milky stars, Remo Williams was invested as the new Sunny Joe.

He stepped out of a hogan wearing buckskin and hawk feathers, muttering, "I feel like Tonto in this getup."

No one heard him.

Sunny Joe Roam led him before a roaring fire and said, "I present to you my long-lost son..."

"Remo Williams," Remo said.

"Remo Williams, who was sent to us by a vision, and who is the next Sunny Joe."

A sea of red sandstone faces regarded Remo, and he had a flash of déjà vu. Their flat faces reminded him of the faces of the villagers of Sinanju, whose lives he was sworn to protect. Except Sinanju faces were the color of old ivory or faded lemons. These faces were distinctly red. But their eyes were identical down to the Mongoloid eye folds. And their lack of appreciation equal.

"Hey," a man in iron gray pigtails spoke up. "He's nothing but an apple."

Remo looked at Sunny Joe quizzically.

"An apple means an Indian who's half-white. You know, red on the outside and white on the inside. Pay no never mind. Been called apple a time or two myself."

"My son is no apple," Sunny Joe told the crowd.

"This is true," a new voice said.

Remo turned. It was the Master of Sinanju. He approached.

"He is a banana," said Chiun.

"Banana?"

"Yes. He is yellow on the outside and white on the inside."

"Don't you mean the other way around, chief?" asked Sunny Joe Roam.

"He is a banana before he is an apple. Do not forget I have taught him the ways of Sinanju. If you teach him the ways of the Sun On Jos for a thousand years, you will not erase his Koreanness."

Sunny Joe regarded Chiun squarely. "Do you have an objection to what we do here tonight, old chief?"

"It is not for me to object," replied Chiun.

Sunny Joe turned to Remo. "What about you, Remo?"

"Let's get it done," Remo said.

"So be it."

They sang the old songs and beat the drums, and as the moon rose cool and clear in a star-sprinkled sky, Remo Williams became the latest Sunny Joe and took the sacred oath to protect his people from all harm.

All this, Chiun watched with unreadable eyes. And when they brought out the corn and fry bread, he slipped away unnoticed.

WHEN ALL HAD DIED DOWN, Remo walked out into the desert, following a set of tracks not even the keenest eye of the Sun On Jo tribe could follow.

He found the Master of Sinanju at the foot of Red Ghost Butte.

Chiun turned. No flicker of emotion crossed his seamed face. "You have found your father, Remo Williams. Congratulations."

"Thanks."

Silence hung between them. Remo scuffed the red earth with his beaded moccasins. A hawk tail feather fell over his eyes. He plucked it out and began stroking the quill.

"And what do you think of your father whom you do not know?" asked Chiun.

"He's a good guy."

"Yes?"

"But he's a stranger. I don't really know him. If I spent the rest of my life here, I might just start to know him."

"Will you?"

"I told you I was through with CURE. I still feel that way."

"You have not answered my question, Remo Williams."

"I've been thinking a lot about what happened these last few days."

"And what do your thoughts tell you?"

"That whole Rite of Attainment, the snotty way you treated me. You were setting me up to find my father, weren't you?"

"Possibly."

"You knew one of the Masters would tell me the truth. And you dumped all over me so that when the time came I could choose my father if my heart told me it was the right thing to do."

"I do not admit this."

"You figured it would be easier for me if I hated your guts."

"Do you despise my guts?" asked Chiun.

"If I hadn't before this, why should I start now, Little Father?"

And Remo smiled.

Chiun's wise visage began to come apart. He forced it to tighten. "Quickly, what is the lesson of the coins?"

"Empires come and go, but gold is forever."

"Close enough. And your visits with the Masters who came before you?"

"Every Master has a different lesson, but the one that stands out is that the Void is what you make it. If you are unhappy in life, you will be unhappy in the Void."

"What else?"

Remo thought a moment. "I think the most important thing I learned is the lessons you are taught when you are young are the ones that get you through life."

Chiun wrinkled up his face. "Who taught you that?"

"Sister Mary Margaret."

Abruptly Chiun lifted a bony finger. "Look to the sky, Remo. What stars do you see?"

Remo gazed upward. On either side of the Silvery River were two very bright stars.

"That's Kyon-u the Herder and Chik-nyo the Weaver."

"Not Altair and Vega?"

"Kyon-u and Chik-nyo," said Remo. "When Chik-nyo becomes the pole star, the House will still be standing even when America has become the ancient Greece of that century."

Chiun's hazel eyes beamed with a radiant pride. "You are a true son of my village."

"Thanks, Little Father."

"And you are the true treasure of Sinanju."

Before Remo could say anything, Chiun lifted two balled fists and held them before Remo's chest.

Remo blinked. "Lodestones?"

"You have met the challenge of every Master except me. This is your last chance to prove yourself to your ancestors."

They circled one another warily, eyes cold, bodies tense, fists upraised, yet hardly moving. No blow was landed. No countermeasure struck. An hour passed. Then two. The concentration on their faces was deep and fierce and intense.

At one point Chiun tried to break Remo's concentration. "You understand that you and I are of the same blood, do you not?"

"I can live with it." Remo frowned. "I didn't meet every Master, did I?"

"No. But the others may appear to you if they feel the need is there. For no Master is ever truly alone."

Remo nodded. "There's one thing I still haven't figured out."

"What is that?"

"Why didn't you tell me about Sunny Joe years ago? Were you afraid of losing me?"

"Not as afraid as I was that Emperor Smith would order me to dispatch your father to keep secret the fact you still lived. For you know that is what he would demand of me should he learn you are no longer a fatherless man."

Remo said nothing. They fell into a tight silence once more.

Somewhere in the third hour the Master of Sinanju abruptly broke off and said, "Enough. You have shamed neither the Master who trained you nor the House you serve."

And stepping back, Chiun bowed deeply, a forty-five-degree bow, and said, "I bow to you, Remo Williams, future Reigning Master of Sinanju."

And Remo bowed equally in return, and for the first time in his life, his heart was full to overflowing.

FLY WITH GOLD EAGLE IN A SPECIAL MONTH CELEBRATING

DON PENDLETON'S THE EXECUTIONER® 200

Mack Bolan has kept action adventure fans riveted to THE EXECUTIONER for over 20 years! Now, his 200th adventure will be published and is sure to become a collector's item!

AND

THE Destroyer 100

THE DESTROYER is synonymous with success. And its 100th volume, with a special introduction written by Warren Murphy, will be a must-have for all action adventure fans!

BOTH AVAILABLE IN AUGUST 1995

Gold Eagle is proud to celebrate the successes of two of our most popular action teams: THE EXECUTIONER #200 and THE DESTROYER #100—TRUE PUBLISHING ACHIEVEMENTS!

Don't miss these two books—available in August 1995.

GESPEC

A perilous quest in a hostile land

JAMES AXLER

DEATH LANDS®

Emerald Fire

In EMERALD FIRE, Ryan Cawdor and his band of warrior survivalists emerge from a gateway into an abandoned U.S. military complex, now a native shrine to the white gods of preblast days. Here the group is given royal treatment, only to discover that privilege has a blood price.

In the Deathlands, you're always too far from home....